Dear

Hero

By Hope Bolinger and Alyssa Roat

INTENSE PUBLICATIONS
www.INtensePublications.com

INtense Publications

Paperback ISBN-13: 978-1-947796-80-5

Dear Hero

Copyright © 2020 Alyssa Roat and Hope Bolinger

Contact@INtensePublications.com.

This is a work of fiction. Names, characters, places and incidents are either the product of the author's imagination or are used fictitiously and any resemblance to actual persons, living or dead, business establishments, events or locales is entirely coincidental.

This edition published by arrangement with INtense Publications LLC. The opinions expressed by the author are not necessarily those of INtense Publications LLC.

www.INtensePublications.com

Printed in U.S.A

Meta Match

Every hero needs a villain.

80C8

Every villain needs a hero.

Private Message
June 21

Hero: 1:43 P.M.

Hey, so saw you swiped right... nice, um, photo. Can almost see that creepy smile under that hood.

Villain: 1:56 P.M.

Your photo is sickening as well. That pure face, noble gaze... bleck.

Hero: 1:58 P.M.

Lol. Guess we're a good match, then. What brought you to Meta-Match?

Villain: 1:58 P.M.

I was looking for carpet cleaning. Did you not read the slogan? "Pairing up villains and heroes for professional combat: Metaaaa-Match!"

Hero: 1:58 P.M.

That's not what I meant. I feel kind of embarrassed about being on here, but my last villain dumped me, and I'm having difficulty finding someone to fight.

1:59 P.M.
Villain: Wow. That's pretty villainous. Cheers to your ex. My last hero died on the job. Guess I got a little too intense.

2:00 P.M.
Hero: Wow. He or she (or it) must not have been that much of a hero then, eh? :) Anyways, glad to hear you're a bit more intimidating than my last guy. He, uh, fell in love with a hero. Cute girl. Really annoying. Love interest material, you know? At least, that's how he described her. Never saw a picture.

2:01 P.M.
Villain: Gross. How unprofessional.

Hero: Agreed.

Hero: Promise me we aren't going to get together, sister? ;)

2:02 P.M.
Villain: Ugh definitely not. I hate you already.

Hero: Ah, I'm blushing... sorry, I'm a bit rusty at this. I guess I should ask you some get to know you stuff, you know?

2:03 P.M.
Villain: Let's start with the basics. Do you have superpowers?

Hero: Besides wooing all the ladies? ;)

Villain: Oh, gross, spare me.

2:04 P.M.
Hero: Wow. Maybe you are as weak as my last villain if that got you. Lol. Umm, I can read minds (not control them, always have to put that caveat) and control technology. But it's not as cool as telekinesis or flying or whatnot. Last dude in the chat room dumped me because "my power wasn't cool enough." Smh. Like his ability to screech like an eagle was any better. He had a beaky nose, too.

2:05 P.M.
Villain: Nah, I like it. You can figure out a villain's true motives and mess with them. I'll clearly win, though, because I just kill people for the fun of it. No motive. Any psychopath is my role model.

2:07 P.M.
Hero: You and every other Mary Sue. How bout you? Got any special abilities? Please don't say you can conjure up spiders. THEY'RE MY ONE WEAKNESS.

Villain: Wow you're a dumb hero. Why would you share that?

Hero: JK, here's a picture of me with a ten-foot-tall spider. Gift from my last villain. Birthday's on February 25 btw. Don't forget :)

2:13 P.M.

Villain: Ooo, he's cute. I suck people's powers and use them myself.

Hero: Wow. I'll make sure not to get too close to you. OK, next question. Backstory. Let me guess. You have a horrible one.

2:14 P.M.

Villain: I guess. Kind of cliché. Parents died horrifically. I was taken in by a villain who used me against her enemies. Eventually killed her. You know.

2:15 P.M.

Hero: Wow. Too bad you're a villain and all because I like it when other villains die and stuff. Not too bad of a backstory. Hardly a monologue at all.

2:16 P.M.

Villain: Thanks. I just kind of kill everyone. What about you? Either you have a tragic backstory or your life was perfect.

Hero: Nah, just didn't want to work retail. So here I am!

2:17 P.M.

Villain: OMG retail SUUUCKS. Managers are the real villains of the world.

Hero: Dude, I know. I kept telling myself, "Bro, you're gonna become a villain if you have to scan one more expired coupon." Store smelled like sawdust and depression.

Hero: Plus, I worked at a store with a bunch of paint. Apparently radioactive paint is a thing and can and will give you superpowers when you clean it up in aisle five.

2:18 P.M.

Villain: Working in a clothing store helped me hone my edge. Folding all those T-shirts for the millionth time... I think I left part of my mind behind in the clothes. Anyway, I "accidentally" killed a coworker and that was the end of that.

2:20 P.M.

Hero: Been there. Didn't do that. I got to go. I have a date with a really cute chick. Here's her photo. Hot, huh? She's blonde and got blue eyes... so I guess the opposite of your, uh, red contacts and dark hair and stuff. Really nice. I feel like even though she's eighteen she talks like she's thirty.

Villain: Dude that's the best power origin story ever. You go have fun being obnoxious. Catch you later.

Private Message
June 21

Hero: 5:37 P.M.

Hey, Villain, just got back. I see you're not active at the moment, but whenever you get a chance to read this, feel free to reply. Or not. You villains are weird with how you reply to things. Here's a nice picture of my date drinking her coffee. Super chill atmosphere. Lots of jazz music. You would've hated it.

Hero:

I was a little wary because her t-shirt has a Great Guy logo. From what I can tell, he's an awful human being, but we had a good chat and all. Says the t-shirt is a hand-me-down, so a keeper for now. I would tell you her name, but then you'd kidnap her because that's what villains do. For now, we'll call her, "Juliet" (Because you know, she's hot, and romantic and stuff).

Hero: 5:38 P.M.

Speaking of, we should probably call each other by names other than Hero or Villain. Obviously I can't give you my real name (secret identity, what a hassle). But you can call me by my superhero alias.

Hero changed name to Cortex

5:40 P.M.
Cortex: I showed Juliet your profile pic and she says she thinks she may know your henchman? Didn't even know you had one. Guess I need to get a sidekick.

5:42 P.M.
Cortex: Hey, I know we're still considering whether we'd be a good villain/hero match, but can you do me a huge favor? Sorry if this sounds vulnerable and all... I sound like a freaking love interest...

5:43 P.M.
Cortex: It's just. I've already lost one girl to another villain. Like, lost lost one. When/If we start fighting, can you please promise me to leave whatever girl I'm dating out of harm's way? You can kill me and all (lol. Not likely) just promise to leave her alone? I mean, I really like her. She already seemed to be finishing my sentences by the end of the date. Mind reader? Lol. No, she says she's too out of shape to even pretend to be a hero. She still jogs every morning, so not really sure what she's talking about.

5:44 P.M.
Villain: Dude, you're blowing up my inbox.

Cortex: Whoa, sorry. Didn't see you pop on. Guess I'm as talkative as a villain who monologues. But seriously, do you promise to leave her out of it?

5:45 P.M.

Villain: I don't care who the heck you date. This is a professional relationship. I don't care about hurting you personally.

Cortex: Whew. That's a relief. Can I call you something other than Villain? How about Soon-To-Be-Dead, or something like that? I'm deadly serious :)

5:46 P.M.

Villain: Ha. So funny. You can call me Vortex.

Villain: Gosh dang it our names rhyme.

Villain changed name to Vortex

Cortex: How cute. All we need is a hashtag now.

5:47 P.M.

Vortex: In your dreams. I have to go feed my cat. Text you later.

Cortex: Say hi to your pet sharks for me!

Vortex: I'll tell them to eat you if they see you.

Private Message
June 22

Hope you're having as miserable of a Friday evening as I am.

Cortex:

If hanging out with Juliet counts, then yes. Second date down, and I already want to marry this girl. Every time we hold hands ... she has freezing hands, btw. And she smells like coconuts ... and that's not bad as scents go.

Cortex: 6:02 P.M.

So should we get to know each other a little more before, like, meeting up to throw a punch at each other?

Vortex:

First of all, let's establish that I don't want to know the details of your pathetic love life. Do you know anything about this girl besides her name?

Cortex: Here's a pic of us kissing. She likes cherry flavored chapstick. And I think she has a dog. She showed me a lot of pics of corgis.

> 6:03 P.M.
> **Vortex:** Gross! Who takes a pic of themselves kissing?

Cortex: She sent it to me, but I thought it would make you mad. I'm trying to build up the animosity, you know?

> **Vortex:** Ah, we'll get along great. You're so awful. Also, you're a one-dimensional character who obviously is not ready for a serious relationship.

6:04 P.M.
Cortex: Awww, I hate you, too. Speaking of one-dimensional, let's flesh out a little bit about ourselves. Like what's your biggest weakness? How have past heroes defeated you? Stuff like that :) :) :)

> **Vortex:** Nice try. How about my favorite way to kill heroes? I love the rack, personally. Watching them writhe as their limbs crack and pop.

6:05 P.M.
Cortex: Rice Krispies. Glad to plan ahead for my funeral... which will never happen, btw. OK, so are you a fan of any rays? Death rays? Stingrays? Rays of sunshine like myself?

6:06 P.M.

Vortex: Well, here's a picture of my pet stingray. But rays are so overused. I like good old-fashioned violence.

6:07 P.M.

Cortex: Well, that's a relief. And your pet is so pale it looks like he's never seen the light of day. Glad you don't have a corgi.

Vortex: He's albino, genius.

Cortex: My name is Cortex. That's a part of the brain :) It's like an outer gray shell that protects all the good stuff. I'm sure you've seen it if you ever dashed a hero's brains out.

6:08 P.M.

Vortex: Wow thank you for informing me. I totally didn't know any basic anatomy. In case you are as dense as you seem, Vortex has to do with sucking things in. Like I suck powers.

Cortex: Vortie (can I call you that? Imma call you that anyway) I live in Indiana. I know a thing or two about tornadoes.

6:09 P.M.

Cortex: Anyway, as for weapons, I am a fan of a katana (family's Japanese). But if you like to fight mano y mano, I'm cool with that, too. And that's the extent of the Spanish I know soooo. I think mano has something to do with hands?

Vortex changed name to Call Me Vortie And Die.

Cortex changed name to I'm Invincible Come At Me Bro.

I'm Invincible Come At Me Bro changed name to Cortex.

Call Me Vortie And Die changed name to V.

6:10 P.M.
Cortex: Love it. I was starting to get our names confused. (And by love it, I mean, hate it)

V: Same.

V: ...

V: What now?

Cortex: Why don't you tell me about your henchman? I'm currently searching internship sites to find someone to be a sidekick.

6:11 P.M.
V: Totally recommend a sidekick. My henchman is the best. His name is Bernard. Eighty-five. Totally evil. They don't come like that anymore.

6:12 P.M.
Cortex: Dang, these interns are older than me. Most are in college already.

V: Yeah, what are you, twelve? That pic with the girl, I mean, dude, you're too young for that.

Cortex: Dude, we're fresh out of high school. What do you think we'd look like? All those movie stars who are 30 who pretend to be 15?

6:13 P.M.
V: Fair. Hey, I just finished high school too.

6:14 P.M.
Cortex: My school was tiny. We only had one rival because they placed us smack in the middle of a cornfield. Take a guess at where Juliet attended (hint: not my school).

V: Kind of like Great Guy ;)

Cortex: Leave. Now.

6:15 P.M.
Cortex: Let me guess. You went to a huge high school, but the overweight bullies who smelled like bologna singled you out and picked on you until you turned to theater and villainy for an outlet.

V: Wrong, actually, Mr. Egghead. I was homeschooled. By Bernard.

6:16 P.M.
Cortex: Makes sense. And Bernard sounds creepy.

Cortex: Yo, just found a sidekick. Gonna send a pic. What D'ya think?

> 6:17 P.M.
> **V:** Is he wearing a fish costume?

Cortex: Looks nice with the red hair. Kind of like Ron Weasley meets Poseidon. He says he wore it for a play. Apparently his "resume" on this thing is just the number of shows he was in.

> 6:18 P.M.
> **V:** Does he at least have superpowers?

6:19 P.M.
Cortex: Apparently he has the superpower of brewing coffee.

> **V:** Hire him. Now.

Cortex: Wait, does Bernard have powers?

> 6:20 P.M.
> **V:** Ha. You wish I'd tell you. I'm not giving you that advantage.

6:22 P.M.
Cortex: Sorry, had to use the little hero's room.

> 6:23 P.M.
> **V:** Heroes. You can't even just use the pot like a normal person.

Cortex: Oh please never refer to it like that ever again. Are there any other questions we need to get out of the way before we decide to... you know... do the do and become hero vs. villain?

> **V:** pot

> **V:** pot

> 6:24 P.M.
> **V:** pot

> **V:** Nooooo don't refer to our battle that way.

6:25 P.M.
Cortex: In what way?

> **V:** Argghh I'm leaving. I have work at 7. Talk to you tomorrow.

6:26 P.M.
Cortex: Ok... can we still be potential hero and villain?

> **V:** Absolutely. You're maddening. Tootles!

Private Message
June 24

Cortex: 5:31 A.M.

Sorry I was out yesterday. Turns out my sidekick lives a city over … everything's twenty minutes away from everything out here. He and I met up at a coffee shop called "Bean There, Done That." It's a popular chain in Indiana. Good spiced lattes. Nice guy … a little obnoxious. Couldn't come up with a sidekick name yet, so we'll call him "Kevin" for now. His name is actually Kevin, but I don't care if you find him and kill him. He seems cool, but his favorite movie is Episode Two of Star Wars, so I won't be too sad to see him go.

Cortex: 5:40 A.M.

I realized you might not be a morning person like me. I'll make sure to get up extra early to message you. Off to a morning jog! Got a late start today. How embarrassing.

Cortex: 8:01 A.M.

You still asleep, V? Don't tell me you've died yet. That would spoil all the fun (not that I kill villains… try not to). Hey … I hope this isn't too soon, but I was wondering if you wanted to maybe meet up and throw a couple punches. Just a little fight. Maybe

even at a coffee shop so it seems more chill.
Nothing like the roof of a skyrise or anything like
that (I'm not one of those fast-moving heroes ... I
take things slow). Let me know!

8:51 A.M.
V: Oh. My. Goodness. You realize
there's a time difference.

Cortex: Nah, brah. You never said where you lived.

V: Sigh. I live in a land as dead as you
will be once I'm done with you. A land
of cactus and sadness. Southern
Arizona.

8:52 A.M.
Cortex: Ah, was gonna say New Jersey but you
beat me to it with the cactus thing. So I guess that's
a bit of a hike for a fight, huh?

V: Not really. Bernard can bring me. It's
only a fifteen-minute ride.

8:53 A.M.
Cortex: Eww, Bernard is chaperoning? Is he gonna
watch the fight, too, and make sure I don't put my
arm over your shoulder when I yawn?

V: No, I'm perfectly capable of cutting
off your arm myself.

8:54 A.M.
Cortex: I mean, I can ask my dad to borrow his
helicopter to ride over a couple times down to you if

needed. Just got my license. No way he'd let me borrow his jet, though. :)

> **V:** Why the heck do you work retail if your dad has a helicopter?

8:55 A.M.
Cortex: Eh, needed something to do. Dad won't let me go for sports because it would give away the whole I'm-a-superhero-thing. I don't really know what mind-reading has to do with sports, but our family ... our family has a history with heroes and we need to be a bit more enigmatic. No retail place takes a high schooler seriously. I tried to apply to food after working a few weeks in retail, but they said I couldn't learn the necessary skills for flipping burgers after scanning coupons for two weeks. Retail and food are nemeses apparently. Gotta love the economy, eh?

Cortex: Anyway, you cool to try to meet up? I know a fun shop where we can grab a cup and then have it out in the parking lot.

> 8:56 A.M.
> **V:** Sounds good to me. Where and when? My next shift is tomorrow evening.

Cortex: Today and tomorrow aren't great. Today I'm watching my sister's tennis match (she can't hit the ball to save her life). It isn't fair because she doesn't have powers, so my parents didn't care if she went out for sports. She's also a younger child so ... they gave up on her. And my dad's having a big gala at his house tomorrow and take a wild guess at who he invited.

8:57 A.M.
V: Me?

8:58 A.M.
Cortex: Lol. No. He's bringing Dimension.

Cortex: My favorite hero.

Cortex: The dude who inspired me to get started when I turned fifteen. Ever heard of him?

> **V:** Sickeningly nice guy. Actually treats women like people. Ugh. Hard to hate. It's so annoying.

8:59 A.M.
Cortex: Ah, man. So you've heard of him? He's kind of lesser known (compared with any heroes featured in major movies, at least). Probably because he sticks around in the fourth dimension most of time. Hardly any news coverage in there.

> **V:** I was supposed to kill him once. Didn't. Killed my master instead.

9:00 A.M.
Cortex: Man, you got a little bit of a hero inside you if you spared Dimension. Didn't know you were capable.

Cortex: Anyways, you cool with the day after tomorrow? I can hop on late tomorrow to tell you about Dimension and all.

> 9:01 A.M.
> **V:** Sounds good. As long as you never insinuate there is anything hero-like about me. I want to hear about the dude. And I want to kick your butt.

9:03 A.M.
Cortex: Sure thing. I'll even tell him about you so he can punch you once. Networking, you know? Although he's getting older. Don't know how strong his fighting is anymore.

> **V:** Wow. Thank you. That would be great for my resume.

Cortex: Gotta do something with all those job employers who won't take us on. Who knows? Maybe things get better after college. Then all those big firms will open up their arms to us.

> 9:04 A.M.
> **V:** Well, I certainly won't get into VillainCorp by fighting you, but it's a start. Get lost, dude. I want to go back to sleep.

Private Message
June 25

Cortex: 11:02 P.M.

Hey, V. I know you want to hear about the gala and all, but I'm not in the mood :(It just ended.

V: 11:04 P.M.

Why not? Wasn't it fun? I'd imagine there were a bunch of cute girls for you to flirt with.

Cortex:

Ugh, no the average age of them was about sixty. Can't unsee Ms. Abarnanthee in that sequin slit dress. Remind me never to go shirtless after I turn thirty.

Cortex: 11:05 P.M.

And the food was a bunch of cold quiches, sour kimbap, and alcohol I wasn't allowed to drink, so you really didn't miss out. Music wasn't even jazz.

Cortex:

Couldn't talk to many people either. Had about five minutes with Dimension, but that was definitely enough. Built him up so much in my mind, you know? After years of reading his comics.

Cortex: V... I dunno if I want to fight tomorrow. And how the heck do you stay up late? I feel like I just crashed from five energy drinks.

> 11:06 P.M.
> **V:** It's only eight here. Why don't you want to fight? This is our big day.

11:07 P.M.
Cortex: Let's not make a big deal about it. It's just coffee... and beating up your face.

Cortex: V, have you ever had a hero who let you down?

> 11:08 P.M.
> **V:** Everyone lets you down. That's why you only look out for yourself. And kill people frequently.

11:09 P.M.
Cortex: Wow. So much for coming to you for advice.

Cortex: V... Dimension... he got older. He must be about fifty now. The purple on his suit's all faded, and he looks like all the scantily clad old women. About sixty. Or seventy, some people reminded me of raisins ... or what happens to your hands when you leave a pool. And... he seemed so weak. It was heartbreaking.

11:10 P.M.
Cortex: And then I realized... that's me. I'm just a small hero now with about 100 Twitter followers,

but in fifty years, I'm going to let some kid down. I mean, even a villain like yourself could take Dimension out with a single punch.

> **V:** Villains never let people down. People expect the worst. And that's what they get. Stop being such a hero and caring about a proverbial kid.

11:11 P.M.
Cortex: Whoa, what does that even mean?

Cortex: V, I don't want to fight because if I continue down this path, one day I have to quit. Maybe I should just stick to mopping up radioactive paint.

> 11:12 P.M.
> **V:** Everything comes to an end. Good life. Parents. Love. Life itself. I guess you just have to live while you can.

> **V:** And Cortex...

> **V:** I need you. I don't have another hero to fight.

11:13 P.M.
Cortex: Now don't get all sappy on me. I guess I can show up tomorrow. It's just casual, right? It's been a while... what do most of your first fights look like?

> **V:** Totally casual. Heck, we don't even know if we're a match yet.

11:14 P.M.
Cortex: True, so I guess I forgot to send some details about the where and when tomorrow. I'm guessing mornings are out?

11:15 P.M.
V: Yes, please.

Cortex: Five in the morning it is! Right after my jog at four.

V: Certainly. Five MY time.

Cortex: Ugh, fine.

11:16 P.M.
Cortex: How about noon? High noon? I'll come in cowboy boots just for you. I think my sister has a pink pair. ;)

V: Gross. I'll leave my deadly weapons at home so I don't kill you too quickly.

11:17 P.M.
Cortex: Wonder if the rack will fit in Bernard's jet or whatever you travel in. How the heck do you fly so fast? And why is an 85-year-old man flying it?

V: I never said he was a man. He's a freaking dragon.

11:18 P.M.
Cortex: Uh huh. Sure. And my dad is a T-Rex.

Cortex: So for place, we have about ten coffee shops in my town alone. For some reason, Indiana has a monopoly on expensive hot drinks.

11:19 P.M.
V: Nothing fancy. Starbucks?

Cortex: I have to give you the list first. Like a waiter. *Puts on black suit, tux, and an annoyed expression at how stupid certain customers can be*

V: This is why I've murdered two waiters.

Cortex: No! They're the victims! Ok... one hot list coming for you:

11:20 P.M.
Cortex: Bean There, Done That. Really homey atmosphere. Low lighting, few customers.

V: No.

Cortex: Joe for Yo, a frozen yogurt and coffee shop. They have cookie dough as toppings for both and lots of screaming children :) have a feeling you'd love it. They play songs from Frozen on repeat. Get it? Frozen yogurt? Lol.

V: I LOVE FROZEN YOGURT but hate children. What else you got?

11:21 P.M.
Cortex: Actually same. Guess we got one thing in common.

Cortex: Cuppa for Cool Cids, really shady place. Coffee tastes like meth. Blinds look like they've got holes from gunshots. Seen a deal or two go down in the parking lot. Sounds like your kind of vibe.

> **V:** I like my coffee questionable. Let's do it.

11:22 P.M.
Cortex: Mmmm shocker. Anything else we should hammer out before we meet up?

> **V:** Nah, we're pros. See you tomorrow.

> **V:** And by the way... look at me using hero tactics to get you to fight me. "Cortex, I need you!" Heh heh heh. As if.

11:23 P.M.
Cortex: That did sound weird, I'll admit.

Cortex: Wonder what that evil laugh sounds like. Please tell me it's not like a musk ox. My last nemesis guffawed like one, and I tried so hard not to break out laughing every time.

> **V:** I don't laugh. Too professional for that.

11:24 P.M.
Cortex: Does it really sound that bad? What dying animal does it imitate?

Cortex: A whale?

Cortex: A hyena?

Cortex: My creepy AP Lit teacher who was about as old as Bernard?

     V: Stop it! My laugh sounds terrifying!

11:25 P.M.
Cortex: Lol. See, now I'm using villain tactics to rile you up. Two can play at this taunting game. So there!

     V: Ugh don't stoop to my level. See you tomorrow, loser.

11:26 P.M.
Cortex: So you admit you're on a lower level. See you tomorrow :)

     V: Man, I really hate you.

Private Message
June 29

Cortex: 12:04 P.M.

So, uh, having a terrible day?

V: 12:35 P.M.

Naturally.

Cortex: 12:36 P.M.

Interesting weather. The sky looks like it can't decide if it's going to rain. But it's like that everyday.

Cortex:

So . . .

Cortex:

What's new?

V: 12:37 P.M.

Not my weather. Freaking sunny. Every. Single. Day.

Cortex:

Why don't you move? You'd fit right in with the vampires in Washington.

V: Eh, I'm vegan.

12:38 P.M.
Cortex: Whoa, didn't predict that with your bloodlust and everything.

Cortex: So... about our meeting... umm, haven't heard since.

12:39 P.M.
Cortex: On a scale of one to listening to jazz music, how much did it suck?

> 12:40 P.M.
> **V:** About as much as a vortex. Heh. Heh. Heh... Dude, have you ever even punched before?

12:41 P.M.
Cortex: It's been a while... my last villain dumped me about six months back. And you get suspended in high school for trying to knock people out for practice. But it's fine when Jerry brings in a lightsaber and whacks some kid on the head in the lunch room for stealing his Pokemon cards.

> **V:** Freaking nerds. That's why I was homeschooled.

12:42 P.M.
Cortex: I mean, you're one to talk about the fighting thing. Sure I missed your face and hit the windshield of a car (thing was crazy dented already, and looked abandoned), but you didn't even use

your powers once. What am I? Your practice
punching bag?

> **V:** I didn't want you to die on the first
> round. And there was probably
> something in my coffee. Or something.

12:43 P.M.
Cortex: I felt so embarrassed because I wanted to
read your mind and stuff, but you didn't use your
powers, and I felt like I would be taking advantage.
And no use controlling electricity when the coffee
shop's power went out.

> **V:** Yeah...

> **V:** So, are we still doing this? I have a
> bunch of other people I could fight, of
> course, but...

12:44 P.M.
Cortex: Yeah, well I got a lot of villains who swiped
right on me, too, you know. Ever heard of Shadow
Sabre? The dude literally uses shadows to choke you
to death. He's fought this one hero I'm following on
Instagram who has about 117K followers. He just
matched with me today.

> **V:** Yeah, right. How boring is that? He's
> been fought before.

Cortex: True. And he HATES coffee! But you
seemed to like it :) Good convo, btw. Almost forgot
about the fight when we were sipping the shady

stuff and eyeing the creepy customers in the corner booth.

> 12:45 P.M.
> **V:** Well, you were cracking me up with your crack jokes ;)

12:46 P.M.
Cortex: Pot

Cortex: Pot

12:47 P.M.
Cortex: Pot, sorry, I'll stop.

> **V:** Omg lol

Cortex: So should we try again? I've never been in this situation before. My last villain and I puzzle pieced well together. It seems like I'm back at square one.

> 12:48 P.M.
> **V:** Well... Bernard has an idea. But I don't know if I like it.

12:50 P.M.
Cortex: I already don't like it. Got one peek of Bernard when I slammed my fist into that windshield. Looks like a tombstone with wrinkles and a condescending frown.

Cortex: And his face was so ashy... maybe he is a dragon, lol. He just burned himself up.

12:51 P.M.

V: I told you he's a dragon. He morphs. Anyway, he suggested we get a choreographer to help us.

12:52 P.M.

Cortex: Ummm, what? Like the dudes who teach you how to dance for weddings and school plays and stuff?

Cortex: Yeah, no thanks.

12:53 P.M.

V: Bernard says we looked awful. He said we should get professional help if we don't want to embarrass ourselves. Apparently we should be, like, running around and spinning and stuff too? I can't even do a cartwheel.

12:54 P.M.

Cortex: That makes literally no sense. You'd get out of breath from all that extra work. What is this? High School Musical?

Cortex: But we do need desperate help ...

Cortex: Did Dimension ever hire a choreographer? Can you ask Bernard?

V: Yeah, hold up, I'll ask.

12:56 P.M.

V: So... plot twist. Bernard was Dimension's choreographer. Back when he was young and spry. I feel a little betrayed...

Cortex: Not buying it. Bernard taught dance and doubles as a dragon? I can't even work both retail and food.

V: It's a generational thing. Old people could do everything before they messed up the economy for us.

12:58 P.M.
Cortex: Preach it, sister.

Cortex: So how do we go about hiring a choreographer? Does it cost a lot?

12:59 P.M.
V: Hold on, let me look up rates.

1:02 P.M.
V: Wow... okay, most of them charge like 60 bucks. The lowest is 35.

Cortex: Dang. A whole shift of cleaning up paint and picking up shattered light bulbs. Maybe skip the choreographer?

1:04 P.M.
V: Well... there's this guy. An old coach of mine. Taught me monologuing.

Cortex: Hate him already.

V: He also teaches choreography. If I asked, he'd probably teach us for free if I agree to help out at drama camp.

1:05 P.M.
Cortex: He a theater dude? Surprised they all don't turn into villains after going through techweek (trust me, I ran lights once for Next to Normal ... because you know, I control technology and all).

Cortex: I mean, guess it doesn't hurt to try. You think you can text him and ask?

V: Sigh. I guess. I'll text him. Hold on a minute.

1:46 P.M.
V: He said yes.

Cortex: Cool. I'm free all week. Anything to get out of watching another of my sister's tennis matches. When you available?

V: Well, I accidentally killed a coworker, so I'm out of retail job number two, and I literally have nothing going on.

1:47 P.M.
Cortex: How have you not been arrested yet?

Cortex: Does tomorrow sound too early?

V: Nah, sounds good.

1:48 P.M.

Cortex: Noon again? And where in Arizona?

> **V:** Yes, noon Arizona time. And there's this sketch bowling alley no one actually goes to that could work. I don't want to go to the drama teacher's studio. Associating with heroes and villains... wouldn't want to make him a target.

Cortex: Good call. Gotta warn you. I bowl a 300 game.

1:49 P.M.

Cortex: Just kidding ... I aim for the gutter every time. Kind of like what villains do with their lives.

> **V:** Jerk. Lol.

1:50 P.M.

Cortex: Heading out for a walk in the park with Juliet. Want me to tell her anything when I see her?

> **V:** Ugh, no. But I can tell you what NOT to tell me: how many times you kiss on that walk.

Cortex: I'll send lots of pics. Hate you, bye.

Private Message
June 30

Cortex: 11:08 P.M.

Hey, V! About to load up to fly to Arizona. Luckily the three-hour time difference won't matter much with how long it takes to get down there. Because I'm up in the air, I probably won't see a reply until after we ... learn to dance. Sadly no pictures from my date with Juliet. She cancelled five minutes after we talked because her grandpa died. Aneurysm. No one predicted it. Too bad too, she had put him down as her role model on her college application. Says she wants to go into Journalism ... guess all heroes need a journalist girlfriend. She's really good at asking questions. Seems to know the answers to them, too. So Mom decided to take my free time from my cancelled date and send me into a hair stylist. Got a nice buzz cut. Not that you'll be able to tell under the purple mask ;) I liked my wavy hair better. Also, hope this isn't too awkward ... talked with my sidekick Kevin (he goes by the name "Corpus" now). He wants to know if he can join us in our next choreography session (dude Snapchatted me during my hair appointment). Feels it could boost his resume to have additional skills. He also wants to try out for the Community Theater production of *Annie* and thinks the choreography background can land him a part. Maybe he'll get the lead with his hair. He seems like the orphan type. See you in a few hours!

Group Chat
June 30

7:08 P.M.
Cortex added V to Group Chat.

Cortex added Corpus to Group Chat.

Cortex added Bernard VII to Group Chat.

Cortex changed Group Chat name to "You Wanna Dance, Punk?"

Cortex:

Just got back. Sorry you missed out today, Kevin. Promise we'll include you next time at the bowling alley.

Corpus: 7:10 P.M.

That's ok. They don't call me the spare for nothing.

V:

Ugh do we really have to bring this dude?

Corpus changed name to The Spare.

7:11 P.M.

The Spare: She seems fun. Single, V? You could be dating the newest Marion Daddy Warbucks in their production of Annie.

> **V:** I tend to kill anyone who tries to hit on me.

7:12 P.M.

The Spare: Still worth a shot...

The Spare: Anyone want to fill me in on what I missed today? Also, does Bernard even know how to operate a computer?

> **Bernard VII:** Pardon me, young sir, but I am perfectly capable of typing upon a digital apparatus.

7:13 P.M.

Cortex: You missed V FAILING at bowling. Seriously, her final score was in the single digits.

> **Bernard VII:** I also feel inclined to admit that this feat was achieved even with bumpers.

V: Bernard!!!

> 7:14 P.M.
>
> **Cortex:** You also missed learning the proper way to punch. Apparently, if you enclose your thumb with your fingers, you'll probably break it. Probably explains why my hand's still injured

from hitting that windshield. V freaked out when she saw it bandaged.

V: Did not. Just wanted to make sure I wouldn't have to find a different hero.

7:15 P.M.
The Spare: Ugh, get a room. Also, V, Cortie sent me a bunch of pics of you dancing with the instructor dude. Let me send them.

The Spare: Got all fifteen?

V: What the heck, Cortex? You creep!

7:16 P.M.
Cortex: What? You looked so happy. Tried not to get too much of Mr. Lefebvre (or however the heck he spelled it) in the pics. No man should ever wear leggings or tights. Not even superheroes.

7:17 P.M.
The Spare: Yeah, and the handlebar mustache on the dude ... nice touch.

V: Yeah, please never wear tights, Cortex. I will refuse to fight you. Also, please delete "happy" pictures. It makes me look bad.

7:18 P.M.
Bernard VII: Miss Vortex, we have many pictures of you smiling in the hall.

V: Bernard!!!

Bernard VII: For example, at your ballet recital.

V: Noooooo

7:19 P.M.
The Spare: Speaking of dancing, did y'all do anything other than that? Srsly what did you learn?

7:20 P.M.
Cortex: A couple basic kicks and all the reasons why Hamilton is the best musical to ever rock the Broadway stage according ... Imma just call him Mr. L. You didn't miss much, Kevin. He says next week we move into spins, so yippee!

V: I mean, Hamilton really is pretty fantastic.

Cortex: It's overdone. Besides, I hate that period of history. Stick me back in Ancient Rome with the lions in the Colosseum.

7:21 P.M.
V: Fight me.

Cortex: I will when you learn to punch.

V: At least I have a body count. How many people have you killed?

The Spare: Body count? That sounds hot.

7:22 P.M.

Cortex: None. Ugh. Why do you think that's an accomplishment? Trying to compensate for bowling? I will say ... your pirouette was on-point. I think you made the instructor cry.

> **V:** He cries a lot. Kevin, I could add you to that body count.

7:33 P.M.
The Spare: Please do, baby. ;)

> **Cortex:** Kevin, tone it down. You're a pasty kid with a whimpering voice. Stop trying to act all cool here.

Bernard VII: Kevin, this is inappropriate behavior toward my ward.

> 7:34 P.M.
> **V:** Dang, Cortex. Harsh. Almost villainous ;)

Cortex: Ugh, no. And where did you pick up Bernard? The freaking 1800s? Who uses "ward" as a word?

> **Bernard VII:** I would like to remind you that I am an eighty-foot-long dragon who does not wish to be insulted by haughty young whippersnappers.

7:35 P.M.
Cortex: Right, and Dimension's my uncle.

Cortex: I will admit ... weird as today was, I did have fun in that sketchy bowling alley. Tried to make it a little bit brighter with my powers, but those dim lights don't un-gray for minimum wage.

7:36 P.M.
Bernard VII: Miss Vortex also had a splendid time. She informed me how pleased she was to find a hero such as young Cortex.

> **V:** Bernard!!! You have no filter!

7:37 P.M.
Cortex: So when do we next meet up for round two?

7:40 P.M.
Cortex: V?

7:44 P.M.
Cortex: We're bringing Kevin next time. Incentive to use him as a punching bag ;)

> **The Spare:** I'm down.

7:45 P.M.
V: Ugh, I don't know. I'm pretty busy.

> **Bernard VII:** Would you like me to retrieve the calendar, Miss Vortex?

V: No! That's okay. I have it memorized. I'm super busy. Work, you know?

7:46 P.M.

Cortex: Ah, my retail place liked to keep me overtime too. Ever have to clopen? Close and open two days in a row?

> **Bernard VII:** Miss Vortex, you were let go once more for killing a coworker.

7:47 P.M.
Cortex: Wait, that's right. V, what the heck?

> **V:** Oh, yeah. Forgot. Anyway, I'm just not super excited to fight a lousy hero like you. Retail sounded more fun.

7:48 P.M.
Cortex: ...

Cortex: OK, well I'll hop on tomorrow and check in again. Been listening to police scanners and apparently Sweet Tooth (a villain I've been messaging) is raiding the Sugar Cube Candy Store a couple towns over. Gonna try and catch him. Have fun.

7:49 P.M.
The Spare: Later, V! Kill me anytime you like :)

> **V:** Ugh

7:55 P.M.
Bernard VII: I am bewildered by this situation. Miss Vortex, are you having a spat with Master Cortex?

V: Private message, Bernard!

Private Message
June 30

7:56 P.M.
Victoria added Bernard VII.

Bernard VII:

What is this? Why don't you wish to spar with Cortex?

Victoria: 7:57 P.M.

I'm getting a little freaked out. Did you have to mention that stuff in the group chat? It makes me look weak.

Bernard VII:

I was of the opinion it portrayed you as human, and thus, more likeable.

Victoria:

No, that's the point. They're supposed to hate me.

Bernard VII:

This may be the reason you have no friends.

Victoria: 7:58 P.M.
I have friends. You. Fluffy. Mr. Flappers.

Bernard VII: The cat and stingray do not count as friends. They are pets.

Victoria: I don't need friends.

7:59 P.M.
Bernard VII: Perhaps you will change your mind. Cortex seems like a fine young man, if a bit arrogant, as heroes are prone to be. However, I find Kevin distasteful. I would be pleased to incinerate him if necessary.

Victoria: Thanks, but I can kill him myself. What's my body count, by the way? I need to brag to Cortex. Make him afraid of me. Especially after that ballet comment.

Bernard VII: Thirty-seven, Miss Victoria.

8:00 P.M.
Victoria: Thanks. I'm going to go see Mr. Flappers. And please, try not to embarrass me in the group chat next time.

Bernard VII: Very well. Tell Mr. Flappers hello for me. And Miss Victoria?

Victoria: ?

8:01 P.M.
Bernard VII: When are you going to tell Cortex who your former master was?

> **Victoria:** Never. And don't you dare tell him. There's a reason I killed that woman.

Bernard VII: I fear he may find out on his own anyway.

> **Victoria:** Good. Then he'll really hate me.

> 8:02 P.M.
> **Victoria:** But please, please don't tell him.

Bernard VII: I will not go against your wishes. I promised your father I would look after you. I do not wish for Cortex to become enraged and kill you.

> **Victoria:** Ha. As if. He's never killed anyone. And this whole "I promised your father" thing makes you sound like that old guy in the movie we watched last week.

8:03 P.M.
Bernard VII: A good man.

> **Victoria:** I guess. Even if that movie was about a hero, though.

Bernard VII: One more question: why does Cortex doubt that I am a dragon?

> **Victoria:** I don't know lol but he's in for a shock one of these days. Speaking of... I really need to feed our new electric eel. Did you name him yet?

8:04 P.M.
Bernard VII: I will leave that to you, Miss Victoria.

> **Victoria:** Cool. I like Mr. Squiggles. But if Cortex asks, he's Shockwave.

Bernard VII: Duly noted. Enjoy yourself.

Private Message
June 30

8:05 P.M.
Cortex added The Spare

The Spare changed his name to Kevin

8:06 P.M.
Kevin:

All right, let's talk smack about all the villains because they can't see us in here! You hear that villains? You ain't nothing outside of these walls!

8:07 P.M.
Cortex:

Don't make me hire someone else from Internship.com.

8:08 P.M.
Kevin:

You wouldn't.

8:09 P.M.
Cortex:

Try me. Or I'll just add all the villains

I'm talking to to this text and they'll see all the nice stuff you have to say about them. I'll put your address in here too for all of them to see.

Kevin: OK, I'll stop. Yeesh.

8:10 P.M.
Cortex: You sure? I'm talking to a really cute villain called Sulfur.

Kevin: :) What's she look like?

8:11 P.M.
Cortex: See the pic I sent? Nice skin that looks like a melted candle, drooping around the eyes. Oh, and the eyes looked burned out of the sockets, so that's a unique feature. They say her breath can knock out even the strongest of men. Smells like rotten eggs. Ready to pucker up?

8:12 P.M.
Kevin: No thanks. She seems like she has a great personality though.

8:13 P.M.
Kevin: So why did you add me to this group text?

Cortex: To see if you're down for the stakeout at Sugar Cube.

8:15 P.M.

Kevin: Bro, you need me to drive over there now? Have to ask Mom to borrow her Odyssey.

> **Cortex:** Nah, Sweet Tooth isn't doing it for another week. Apparently he sliced his hand on a sugar bowl he shattered. I was just lying on the Group Message to make her jealous. Since she's playing all hard-to-get now.

8:16 P.M.
Kevin: Rough stuff. So you gonna ask her for her number?

> 8:17 P.M.
> **Cortex:** Sweet Tooth is a dude, and not really my type. I'm not into middle-aged men with beer guts that burst out of red spandex.

8:18 P.M.
Kevin: That's hot.

> **Cortex:** Dude, I've heard you talk. Also, since when do theater kids do well in frat houses? You are an anomaly. And V isn't in here. Please go back to normal now.

8:19 P.M.
Kevin: Fine.

Kevin: And I meant V's number.

> 8:20 P.M.

Cortex: So I can use it to give to the police to track down her phone and arrest her?

8:21 P.M.
Kevin: ...

Kevin: Bro, seriously?

Cortex: Kevin, I'm dating Juliet. You know, the blonde chick who loves sparkles more than Bella in Twilight? Just kidding. She hates that kind of stuff. Too mature for it.

8:22 P.M.
Kevin: Yeah, but V, man. V.

Cortex: V stands for Villain. And this has been the ABCs on a disturbed version of Sesame Street.

8:23 P.M.
Cortex: What's wrong with Juliet?

8:24 P.M.
Kevin: Bro, we can call her by her real name in this chat.

8:25 P.M.
Cortex: All right. What's wrong with Tamora?

8:26 P.M.
Kevin: Let's start with her name.

Cortex: Let's not.

Cortex: What's wrong with her name?

8:27 P.M.
Kevin: Also, her hair is bleached. No way that's natural blonde.

8:28 P.M.
Cortex: You never answered the name question.

Kevin: What's in one?

Cortex: What?

Kevin: What's in a name. Shakespeare, bro.

Cortex: If you bring up any theater references in this, I'm banning you from all future chats.

8:29 P.M.
Kevin: I don't know, something about her seems off. Like from the videos you've shown, her laugh sounds super fake. And her smile ... she sort of squinches her eyes like she's wincing whenever you kiss.

8:30 P.M.
Cortex: Way to make me feel super insecure.

8:31 P.M.
Kevin: Sorry, man.

8:32 P.M.

Cortex: Whatever, if you wanted to ask about Sweet Tooth, PM me next week. I'm going to binge that new Netflix hero show.

8:33 P.M.

Kevin: Fine, I see you.

Kevin: But a certain blind superhero won't.

Kevin: :)

8:40 P.M.

Kevin: Cortex?

Private Message
July 1

10:04 A.M.
*Cortex changed Private Message name to Potential
Nemeses*

Cortex:

Listened to "Heathens" by Twenty-One Pilots today
on my early morning jog, and you popped into my
head.

Cortex: 10:06 A.M.

Soooo you got a favorite color? Please say orange.
Orange goes great on jumpsuits for prison you
know. It would make your red contacts pop.
Speaking of contacts, Juliet got new ones, green this
time. Saw it in a picture she took at her grandpa's
funeral. Haven't heard much from her lately. I think
she looks better with the blue ones, but whatever.

Cortex: 10:40 A.M.

Let me guess. Your favorite color is black.

Cortex: 11:03 A.M.

Seriously, how can you sleep in so late?

11:35 A.M.
V: Arggh dude how long will it take you to remember the time difference? It's only eight thirty here. And my favorite color is NOT black. It is purple.

11:36 A.M.
Cortex: Like my mask? Man, what is with people and purple?

11:37 A.M.
Cortex: Sorry about waking you up. Is there an ideal time to start messaging? Tell me in EST because I hate math. Lol.

V: You're Japanese. Shouldn't you be good at math?

11:38 A.M.
Cortex: Mmm I'm fine with you being a murderer and all, but maybe not a racist? Lol. My favorite subject is graphic design. It involves technology, so big shocker there.

Cortex: Did you know I'm not even using my fingers to type this. I'VE BEEN USING MY MIND. Gasp!

V: Just kidding. I'm glad you're not good at math. Too cliche. It is a little weird though since a lot of tech is math. Also, that seems like a waste of your powers to mind text.

11:39 A.M.
Cortex: You don't really need math skills to operate Photoshop. Like this photo I just sent with your face on a stingray. Cute, right?

> **V:** Is that from the picture I sent you of Mr. Flappers?

> **V:** I mean my scary albino stingray?

11:40 A.M.
Cortex: Mr. Flappers? Have you had him since you were six? And yes. I can whip out Photoshop projects in about thirty seconds. Pretty easy when you can control it with your mind.

> **V:** Who says I named him? Anyway, that's pretty neat. Why are you in the hero business? You could make lots of money at that.

11:41 A.M.
Cortex: Well, Bernie probably would name him something posh, so who else?

Cortex: Who says I can't work three jobs? In this stupid economy.

11:42 A.M.
Cortex: So do you still want to meet up for fun-spin-time-with-Mr.-I-need-to-stop-wearing-tights?

> **V:** Ha! Yeah, I guess. He's free kind of whenever. Calm before the storm of

drama camp next week. Which we're
signed up to help with, by the way.

11:43 A.M.
Cortex: .... you mean you're. As in you're. Not
we're.

V: Um... no. I mean we're.

Cortex: WHAT?

11:44 A.M.
Cortex: I didn't agree to this!!!!

Cortex: You mean I just spent the last
"choreography" session learning how to plie and
sway and anything else that ends in an ay and
sounds French for him to sign me up to help with
drama camp?

Cortex: How long have you known about this?

V: Wow, chill. I thought you were a
hero. Heroes love helping the kiddies.
Good publicity. This was the plan the
whole time, dude.

11:45 A.M.
Cortex: Do you not remember that I don't like
kids?

V: I hate them more than you do. But if
we both help, it only has to be for one
week, not two. And I wasn't doing two.

11:46 A.M.

Cortex: Sigh. OK, what are they going to have me do? I'm fine with running lights if that means talking to normal people. AKA taller than four feet people.

> **V:** Actually we're both counselors. He put us in a group together. Whoopie, right?

11:47 A.M.
Cortex: Wow. Worse than Kevin. The dude wanted me to get together with you and get your number and stuff. Bet he likes Nicholas Sparks movies, too. He's auditioning for Annie tonight.

> **V:** Gross!!! Ugh I hate Juliet less now.

11:48 A.M.
Cortex: That's good...I guess. Also, why are you now cool with us meeting up for choreography? Didn't you freak out the other day?

> **V:** I didn't freak out.

Cortex: Well, weren't you busy all of a sudden? And then you remembered you'd murdered someone and that kind of cancelled that excuse?

> **V:** Well... I just don't want to move too fast. My last nemesis and I were only together for a month. Then I killed her. I'd like to have a longer relationship this time before you die.

11:49 A.M.

Cortex: I mean, I get that. I guess we got to set up boundaries ... or whatever the heck my Catholic parents liked to call it when they gave me the talk in sixth grade.

Cortex: So what is off-limits?

> **V:** Basically, let's just put killing out of bounds. Probably maiming, too. It's not good for resume building if you can't keep a nemesis.

11:50 A.M.
Cortex: I'm down for surviving for a while longer.

Cortex: How about powers? When can we use those more? Give me like a month count.

> **V:** Um.

> 11:51 A.M.
> **V:** Well, your powers are weird. I don't really want to read your mind. And I'd rather you didn't read mine, either. So why don't we stick to just the technology stuff, and I can steal that from you.

11:52 A.M.
Cortex: Don't want to read my mind, eh? 'Fraid what you'll find? ;)

Cortex: I think that's fine. Are weapons even in the question now?

V: Absolutely. Just, if it gets too intense, we can back off. No killing or maiming, you know? But I really love my throwing knives.

11:53 A.M.
Cortex: How can you use them if you don't maim someone? Here's a pic of one of my last villain flings (just a two-fight thing back during my sophomore year). He had a throwing star, and check out what it did to my leg.

V: Oh, dude. Great pic. But you're just supposed to deflect them with your katana. We can practice with wiffle balls and bats if you want.

11:54 A.M.
Cortex: Sure, bring it to the next choreography sesh. Better that than spinning like whirling dervishes.

V: Cool. Mr. L can probably come up with a cool fight for us with them.

11:55 A.M.
Cortex: Let's leave a little room for improv. Some fights look sooooo fake.

V: Yeah, it's more fun that way.

Cortex: Noon tomorrow?

11:56 A.M.

V: Heck yeah. I'm looking forward to throwing things at you.

11:57 A.M.
Cortex: Your state or mine? ;)

V: Idiot. I'm not letting Mr. L ride a dragon. Peace! (Or violence. lol)

Potential Nemeses
July 2

Cortex: 9:03 P.M.

Wow. So you kill really violently ...

V:

Honestly it was a little gross. He started oozing sugar or gelatin or something when I ripped open his guts.

Cortex: 9:04 P.M.

Oh. My. Goodness. Please don't make me relive it. The stench is still stuck in my nose.

Cortex:

The only reason I didn't call the cops was because you saved my shoulder from getting hacked off by his glass-sharp hands.

Cortex:

And, because, I'm a hero and I don't call the police.

I save the day.

9:05 P.M.
V: Yeah, I don't call the police either lol. What did you do to make Sweet Tooth mad? He had the death look in his eye.

9:07 P.M.
Cortex: Brah, I don't even know what he was doing there. I planned to stake out a heist a couple days from now. And he lives in Indiana. All I know was I landed my helicopter near that bowling alley, I was just reaching in to get my bag with my tennis shoes, and the next thing I know, a flash of glass strikes against my cheek. Wanna see a picture of the scar? Oh, and thank Bernard for stitching up my face and all. Looks like a spider's sticking out of my cheek. Too bad he saw my face, though. I covered my eyes in the picture so you wouldn't have to.

V: Yes, send me lots of pics.

9:08 P.M.
Cortex: There, sent ten. Enough?

V: Wow, I love looking at ripped flesh. Very nice. Anyway, you totally had your guard down. I had to kill the dude.

9:09 P.M.
Cortex: Well, you didn't have to. You could've maimed him, but he probs would've gutted me by the time you did any actual damage.

Cortex: I loved how high Kevin screamed when he saw everything from his seat. So useless. The dude burns coffee, too. What an intern...can't blame him for being out of it. He's a bit shocked that the Annie auditions tanked.

Cortex: Remind me why you spared my life and all. Not that I'm grateful. But it's kind of embarrassing.

> 9:10 P.M.
> **V:** We had stuff to do. Hard to practice fighting when you're dead. And it's a pain looking for a new nemesis. I told you I didn't want you to die yet.

9:11 P.M.
Cortex: You could've practiced with Kevin ;)

Cortex: Well, thanks I guess. Sorry we didn't get to choreograph much afterwards. I kind of threw up all over your carpet since Sweet Tooth's razor sharp hand injected me with something poisonous and all.

> **V:** Nah it was fun watching you go all pale and puke-y. Very non-heroic. As if it was poisoned. You just don't like gore.

9:12 P.M.
Cortex: Did you not see the pic I sent the other day of my sliced up leg? Nice house, btw. Why do you work retail again?

Cortex: Also, cute eel. And Bernard definitely calls it a different name than you.

V: Isn't he precious!!! Oh, and yeah, I work retail same reason as you. Bernard says it's good for me. Mr. Squiggles is amazing. He could easily kill us all.

9:13 P.M.
Cortex: Aww, the things I read in this are straight out of a horror movie. My parents don't let us have pets. Mom's allergic to anything with hair ... even her own hair. That's why she's bald.

V: Omg hahaha

Cortex: Just kidding, she's in chemo.

V: Oh... I'm sorry.

9:14 P.M.
Cortex: Nah, it's fine. She's been battling it for five years. If anything, she's more of a hero than I am. She'd look terrible in spandex. Way too skinny at this point.

V: Cortex. I'm so sorry. I don't have a mom, but if that was happening to Bernard... Sorry, man. Just let me know if you ever need a day off or something.

9:15 P.M.
Cortex: Wow. Ummm are you okay? I think you've been replaced by something called compassion. It's scarier than all the other stuff you've said.

V: Ha. Nah. Just making you get too comfortable, you know? Let your guard down. That's all. Loser.

9:16 P.M.
Cortex: OK, whew that makes me feel a little better. Also, how many secret layers does your house have? I must've counted at least nine hidden passages.

V: Oh, dude, I don't even know. We should totally explore sometime. Or, at least, we would if I would ever let you come over again. Which I won't.

9:17 P.M.
Cortex: Great! So tomorrow it is. We needed a rain check on the choreography anyway. I still have my hands and legs, so I'll bring the katanas.

V: Okay, fine. Meet me at the bowling alley for a blindfold. You know you can't actually know where I live. Maybe I can show you the shark tank.

Cortex: So I can pitch some of my inventions? Great. It's a date.

9:18 P.M.
Cortex: I mean, get together. Thingy. You know what I mean.

V: I love that show! Mr. Wonderful is brutal. But, yeah, obviously not a date. Blech.

Cortex: Tomorrow then. Make sure the blindfold is purple.

V: I'll make it orange. Just for you.

11:18 P.M.
Cortex: You're probably not on at the moment, but I just realized why Sweet Tooth showed up today. Turns out, I sent part of a PM to him instead of you. That would probably explain why you were confused why I wore my cowboy boots when I showed up (info that was included in that message). Lol. My sister's, I mean; that's why they were pink. Definitely not showing you that chat for the reason why you saw them (dodged a bullet there... or throwing knives in your case), but I guess it makes sense now why he sprung up in the desert. Hopefully we won't mix our lives with other heroes/villains any more after that. At least, it won't be a problem if we do end up being matches ;) Ok, see you tomorrow!

12:08 A.M.
V: What the heck? Now I really want to know the tale of the pink boots. I guess I was too busy saving your life to notice your footwear.

Archived Message "Bittersweet": July 1

Sweet Tooth: 7:38 P.M.

yaeh, man. Broooke my keybaord with my galss hands. Btu I mihgt be able to figgghht earrlier than nexxt weke. Wan~na go sooner/=?

Cortex: 8:37 P.M.

Oh, one more thing, V. I know you don't like cowboy boots and all, but my sister stole my shoes for JAFAX, an anime convention in Michigan. Apparently her costume needed my purple boots more than I did. And she doesn't get back until late afternoon tomorrow (staying with a friend in Grand Rapids). To get back at her, I'll steal her favorite pair of shoes. Sparkly pink cowboy boots. And yes, we wear the same shoe size (she has big feet for our family... probably gets it from our white mom). So be prepared to lose to a guy in pink shoes tomorrow.

Cortex: 8:40 P.M.

Hey ... I know this may seem a little soon, but do you want to fight again sometime? I had so much fun the first time, even if we had no idea what we were doing. And think of how much better we'll be with these lessons (I keep picturing me decking you in the stomach as you pirouette). I don't say this to a lot of villains, but I think we have something special going. Like, punching you in the face comes so much easier. And we honestly would have talked for hours if the power didn't go out to the sound of smashed glass at Cuppa. I really feel like they matched us well.

Cortex: So, round two? ;)

8:41 P.M.
Cortex: You know what, don't tell me on here. I like my rejections in person. Even if you say no, I have plenty of other villains I can hash it out on Meta-Match. Forget I said anything.

8:42 P.M.
Cortex: I'll see you tomorrow. Also, you sure you don't want to try out Fiesta Lanes when we meet up at noon? It's also in Tucson. The bologna smell from Split Decision Lanes kind of spoils the fighting mood, you know?

9:03 P.M.
Sweet Tooth: Umnbmmm? Waht? You wanna fihgt tomorrrrow? Lemme chekc my schedle.

9:05 P.M.
Sweet Tooth: I"m feree tomorrow. See yuo then, punk. Be rrady to die@!

Archived Message "Bittersweet" reopened July 2

11:15 P.M.
Cortex: Crap.

Potential Nemeses
July 2

Cortex: 12:03 P.M.

V, I don't think I'm gonna come today. Juliet's acting all weird over text. Kinda worried about her.

V: 12:05 P.M.

I just woke up. What do you mean weird?

Cortex: 12:06 P.M.

Well, she usually sounds really peppy over text. But I know she has depression and stuff and she was really close with her grandpa. I just am going to visit her house and see if she's okay.

V:

That makes sense I guess. Besides. I could use a day without your annoying face.

Cortex: 12:07 P.M. Glad to see you're not heartbroken. I just don't want anything to happen to her, you know? I already lost my last gf and all.

> **V:** About that... what was her name?

12:08 P.M.
Cortex: Ummm why?

> **V:** I think I might have known her.

12:09 P.M.
Cortex: Really? Well, I guess she's dead and all so it doesn't really matter if you know. Name's Regan. Attached a pic. Beautiful right? Green hair and tan. Odd combo, but I dig it. Or dug it.

> **V:** Yeah. Um. About that. Pretty sure she was a villain named Stroke.

12:10 P.M.
Cortex: I'm going to pretend like you didn't say that.

12:11 P.M.
Cortex: Actually, no. Are you freaking kidding me? This girl I date for two years which my ex-villain Seizure stabbed twenty-three times (really bloody. Sent pics and everything. I couldn't recognize the body), is a villain. Seriously leave this chat if you don't apologize in five seconds.

> **V:** Twenty-three times? Like in Llamas with Hats? Dude, I know it's touchy, but I had a professional relationship with

her. She always bragged about how she had this hero going for two years. Just saying, maybe you should be careful with Juliet.

12:12 P.M.
Cortex: Ummm ever heard of evil twins? Because about ten of them on this site swiped right. Having a nice little chat with one now.

Cortex: And what the heck do you mean "be careful with Juliet?"

Cortex: And seriously? No apology?

12:13 P.M.
V: That girl seems sketch. Kind of fake-looking in the pictures. And with your track record...

12:14 P.M.
Cortex: Never did track. Wasn't allowed to.

Cortex: And you know what? I'm happy I'm not showing up to your house today. I might break the no-killing rule.

V: Well, sorry you have poor choice in women. Maybe I don't care if your girlfriend wants to kill you. Good riddance.

12:15 P.M.
Cortex: Well I'd rather she kill me than you. You're not even worth it.

Archived Message "Bittersweet": July 1

Archived Message "Bittersweet": July 1 reopened July 3

Cortex: 12:20 P.M

So, since you're dead and all Sweet Tooth, maybe this can help me out. No way in heck I'll talk to Kevin about this. I swear they stuffed the mind of a three year old into a pimply nineteen-year-old body.

Cortex: 12:21 P.M.

But I gotta talk to someone. No way I can go to Dad. And Mom ... Mom probably can't handle much at the moment.

Cortex: 12:22 P.M.

Sweet Tooth, I'm afraid of losing. People, I mean. Regan did seem a little sketch. There was that one time she showed up to my house with blood on her hands. Reminded me of when we read Macbeth in AP Lit that one time. And she said it was paint. But paint isn't sticky and doesn't smell like blood, you know?

Cortex: 12:23 P.M.

The last thing I said to V was harsh.

12:24 P.M.
Cortex: I should apologize, shouldn't I? I mean, I could lose the only good villain I got a thing going with on this stupid site. All the others are looking to tase you with a beam once and that's it.

Cortex: But she's good at fighting, you know? Like, she's a fighter. And not just in the nutcracker choke kind of way. You can tell she's seen some dark stuff but is still fighting.

Cortex: Juliet's not much of a fighter.

12:25 P.M.
Cortex: I mean, because it's just you and me (and really just me) I guess it doesn't hurt to use real names, huh?

Cortex changed name to Caleb.

12:26 P.M.
Caleb: Listen, I'm going to head to Juliet's house (I mean Tamora's; I can use her real name in here, too). I'll keep you updated.

2:04 P.M.
Caleb: Remind me never to talk to girls.

2:05 P.M.

Caleb: And remind me that your nose hurts when they slam a door against it. Seriously, must've made the thing out of mahogany.

2:07 P.M.
Caleb: I don't know what happened, Sweetie (can I call you that?). We were curled up on the couch, her snot running all over my Chamber 5K t-shirt. She told me all about how she and gpa were really close and how she saw him as this great role model. And how life goes so quickly and she wanted to end it all and stuff like that (she says this sort of stuff a lot).

Caleb: So I told her she had to fight.

2:08 P.M.
Caleb: I said her grandpa would want her to keep going and be strong and keep fighting for him.

2:09 P.M.
Caleb: It was going great. She looks at me with this puffy face, eyes bloodshot from crying with green contacts in. She kind of slurs in a really thick drunkish voice, "You really think so?" Her lips kind of quivered, and I wanted to kiss them. So I did. They tasted salty. Because, you know, tears. She kind of frowned, licked her lips, and replied, "How do you keep fighting when the thing you loved most dies?"

Caleb: And I said, "Well, take my new nemesis (fingers crossed that we'll make it official soon) for instance. V had lots of tragedy happen in her life with her parents dying early on and—"

2:10 P.M.

Caleb: Next thing I know, she shoves me off the couch and out the door and shuts it before I can get through the sentence.

2:11 P.M.
Caleb: Girls are weird.

2:12 P.M.
Caleb: Be happy you were incredibly ugly. You never had to deal with them.

Private Message:
July 2

Bernard VII: 12:39 P.M.

Miss Victoria, when is young Cortex arriving?

Victoria:

He's not.

Bernard VII:

Has something occurred?

Victoria: 12:40 P.M.

We kind of got in a fight. Like, a word fight. Not a battle.

Bernard VII:

Miss Victoria. What has transpired?

Victoria:

He started talking about his ex-girlfriend, and I told him she was a villain (not the other stuff though) and he got all mad. So much for being helpful.

12:41 P.M.

Bernard VII: Pardon me, but knowing you, Miss Victoria, I doubt your phrasing appeared... helpful.

> **Victoria:** Ugh. I guess. I mean, it sucks that she died from his perspective. I guess I should apologize. But villains don't apologize.

12:42 P.M.

Bernard VII: Villains who wish to keep their nemesis may have to.

Private Message
July 3

Kevin: 4:18 P.M.

So, boss, can I get you anything? A cup of watery Keurig coffee? A new villain to fight, perhaps, since V killed Sweet Tooth?

Cortex: 4:19 P.M.

You're literally in the other room Kevin. I let you stay in our house as part of your internship.

Kevin:

Riiiiiiiight, but the University says I need to get a number of hours in for this semester, and I can't get you cups of coffee for literally 160 hours straight. I already burned my hand on the last batch.

Cortex: 4:20 P.M.

Wanna trade with my scarred up face?

Kevin: 4:21 P.M.

I mean, V might think it's HAWT.

Cortex: OK, you're officially banned from using that word.

4:22 P.M.
Cortex: And please turn off that god-awful music you have going in the study. You're disrupting the feng shui.

Cortex: Oh. My. Gosh. Is that the Annie Soundtrack? Turn. It. Off. You didn't make that play. Get over it.

4:23 P.M.
Kevin: It's the Hard Knock Life.

4:24 P.M.
Cortex: I will throw your phone out the window. Wait a minute. I can control technology.

Kevin: Hey!

Cortex: There. I've disabled access to your music.

4:25 P.M.
Kevin: Wow. You're more villainous than V.

Cortex: Take it back. And I don't want to talk about her.

4:26 P.M.
Kevin: Oooooooooh Cortex is in looooooooove

Cortex: What are you? A middle schooler? The only reason I haven't fired you yet is because V hates you more than me. So that lowers my risk of mortality.

Kevin: Glad to know my college degree made me useful.

4:27 P.M.
Kevin: So why you no want to talk about the lovely psychopathic lady?

Cortex: Kevin, I swear, stop singing the songs from Annie. I can control minds too, you know.

Kevin: No, you only read minds. *Pushes up nerd glasses* I know my comics!

4:28 P.M.
Cortex: If you stop singing, I'll tell you why I'm mad at her.

4:29 P.M.
Kevin: Broadway will have to wait. What's up?

Cortex: She said my last girlfriend was a villain who went by the name of Stroke.

4:30 P.M.
Kevin: Ah, Stroke! Cute chick. She had the nice green hair and skin tanner than Florida.

Kevin: Yeah, too bad she died and all.

> 4:31 P.M.
> **Cortex:** Ummm what?

Kevin: Earth to Cortex. Have you ever visited a comic book store? You have one about five minutes from your house.

> **Cortex:** Did you say green hair?

Kevin: Seriously just Google Stroke.

> 4:32 P.M.
> **Cortex:** All I'm getting is the seven warning signs you're about to have one.

4:33 P.M.
Kevin: *Sigh* Google: Stroke, Villain.

4:40 P.M.
Kevin: Well?

> 4:41 P.M.
> **Cortex:** Crap.

4:42 P.M.
Kevin: Duuuuuuude, you have terrible taste in women.

> **Cortex:** I should apologize. I'll hop into that chat and see if she hasn't deleted me yet.

Potential Nemeses
July 3

V: 4:42 P.M.

Hey, Cortex... I was talking to Bernard. I guess I was a little harsh. Losing people is hard, even when they are villains. I should know. My parents were supervillains. You might have heard of them. Dustdevil and Firewhirl. Super sucked when they died. I was only ten, though, so...

V:

Anyway... I guess I'm trying to apologize.

Cortex: 4:43 P.M.

Oh, gosh, V ... I was hopping in here to say sorry, too.

Cortex:

I, uh, Googled Stroke. I guess you were right.

Cortex:

There are more than 200,000 cases of

it diagnosed each year...and I guess one of those cases happens to be a psychopath who implants clots into the brains of all her enemies until they die. If it's any consolation, she was a terrible kisser.

4:44 P.M.
V: Wow. What have I said about telling me about your romantic details?

4:45 P.M.
Cortex: I mean, she was even worse than my first kiss. Super wet. Wetter than a burrito. Probably worse than your first one, too.

V: That's a disgusting description. As if I've ever kissed a dude. Gross. Too evil for that.

4:46 P.M.
Cortex: Well, fine, your first kiss with a girl, then.

V: Just because I've never kissed a dude doesn't mean I'm a lesbian, smartypants. Some people just don't kiss everyone they see.

Cortex: I don't do that. No way in heck I'm smooching Bernard. His wrinkles have wrinkles.

4:47 P.M.
V: Ha! Dork.

4:48 P.M.

Cortex: So are we cool? Can we go back to being enemies again and all that? This is my first word fight with a villain.

V: Yeah, me too. They usually die first... but, yeah. We're cool.

4:49 P.M.

Cortex: Hang on a sec, Juliet is calling me. But I wanted to ask you something, so remind me in like ten minutes to hop back on.

V: Okay. Tell her hi from me. She's probably not a villain. I just got worked up.

Cortex: Will do!

5:00 P.M.
V: So... what did you want to ask?

5:05 P.M.
Cortex: ...

Cortex: How soon can you find a different hero to fight? I'm done.

V: What? I thought you said we were cool.

5:06 P.M.
Cortex: Yeah, well, Juliet just called and broke up with me. And when I

asked her why, she said I talked about you too much. She thinks I can do better and to call her up when I've found a different villain.

5:07 P.M.
Cortex: Do anything in particular to piss her off?

V: Freaking exist, I guess. I take back everything nice I said about her. You're really going to dump me to impress her? What kind of nemesis are you?

5:08 P.M.
Cortex: I'm not buying it. She seemed like she knew you or something from before. What did you do? Kidnap her? Kill her family? Force her to listen to Broadway showtunes? All you villains are the same.

V: What! What is wrong with you heroes? Villains literally don't have time to be evil to everyone. Besides, she's not worth my time.

5:09 P.M.
Cortex: Then, you're not worth mine.

V: Fine. Want to know my body count? Thirty-eight. I have heroes lined up to fight me. Better heroes than you.

5:10 P.M.
Cortex: Let me take a guess, some of her family members are a part of that

body count. They were very vague about how her grandpa died. It happened suddenly. Unexpectedly. Care to explain?

V: I have no freaking idea who her grandpa is. I don't even know her real name, remember?

Cortex: Fine. I got at least ten other villains I'm PMing. I've been spending most of my energy in this one, but I might as well give those others a try.

V: Good riddance. You're too much work, anyway.

5:11 P.M.
Cortex: I hate you.

Private Message
July 3

Cortex: 5:14 P.M.

Hey, Insanity. Sorry I haven't messaged in a while (I saw you swiped right about five days ago). I've been a little busy, but my schedule just opened wider than most people's minds, so wanna meet up and have a go? Not to brag or anything, but I have learned a couple new moves from a choreographer.

Cortex: 5:16 P.M.

I also noticed your photo looks stark white. Reminds me of Indiana's winters. The wind blows so hard, it turns your lips a hypothermic blue. You from someplace cold?

Insanity: 5:18 P.M.

harotua E[0ta 0nt2 9unre tiio g u ag i[ag yu a iopa yioewr iopr ioaw io hsdf iag iopg

Cortex:

Ummmm, did something happen to your keyboard?

Insanity: grjir tqor ey 93 m9-=5 3 0-y5 -jkkt hu u3u9t urhg gopt iot hi ertui !

5:19 P.M.
Cortex: Maybe you fell asleep on it?

Insanity: :)

5:20 P.M.
Cortex: Oh... that's a very, umm, interesting picture of your last victim.

Cortex: Very, ummm, Silence of the Lambs-esque. Ummm. Not really sure how to respond to that.

Insanity: wt akht io gfjkl j

5:21 P.M.
Cortex: Right, so. You want to meet up? We can just share Google maps of places we can fly to (I'm guessing there's a language barrier).

Insanity: I speak English just fine; here's where I'd like you to land your vehicle.

5:22 P.M.
Cortex: Insanity, you just sent me map of a red dot in the middle of the ocean.

Insanity:heeehehehehehehheeheheh ehehehheehhehehehehehehehhehehee e

Insanity: Why is a writing desk like a mad hatter? Quoth the Raven, I'm just a poe boy from a poe family, bismillah!

5:23 P.M.
Cortex: ...

Cortex: All right, I suppose we can do a couple get to know yous before picking a location. Do you have any powers?

5:24 P.M.
Cortex: Insanity.

5:25 P.M.
Cortex: Insanity, I swear, if you send me one more cat photo, I will report you. You've sent the same one 1,000 times in the past three minutes.

Insanity: heeehehehehehehehheeee

5:26 P.M.
Cortex: OK, Insanity. You know what that trash icon by your profile pic does?

Insanity: No, what?

Insanity: Oh.

Insanity: :(

Insanity:hehehehehehehehehheheh hehehehehehehehehehehehe

Private Message
July 3

Victoria: 5:20 P.M.

Bernard? Where are you? I've looked all over the house.

Bernard VII: 5:23 P.M.

Pardon me, Miss Victoria. I'm out for tea with one of my colleagues. Am I needed at home?

Victoria:

No, I'm okay. Cortex broke it off with me.

Bernard VII: 5:24 P.M.

I was under the impression you intended to apologize to him.

Victoria:

I did apologize, and so did he, and we were good, but then his stupid girlfriend broke up with him because she doesn't want him fighting me. She says he talks about me too much. So he broke it off with me! How stupid is that? Why does she even care? She doesn't know me!

5:25 P.M.
Bernard VII: Perhaps she is jealous.

Victoria: Jealous? Of what? We're literally enemies.

Bernard VII: He talks about you, and you spend a good deal of time together.

Victoria: Ugh. I hate this girl. Anyway, Cortex sucks. I'm going to start looking for a new hero.

5:26 P.M.
Bernard VII: That is unfortunate. I thought you two were a good match. Best of luck, Miss Victoria.

Private Message
July 3

Cortex: 5:30 P.M.

Hey, Gloom. I see you made Sadness from Inside Out your profile pic, but I have a feeling that you don't look much like that (because... it's an animated cartoon). You got blue hair and square glasses and a rain cloud above your head like her?

Cortex: 5:31 P.M.

Oh. You do.

Cortex:

Now that I'm looking at your pic, I realize it's actually a photo of you. Even looks a bit different than the character. For instance, you have purple hair and purple glasses (I dig purple, btw.). Just looks kind of cartoonish in the small corner of my screen. Had to enlarge it.

Cortex: 5:32 P.M.

Anyway, wondering if you wanted to get acquainted and maybe throw a punch here or there.

5:33 P.M.
Gloom: I meant to swipe left.

Cortex: Oh, well. Happy accidents, I guess. Still want to get to know each other?

Gloom: :(

5:34 P.M.
Cortex: You sad? Something bad happen today?

Gloom: I don't know if I want to fight :(

Cortex: What? Why not? Had to block a couple villains because they wanted to fight nonstop.

Gloom: :(

5:35 P.M.
Cortex: Gloom, that doesn't answer my question.

Gloom: I'm just, you know, thinking about my backstory, and it makes me feel like someone filled my veins with lead. I just don't feel much like tossing a hero into a bunch of spiked grinding gears when I think about my difficult past.

Cortex: Why don't you tell me about it? I hear monologuing helps.

5:36 P.M.
Gloom: :(

Cortex: :)

5:37 P.M.
Gloom: All right. Even my henchmen won't listen to me, so worth talking about it, I suppose. Sigh. :(

5:40 P.M.
Gloom: So there was this play I really wanted to try out for during high school.

Cortex: It already sounds like a depressing story.

Gloom: :(

Cortex: Sorry. Go on.

5:41 P.M.
Gloom: For the show, Much Ado About Nothing, I really desired the part of Hero. We had read the script in English class, and she sort of spoke to me.

Cortex: Shakespeare. Tragedy. Got it.

Gloom: So I auditioned. And they cast Sarah Hinklestaub instead.

5:45 P.M.
Cortex: ... and?

Gloom: And, Sarah Hinklestaub couldn't do a British accent to save her life, even if Benedict Cumberbatch himself brewed her breakfast tea.

Gloom: Didn't even look British with her ripped jeans and pixie cut and Winter Noelle scented lotion. Everyone knows the classic British winter scent is wassail.

5:46 P.M.
Cortex: I mean, what else happened?

5:47 P.M.
Gloom: What do you imply? :(

5:48 P.M.
Cortex: Like, did your parents die? Did you have a brother or sister who outshone you in anything you tried? Did someone steal the love of your life from you and date them instead of you?

Gloom: No! :(

5:49 P.M.
Cortex: ... ummm

Cortex: How long ago was high school for you?

Gloom: Ten years ago, why?

5:50 P.M.
Cortex: So that's it? That's your whole backstory? You tried out for one play and didn't make it. You're forever stuck in something minor that happened ten years ago. Even those who went to watch that

performance probably forgot who played Hero. Ugh. Remind me never to attend class reunions if they're mostly made up of people like you.

5:51 P.M.
Gloom: I don't want to talk to you anymore. :(

Private Message
July 3

Vortex: 5:35 P.M.

Hey, Great Guy. Heard a little about you. What's your power?

Great Guy: 5:40 P.M.

Well, babe, I'm just naturally great. At everything. *dazzling smile*

Vortex:

Okayyy... Um, how do you like to fight?

Great Guy:

Well, I'm just a great guy, you know? The sort of guy you want to bring home to your parents. I win people over until they don't even want to fight me.

Great Guy: 5:41 P.M.

Vortex?

Great Guy: 5:43 P.M.

Um... Vortex?

Private Message
July 3

Cortex: 5:54 P.M.

What's up, Shadow Sabre? Huge fan. I follow all your Instagram posts. Thanks for swiping right, bro. You down for a foiled scheme or two?

Shadow: 6:03 P.M.

Sorry, Cortex. I have about twenty heroes I'm juggling at the moment.

Cortex: 6:04 P.M.

Oh, did I come too late? I know you swiped right a handful of days ago. To be honest, I was having a bit of a fling with one of the other villains on this site, but we broke it off, so can you put me down on the waiting list or something?

Cortex: 6:05 P.M.

Seriously, your YouTube videos of you manipulating shadows are sick. I don't know who does your videography, but it looks professional. Who knew silhouettes can look so cool against a brick building?

6:20 P.M.
Shadow: ... sorry if this is awkward, but you looked like another hero I knew.

Shadow: Dimension. You guys got the same purple mask. Otherwise, I would've slid my thumb left if I had known.

Cortex: Oh.

Shadow: Yeah. Sorry about that. I love to help little heroes out, but have to do most of my hashes with heroes with significantly larger followings, you know what I mean? Platform building is a hassle.

6:25 P.M.
Shadow: I did see one of your photos on your profile slideshow with you posing next to Dimension in a fancy house. Do you know him? Been trying to get a hold of him.

Cortex: He retired.

Private Message
July 3

Vortex: 5:50 P.M.

Saw that you swiped right a few weeks ago. Still looking for a villain?

Aquagirl:

Blub blub.

Vortex: 5:51 P.M.

Um, translation?

Aquagirl:

Squeee swish blubble

Vortex:

For evil's sake. Ugh.

Aquagirl: 5:55 P.M.

Blurgle gurgle?

Private Message
July 3

Vortex: 6:05 P.M.

Hey, Superman. I hear you got rid of Lex... and the alien guys. And literally everyone. You looking for someone else?

Vortex: 6:13 P.M.

I'm a relatively young villain, but I've had a winning streak... well, my entire career. I kill people pretty quickly. I know you like to fight hard. Maybe we could spar sometime? You know, you can practice, I can boost my resume. I know you go through villains fast. Must be why you're on Meta-Match.

Vortex: 6:15 P.M.

Oh. This is a sample profile. I guess that makes sense. You don't exist in our universe.

Vortex:

Got it. Well, it was fun thinking you were real for about fifteen minutes. Copyright, I guess.

6:16 P.M.
Vortex: Nice talking to you.

6:17 P.M.
Vortex: Gosh dang it all.

Private Message
July 3

Cortex: 6:26 P.M.

Well, well, well, look who swiped right. Somebody put on weight and lost all their arm muscle. Also, hate the haircut. What happened? Did a mullet marry an afro?

Seizure:

Yeah, well, if we're messaging on this thing, that means you also swiped right. The only other way you could PM me was if you decided to be a sidekick or henchman. And even you wouldn't stoop that low (even as short as you are).

Cortex: 6:27 P.M.

What brought you to Meta-Match? Got bored with that girl you picked up and dumped me for?

Seizure:

Just weighing my options.

Cortex:
Is she at least good looking? You never sent any pics.

> 6:28 P.M.
> **Seizure:** That's because I deleted your number. And it's been six months since we last fought, so I don't want to get chummy yet.

6:29 P.M.
Cortex: Seiz, what are you doing on Meta-Match? We had a good thing going. Tell me, have you met any heroes that fought you as hard as I did?

> 6:30 P.M.
> **Seizure:** Not my fault you flipped out when your girlfriend died.

Cortex: Regan? Yeah, well, newsflash, you screwed yourself over, man. She was a villain. Yes, you killed a villain called Stroke. Google it.

> **Seizure:** Whatever, Cort.

6:31 P.M.
Cortex: And also you got really sloppy with her murder. Seriously? Twenty-three stab wounds? You're usually a lot more clever than that. Aren't you the one who can control people's bodies against their will? Why use a knife at all?

> 6:32 P.M.
> **Seizure:** What are you doing?

6:33 P.M.
Cortex: Come on, man. If you joined Meta-Match, you obviously need a new nemesis. Why not give us another go? I even learned to punch better. See the pic I just sent?

> 6:34 P.M.
> **Seizure:** That's you kissing a girl who clearly bleached her hair blonde.

Cortex: Oh, clicked the wrong one. Sorry. Here's the one. Ignore the girl with the dark hair and red eyes in the corner. She made her henchman take the photo when the choreographer showed me how to punch.

> **Seizure:** You have horrendous taste in women.

6:35 P.M.
Cortex: Thanks? Both are out of the picture. Tamora broke up with me, and I no longer fight with V.

> 6:36 P.M.
> **Seizure:** Tamora?

Cortex: I usually call her Juliet in these PMs. Code names you know? And Juliet is a romantic name and all.

> **Seizure:** Ugh, that makes me want to vomit.

6:37 P.M.
Cortex: Good. Want to do it after I shove my foot into your abdomen?

> **Seizure:** Cort ... I don't know if I want to face you again for a while. Got plenty of heroes to distract myself at the moment. One can manipulate time. So I can fight her over and over again and get my fill.

6:38 P.M.
Cortex: Oh. Ok. Let me know if you change that mind of yours in your stupid dented head.

> **Seizure:** Not my fault you hit the middle of my skull with a hammer.

> 6:39 P.M.
> **Seizure:** Cute chick, by the way.

Cortex: Tamora. She's free, bro. Dumped me the other day. Don't really think villains are her type, though :)

> **Seizure:** I didn't mean her.

Potential Nemeses
July 4

Cortex: 11:04 A.M.

Happy Independence Day ...

Cortex: 11:34 A.M.

Nothing like good ol' independence.

Cortex: 12:04 P.M.

Freedom. What a word. Some people truly take it for granted. I'll send a pic of the American flag in case you forgot what it looked like.

Cortex: 12:34 P.M.

Independence and freedom. What a pair. Like villains and heroes. Oreos and literally everything else. Peanut butter and nutella.

V: 12:36 P.M.

Are you freaking kidding me. We broke up and you're still going to wake me up in the morning?

Cortex: Whoa "broke up"? Dude, were we ever together? It was one fight.

Cortex: Speaking of freedom, I uh might need your help with something *winces*

> **V:** Change one letter in "help" and that's where you can go.

12:37 P.M.
Cortex: I'm not sure Yelp is going to help me get back my ex girlfriend who was just kidnapped by my ex-nemesis. Lot of exes in there.

> **V:** That sucks. Loser. Bye.

12:38 P.M.
Cortex: OK, listen, you're obviously not the first person I wanted to go to. I tried to see if Kevin could figure out some clues for Seizure's whereabouts when I got to Juliet's house and found he left one of his syringes behind (but Kevin is freaking useless; has a hard time boiling water). It's imprinted with a golden S. Clearly drugged her and took her to wherever the heck he's staying now.

> 12:39 P.M.
> **V:** So... let me get this straight. You want me to help you get back the girl who told me you needed to dump me.

12:40 P.M.
Cortex: Maybe.

Cortex: But it's more complicated than that. I can't track him down. He doesn't use Meta-Match at home, so even if I use my powers to track the computer, he could be at some town library for all I know. I can get the town, but he sort of is in a big city... it's called Muncie. No way I can find him with just a syringe and nothing else to go off of.

12:41 P.M.
V: Big city? You're obviously from rural Indiana. It's basically a town. Anyway, I've been to his place a couple years back. Big party. But you need to give me a reason to help you.

12:42 P.M.
Cortex: Anything in particular you want besides a coroner for me?

V: Your dad's a big shot. Does he have any hero connections? Resume builders?

12:43 P.M.
Cortex: Oh, goodness, too many to list. I'll just start with some big ones I guess...

Cortex: Basically anyone you've seen in a recent superhero movie if a villain didn't get to them first ...

Cortex: Anyone but villains. We have a, what my dad likes to call, dearth.

12:44 P.M.

V: (What the heck is a dearth?) Does he know Hypnotica?

Cortex: She's B-list, so I imagine so. I think they met at a writer's conference in Upland once.

12:45 P.M.
Cortex: Like, dude. All I need's an address. But if you want me to help set up a fight with her, I guess that's fine. It feels weird setting up a fighting date with someone else.

V: She's a good one for me. Not too big, but big enough. Okay. I'll send you a pic of the address.

12:46 P.M.
Cortex: Dang that looks fortified. Even if I deactivated any electric barriers, no way I can sneak past the guards at the front, and who knows what else I have to deal with inside. Nice bush cut into the shape of an otter though. Cute touch.

V: Yeah, he's got some pretty cool booby traps. Showed them all to me. Good luck.

12:47 P.M.
Cortex: Wanna hint at some, and I'll let you duke it out with some strong bois in the Sun Devil Stadium?

V: I have a big ego, but not that big. I don't want to die. But I mean, if you're going to go in there...

Cortex: Cat caught your keyboard or something? You gonna give me some tips or not?

> 12:48 P.M.
> **V:** I was trying to type it out, but it was too long. I'd literally have to go with you.

Cortex: Oh.

Cortex: And obviously you wouldn't want to. Maybe I can try seeing if Kevin has any more ideas. I kind of liked his most recent one: show up in fish costumes and pretend to be a part of his shark tank.

> 12:49 P.M.
> **V:** Oh gosh. Fine. I'll come. Obviously you're incompetent without me.

> **V:** But we're going to need help. Know any techies?

12:50 P.M.
Cortex: BESIDES me you mean?

> 12:51 P.M.
> **V:** Seizure has his place you-proof. You were nemeses, remember? You can't do that stuff inside.

Cortex: No... you mean he pulled the freaking Granite Maneuver again? Seriously? That stuff's expensive.

V: I can't believe granite is your weakness. That's so lame.

12:52 P.M.
Cortex: *Eye roll* It's not a weakness. It just so happens to be the fact that if you cover any piece of technology or, I guess in this instance, a whole freaking house, that means I cannot penetrate it. But no, I don't get an allergic reaction around countertops.

V: Okay, sure. Whatever you want to call it. But someone else will have to hack his system to give us directions. The halls change, you know? I already have headsets. Killed an IT guy.

12:53 P.M.
Cortex: Of course you did. And what is this? Harry Potter? Do the staircases move, too?

V: He likes that series.

12:54 P.M.
Cortex: Yeah, laughed a lot during the seventh book. He's really a villain. Anyways, so you'll find a hacker. Do we need anyone else? Shall we bring the whole Scooby Doo gang while we're at it?

V: Let's just make a group chat with Bernard, Kevin, and this hacker I know, Juan.

Cortex: Fine, I'll set it up.

Super Secret Squad
July 4, 12:58 P.M.

Cortex added V.

Cortex added Kevin.

V added Juan.

V added Bernard.

Kevin:

What's the secret? I'm not very good at keeping them.

V:

What's NOT a secret is that Cortex is stupid. Honestly? Awful name.

12:59 P.M.
Cortex:

I'm sorry. Kevin's the intern. He's supposed to be coming up with the group names while the rest of us do the real work.

Kevin:

I'm not even offended. Haven't done real work since third grade.

Juan changed his name to Some Juan.

1:00 P.M.
V: Makes more sense, now. Great name, Juan.

> **Some Juan:** Had to make the joke before someone else did.

Kevin: Nah, I'm not that clever.

> **V:** We know.

1:01 P.M.
Cortex: OK, Kevin, you're limited to talking once every ten minutes because literally nothing you say is productive. All right, gang. Everyone here?

> **Bernard:** Present.

Kevin: No.

> **Cortex:** Kevin! Fine, your time starts now.

> 1:02 P.M.
> **Cortex:** All right. What's the plan? Has Juan been filled in about the situation?

Some Juan: Yeah, I'm all bueno. Looked over your and V's texts. Surprised you're not proclaiming your *amor* yet.

> **Cortex:** Yeah, Juan, I took Mandarin Chinese in high school, so unless you

say words like taco or amigo, I will not comprendo.

Some Juan: Mandarin it is. Surprised you haven't proclaimed your *ai*.

V: Juan knows ten languages.

1:03 P.M.
Cortex: Of course he does. Does he also know how to get us into Seizure's house? Like today?

Some Juan: *Oes.* (Northern Welsh.)

Bernard: I shall fly Miss Vortex to Indiana and meet you in Muncie.

Some Juan: Then I'll give you instructions through your headsets. V knows the basic booby-traps, but I'll tell you which way to go in the changing halls. And disable the security system.

1:04 P.M.
Cortex: Anyone have an idea what day/time would be best? Also, my neighbors just lit a bunch of firecrackers and some dogs are going berserk.

V: Thanks for that irrelevant information. I thought we were literally doing this now. Cause, you know, kidnapping is kind of important?

Cortex: Agreed. But you have to realize I've fought this dude a long time. If we want to pick a time best to stop by his house, we need a day when he's not there (he can literally control your actions if he sees you). Maybe a day he's fighting another hero on Meta-Match. He's been searching around, you know.

> **Some Juan**: I can hack his security cameras and let you know when he leaves. But you'll have to be ready at a moment's notice.

1:05 P.M.
Cortex: I could stay at Kevin's frat house at Ball State. Some dudes live there in the summer right?

Cortex: Kevin. Come on.

Cortex: Fine. Your ten minute rule is over.

> 1:06 P.M.
> **Kevin:** Yeah, know a guy or two who can give us a place to stay until we break into the house and stuff.

V: Yeah, I'm NOT staying in a frat house, so Bernard will get us there in fifteen minutes when it's time. Dragon perks.

> 1:07 P.M.
> **Cortex:** Uh huh. So while V's stranded in Arizona with the delusion that Bernard is a dragon, I guess I'll be listening to you, Juan, for your signals. Let's hope I survive without her there.

1:08 P.M.

Some Juan: He's actually a dragon, hermano.

> **Cortex:** Didn't catch that last word. Was it psych?

Some Juan: ...

Some Juan: Gringos. Y Americanos.

> 1:09 P.M.
> **Kevin:** I know, right?

Some Juan: Gracias, Kevin. No eres que estupido si ellos dicen.

> **Kevin:** DONDE ESTA EL BANO?

Some Juan: Eres un idiota.

> 1:10 P.M.
> **Cortex:** Agreed Juan (saw idiot and assumed you meant Kevin). Now, are we all set folks? Anything else to figure out before I pack my duffel with mine and Kevin's stuff, since Kevin travels with all his stuff in grocery bags?

V: Classy. Nah, I think we're good.

> 1:12 P.M.
> **Cortex:** We'll message you guys when we get to the frat house. Should be about a 35-minute drive away.

V: K. Don't die. Or do. Don't really care.

1:13 P.M.
Kevin: I'll try my best to stay alive for you, sweet thang. :)

Bernard: Do not force me to incinerate you, young man.

Potential Nemeses
July 4

Cortex: 2:04 P.M.

Lol. Bernard, I saw your text after I dropped my stuff off. If you really are a dragon, dude, please roast my friend. And all of his friends. This place smells like socks.

V:

So Kevin is your friend now? Awwww. And you're so dumb. Bernard is a dragon. And this is the PM.

Cortex: 2:05 P.M.

Oh. Whoops. See when you mind-type sometimes you open the wrong message. Like a glitch in my system.

Cortex:

This isn't the first time it's happened. You remember when I said the thing about Sweet Tooth and me accidentally telling him about the pink boots? Oh. God. One of the frat guys is wearing something similar, and absolutely nothing else.

V: I am so glad Bernard is a dragon and I don't have to stay there. You probably like it, though. Party scene.

2:06 P.M.
Cortex: Actually, no. I'm a bit more of a introvert. Parties really aren't (as Kevin would say) "ma thang." My dad's had so many of them that they're actually really boring to me now.

V: For the love of all that's evil, never quote Kevin.

Cortex: See, I'm at a conflict here because if I quote him, that will make you more mad, and then things could be sort of like they were before all the stupid stuff that went down before.

2:07 P.M.
Cortex: Oh, dang. Was that yesterday? Feels like a month ago.

V: Yeah, no, feels like yesterday. You know. When you dumped me.

2:08 P.M.
Cortex: Maybe it's because I haven't fought a lot of villains long-term, but I'm not used to this terminology. Do people always say "dumped?" Movies make it seem like the villains are a bit more casual about picking up heroes here and there.

V: I don't know the correct "terminology." You're the first one I haven't killed yet.

2:09 P.M.

Cortex: OK, well then maybe we can create some terms. For example:

Cortex changed PM name to Can We Still Be Enemies?

> **V:** I thought you didn't want to be enemies anymore. You ended this, not me.

2:10 P.M.

Cortex: Oh, right. Sorry, don't have a lot of girlfriends. Guys usually knock each other's teeth out one day and then smile at each other (with gaps in their mouths) the next.

> **V:** Um... You do have a lot of girlfriends. Player.

Cortex: Not like that. Besides dating them, I don't hang out with them a lot. But I can see why you're mad. So, I'm sorry. I overreacted.

> 2:11 P.M.
> **V:** I mean, I guess I still hate you. I might be able to kill you still.

Cortex: Ah, beer pong is alive and well in the summer. I hope Juan messages soon. Don't know if I can stay the night in this place. Even the hardwood floors are sticky.

> **V:** I don't think that's actual hardwood.

2:12 P.M.
Cortex: Yeah, Kevin's told me plenty about college, and from what I've heard, I want to take like five gap years before undergoing that torture. You signed up for classes in the fall, too?

V: Yeah. What are you majoring in? Graphic design?

Cortex: Undecided. But that sounds like a plan. Problem is most heroes... well. They do heroing. But like, what do they do afterwards? Sure, Great Guy's got a gig at a newspaper. But most, like NBA players, get crazy depressed when they hit their fifties.

V: Yeah. I'm just going to Pima Community College for now. Get my gen-eds out of the way.

2:13 P.M.
Cortex: Gonna major in criminal law? Lol.

V: Nah, maybe political science. That's where the real villainy is.

2:14 P.M.
Cortex: Yeah, that or theater. Gotta work on your monologues.

V: Can't stand theater. You have to just *pretend* to kill people.

Cortex: I mean, you do have the last performance! Then, you don't have to deal with those cast members after that. Oh goodness. Sometimes I think like a villain. Definitely have thought of about sixty ways to kill Kevin.

2:15 P.M.
V: Wow. Ever thought of turning to the dark side? We have cookies. Legit. We have like, the evil Girl Scouts.

Cortex: I'm gluten free. Also R.I.P. Boy Scouts.

V: I think they just came out with gluten free. But the real villainy is that a tiny box is five freaking dollars now.

Cortex: Wow. The madness.

2:16 P.M.
Cortex: Oh, I think Juan's messaging us. Should we pull up the group text?

V: Yeah. But, um, one last thought. Are we, like, nemeses now? Or at least, back to where we were?

2:17 P.M.
Cortex: Oh, right. Yeah, we didn't really use much of a label. Do you, um, like, want to call us that now? Or do you still want to take things slower?

V: Ummm... what are you thinking?

Cortex: I'm thinking if Kevin loses one more round of beer pong, I'm the designated driver.

V: I can't believe they've got beer pong going at two in the afternoon. So are you capable of saying anything serious?

2:18 P.M.
Cortex: V, I'm fine with it if you are. I think we pair well together. We can still take things slowly. Like, don't kill me right away until we've rescued Juliet and all.

V: Sounds fair. Gosh, those other heroes on Meta-Match are the literal worst. Glad we have this figured out.

2:19 P.M.
Cortex: You have no idea. Please tell me you've never met Insanity.

V: Oh gosh. So sorry.

Cortex: There are some bad heroes. This dude named Great Guy stole one of my good friend's villains. Tried to change her and everything. It was like a horrible chick flick. But with french kissing (worse than the Mr. L kind).

V: Oh. Oh gross. Yuck yuck yuck. Yeah... blocked him.

2:20 P.M.
Cortex: Honestly, I did, too. But seriously Juan is getting frantic. He sent like 63 exclamation points. We should hop over there.

V: Right. Violence out.

Super Secret Squad
July 4

Cortex: 2:21 P.M.

OK, Juan. I swear you're going to break your keyboard. Tell us what's happening and stop using all caps.

Some Juan:

Seizure just left. Looks like he's going to a 4th of July party. But the girl didn't leave with him. She's still in the bathroom. I have no idea what she's been doing in there for an hour.

Cortex: 2:21 P.M.

Probably thinking of a way to escape. He's got the place loaded with guards and booby traps. You're positive he was leaving?

Some Juan:

I saw a party bus show up in front. I had to use the bathroom, but when I got back, I didn't see him on any of the cameras, so I figure he left on it.

2:22 P.M.

Cortex: All right, I'm piling into the car. I think I'll leave Kevin behind. He has a losing streak going that I don't want to mess up. I'll message you guys when I get there. He lives about ten minutes away, and I'll wait another five for V to show. Meet me about a block away. Figure his guards will notice a car.

Cortex: And an eighty-foot dragon.

> 2:32 P.M.
> **Bernard:** Pardon me, but I regret to inform you that we haven't left yet.

Cortex: Bernard, what the heck! I look like a freak sitting here on the curb blasting the Guardians of the Galaxy album. I literally saw a mother pull her son closer to her on the sidewalk. That. Does. Not. Happen. To. Heroes.

Cortex: What's the hold up?

> 2:33 P.M.
> **Bernard:** Miss Vortex is using the commode.

Cortex: She couldn't hold it for fifteen minutes? He has a nice line of shrubs she can use here. All cut in nice animal shapes.

> **Bernard:** I fear she would not be pleased with that option.
>
> 2:34 P.M.

Bernard: I have been told to inform you that her supervillain suit is ripped and she is attempting to mend it.

Cortex: Tell her some supervillain designer can fix it later (ask the Project Runway folks). No one cares what she looks like. We're literally trying to hide from the sight of everyone here.

2:35 P.M.
Bernard: It appears it has torn in an unfortunate place.

Cortex: Can she just come in civilian clothes? I mean, we probably will have to do that for drama camp anyway.

Cortex: Oh crap. Forgot about that.

Bernard: Evidently she had also forgotten. Miss Vortex will be ready shortly. With a mask only.

2:36 P.M.
Cortex: Make sure she's wearing other clothes too. We don't want to draw too much attention.

V: Shut up, freak. We'll be there in a few.

2:40 P.M.
Cortex: I foooooooooooooooled around and felllll in love. Seriously, I've been through like five tracks already on this thing. You guys planning on arriving this century?

Cortex: Oh, crap. The sky went all dark.

Cortex: Dang, Bernard looks scary. Even his grayish scales have a glow of fire underneath him. Why doesn't he go more places like this?

Cortex: Also, Juan? You still alive, bro? We're go time as soon as they land.

> 2:41 P.M.
> **Some Juan:** I didn't want to interrupt your argument about V's bathroom habits. And we kept telling you he was a dragon. I'm on standby. I'm going to put everyone on text-to-voice and voice-to-text mode, so you can do either if you're in a situation that calls for silence.

2:42 P.M.
Cortex: Just plugged in my headphones. They landed at a nearby park with tree cover.
First plan to get inside? Past, you know, all these freaking dudes in sunglasses and suits?

> **Some Juan:** There's an area that is unguarded for twenty seconds every ten minutes around back. Head for the rear left corner. South corner.

2:43 P.M.
Cortex: What am I? Sacagawea?
South? Fine, I'll just head for the back.

> **V:** do i look okay bernard

V: oh crap voice to text is really strong

Cortex: yeah try not to talk too loudly while we're inside

Cortex: oh dang you weren't kidding

Cortex: glad we didn't bring kevin

2:44 P.M.
Cortex: OK, we're heading back as I'm typing this. Trying not to use my mind to text because I can't make use of that inside. V will let you know when we've made it in.

Some Juan: Okay. Remember. South corner.

V: Got it. I, at least, know my cardinal directions.

2:45 P.M.
Cortex: I know cardinals are little red birds. So there. We're about to head in.

V: what an idiot

Cortex: Wow. It picks up whispering, too.

V: gosh dang it

2:46 P.M.
V: clunk ug thwap

Cortex: If you couldn't get it from those onomatopoeia-to-text things, we just went through a very rough entrance. Wish you guys would've told us we were going spelunking. It looks like a cave in here. All that jagged granite.

Some Juan: My bad. Anyway, the girl is in the west wing of the house.

2:47 P.M.
Cortex: Juan, do I look like a compass to you?

V: compasses are prettier

Cortex: OK, what next, bro? Smells like Axe in here.

Some Juan: There are two guards at the door. You have to go through that window straight ahead of you without them seeing you. You need a distraction.

2:48 P.M.
Cortex: quick v just wear your mask and nothing else

Cortex: oh my gosh dude i'm joking don't kill me

V: Ugh. I'm going in. You get the girl, I'll distract the guards. I'm taking my mask off AND ONLY MY MASK OFF so don't look.

2:49 P.M.

Cortex: fine i'm looking away but we're gonna see each other for realsies at drama camp you know

V: nah it's heroes and villains themed hahaha

Cortex: Did you help Mr. L pick the play or something? Never mind. Not important. Go distract them.

2:50 P.M.

Cortex: Oh, whoops. I'm looking as she's going up to them. Can't see her face, so hopefully she won't zap me dead. Whoa dang. What hip sways.

V: hey guys what's up haha

2:51

Cortex: Should I head for the window, Juan? Oh, goodness. She's twirling her fingers in her hair. What is this? Pride and Prejudice?

V: hey babe haven't seen you round before yeah im new in the neighborhood looking for some friends

Cortex: How are they buying this crap? Juan. Seriously, bro? Is it time?

Some Juan: Sorry. Got distracted. Yeah, go.

Cortex: distracted by what we're in the middle of a heist

Cortex: ugh ugh ugggggh

2:52 P.M.
V: haha yeah sure id love to

V: what yeah of course we can talk until after your shift

> **Cortex:** So is V just gonna flirt the whole time? Made it through the window if you couldn't tell from the ugggggghs.

V: whoa let's not go to fast eh babe oh gosh haha

> 2:53 P.M.
> **Cortex:** Ugh, is there any way we can turn off her mic, Juan? Also which way is west?

Some Juan: Yeah, working on it. This is uncomfortable enough to watch, let alone hear. Ummm west is to your left.

> **Cortex:** Got it.

> 2:55 P.M.
> **Cortex:** yeessh how many rooms does this house have

> **Cortex:** Seriously, guys? I've passed through a dining area, ballroom, and even a room for fresh squeezed juices. Smelled delicious. But honestly, how far

is the west end? Everything smells like a middle schooler trying too hard.

Some Juan: Five more rooms, then there's a bedroom. Juliet is in the guest bathroom there. Hold on, I think V is trying to talk.

> **V:** die you arrogant awful womanizing beast thunk you too thwap bang ugh

2:56 P.M.
Cortex: If a guard falls on speech-to-text, does he make a sound?

> **V:** obviously cortex im coming in the front door couldn't stand it anymore it might give us away sooner but those guys were perverts

Cortex: Welcome to men. Also, why did you make me go through the window, Juan? I could've just waited it out.

> **Some Juan:** I'm a pacifist.

2:57 P.M.
Cortex: You entered the wrong business, bro. Oh wait, I think I hear something bouncing off the smooth stone floors. It echoes a lot on the west end of the house.

Cortex: Sounds like Juliet. Hear sniffling. Definitely her. You almost here, V?

V: What the heck is she bouncing? I'm right behind you, dork. Quick, let's get in the bedroom.

V: i didn't mean it like that stop making that face

2:58 P.M.
Cortex: ah look at that huge king sized bed and i forgot my american printed bro tank in my bedroom

Cortex: ummm that last part wasn't me and i had to turn the bus all the way around just to grab it but no everyone in the family picture had to look patriotic and my green dress shirt would not do

V: oh crap it's seizure

Cortex: Do you have the symptoms? Frothing at the mouth? Uncontrollable muscle spasms?

2:59 P.M.
V: Get your head in the game. Seizure is in the hall. What are we going to do?

Cortex: Great question. Here's another one. Why did we pigeonhole ourselves into the bedroom in the first place?

V: Juliet is in that on-suite bathroom, genius.

V: creak did you say something oh my god

V: oh hey juliet

Cortex: who's juliet

3:00 P.M.
Cortex: that's you babe remember the code names

Cortex: cortie what are you doing here if he finds you

V: still in there tammy

Cortex: Oh, crap! Seizure's in the bedroom now. And seriously? Tammy?

Cortex: Juan, any way you can differentiate voices on the speech-to-text thing? This is getting confusing. Ugh, and why does he use lavender shampoo? What is he? A walking, talking hair salon?

Some Juan: Working on it.

Ceasar: so we meet again cortex

3:01 P.M.
Cortex: sup bad guy

Scissors: what are you doing here

Cortex: oh juan keep the bad nicknames for him coming what a great way to die

Sea Turtle: who the heck are you talking to

V: you stole his girlfriend now can we fight and get this over with

Cortex: mmmm not the best idea v he can control oh see he's already got hold of your arms you have no control over them now

Girlfriend? It's complicated?: aaaahh

V: what the frick he literally gives people seizures blurgh what is going on with my mouth

3:02 P.M.
Cortex: and if he holds on much longer you could die horrifically ah stop choking me

Cortex: Can still text with free hand. Got to get you to touch him to drain powers. I lean forward now.

Girlfriend? It's complicated?: aaaahhhhhhhhhhh

Cortex: ah good you touched him so touching

V: gah how does it feel to have your powers used against you you freak quit choking my hero ha you look stupid foaming at the mouth seizure

3:03 P.M.
Seal Hurt: blurghlblurghlblurgh

V: got him crap is he dead

Cortex: not if you release him

Cortex: v let him go

Cortex: v

V: there he's really actually dead now had to make sure

Cortex: oh juliet's crying it's ok babe everything's over now

3:04 P.M.
V: yeah its cool juliet he's like really dead look at his purple face

Cortex: i don't think that helped she's crying harder

Cortex: oh gosh this is hard he was like my number one nemesis for two years you know

V: sorry wow i didn't think about that

3:05 P.M.
Cortex: it's fine it happens to every villain and hero

Cortex: that's gonna be one of us someday you know

V: gosh morbid much

Cortex: i thought you liked that stuff

Cortex: all right gang let's head home

3:06 P.M.
V: Update to everyone else: we're getting Juliet out.
Also, her hair is definitely not naturally blonde.

> **Some Juan:** Well done, team. Over and out.

Kevin: Where is everyone?

> 3:10 P.M.
> **Bernard:** Miss Vortex has just shown me that my apparatus was not functioning. It seems none of you received my advice or admonishments during this escapade. I deeply apologize.

V: Violence out, all!

Can We Still Be Enemies?
July 5

10:09 A.M.
Cortex changed PM name to Now Nemeses :)

Cortex:

So, V, you wanna tell me when this drama camp thing-y is? My parents need to schedule my summer orientation at Ball State, and we need to know which weeks I'm not available.

Cortex: 11:03 A.M.

Still tuckered out from yesterday Miss I Kill All of Cortex's Nemeses Even Though He Fought Them For Two Years And By All I Mean Just Seizure And Sweet Tooth (Who Was More Of A One-Fight Fling) But I'm Still A Little Bitter?

Cortex:

That would be a pain to put at the top of papers in elementary school. Or at graduations.

V: 11:15 A.M.

Every freaking morning. Why.

11:16 A.M.
Cortex: Because we're nemeses now! Awwwwww.
Don't you hate me?

> **V:** Stop being so hateable. I can't stand it. Anyway, we have orientation tomorrow for counseling, and then camp starts on Monday.

Cortex: Since when are you going to Ball State?

Cortex: Oh sorry didn't read the second part. Sorry just so excited. I got a message from my nemesis. Nem-e-sis, people! I have one! I'm going to shout it from a rooftop!

> 11:17 A.M.
> **V:** You're such a dork. It was fun killing people with you yesterday. It will probably be even more fun killing you.

11:18 A.M.
Cortex: My dying words will certainly be the best you've ever heard. So what does this orientation entail? Besides clawing our eyes out for volunteering in the first place.

> **V:** As if I know. I've never done these things. He just said show up at eight.

Cortex: Ooooooh, so you'll show up at noon, right? Given your sleep schedule. :)

> **V:** IT IS FREAKING EIGHT IN THE MORNING RIGHT NOW

11:19 A.M.
Cortex: 8:19. You're nineteen minutes late, young lady. Here's a detention pass. Wanna have a breakfast club?

Cortex: Also, they never eat breakfast in that movie. So sad. What is your favorite movie?

> **V:** You're so dumb. Um... I don't really watch movies that often. They make me sad.

11:20 A.M.
Cortex: Oh yeah. Anchorman and Deadpool make me depressed every time I watch them.

Cortex: Seriously, you know there are comedies, right?

> **V:** All these good guys always end up winning. It's depressing.

11:21 A.M.
Cortex: Guess you picked the wrong side. I love movies. Could watch them the rest of my life.

> **V:** I just got coloring books as a kid and killed the princesses with red crayon. Speaking of princesses, how's Juliet?

11:22 A.M.
Cortex: Still shaken up. Don't worry. We're not getting together any time soon, so I won't be sending any kissing pics anytime soon. She needs a lot of time to process the event. And, it's sort of my

fault she got kidnapped since I sent Seizure a pic of her.

> **V:** Dude, why would you do that?

11:23 A.M.
Cortex: I sent the wrong one to him. I seriously need to stop using my mind powers with this software. It clashes constantly and sends all the wrong stuff.

> **V:** Let me guess: you meant to send it to me to make me mad.

Cortex: No I think I meant to send another pic. But, I will make sure to keep in mind that still makes you mad :) you still hate her?

> **V:** Jerk. I don't actually care. And yeah I guess. She's obnoxious. Fake. Not that it matters to me if you date imbeciles.

11:24 A.M.
Cortex: Well, if it makes you feel better, when I took her home yesterday she told me to thank you for looking out for her. She says you seem ... good! Gasp. The horror!

> **V:** Yep, okay, really hate her now.

11:25 A.M.
Cortex: Uh huh. Well, she wants to send a gift (she's a huge fan of giving gifts) to everyone who helped out with the operation. Have anything you'd

like in a basket? Fruit? Chocolate? Arsenic tainted wine?

V: Severed heads of my enemies?

Cortex: I'll tell her you like movies. Especially when the good guys win.

V: I wish this stupid program let us send emojis. Oh, wait. Here's a pic of my face, sticking my tongue out at you.

11:26 A.M.
Cortex: Cute. I just photoshopped it to a movie poster. Recognize it? It's a recent superhero flick with 20 heroes in it. You're on all the bodies now.

V: Actually, I like that movie. A lot of people die.

11:27 A.M.
Cortex: Yeah, the only superhero movie I've hated so far. Fine, you may hate movies, but no way you can hate songs. Got a favorite one?

V: I have a pretty great remix of death cries set to heavy metal.

Cortex: Ooooh that sounds fun. You got a link to it? I think we can send music files on here.

V: Yeah, definitely. Here's a link *sends virus*

11:28 A.M.

Cortex: Yeah, I might not click on that. But here's mine :) :)

> 11:30 A.M.
> **V:** AHHHHHHHH my ears! Did they say say sunshine? bleeeegrhghghrgh

Cortex: Well the literal title of the song is, in fact, Sunshine, so no they absolutely did not mention that word :)

Cortex: I'm off to help my parents set up a party for a couple B-list heroes who are being inducted into larger leagues. Just think, that could be me in a couple of years. :)

> **V:** Can I come? Sounds like fun.

11:31 A.M.
Cortex: Only if you promise not to kill anyone.

> **V:** Never mind then.

Cortex: Lol. I can take pictures. Any B-list heroes you want me to look out for? We invited at least fifty.

> **V:** Besides Hypnotica... I've always wanted to kill a person who pops like a balloon. Any like that?

11:32 A.M.
Cortex: Let me ask Mom. She has the guest list on her phone.

V: Hi, Cortex's mom!

11:34 A.M.
Cortex: We do have someone named Helium, so maybe? Other than that, none of the names sound like something that comes from a balloon or something that floats.

Cortex: I would say hi, but she doesn't know about you. My parents think I'm fooling around with a couple of villains.

V: They don't know about me?

11:35 A.M.
Cortex: Do heroes introduce villains to their parents?

V: I don't know, they always die first.

11:36 A.M.
Cortex: Do you want to meet them today? Mom's nice. Dad ... he makes Greek statues look lively (but thankfully he's a bit more clothed than them).

V: I mean, I don't know if that's kind of weird...

Cortex: Let me know. The event happens at five, so if you want to pop by earlier. My sister has a fascination with henchmen, so I would suggest bringing Bernard, too.

11:37 A.M.

V: Oh, Bernard loves having fans. Not many, you know. He acts all cool, but really he's melting inside. Yeah, for him, I guess. Not that I really want to meet your stupid family. But maybe I can get some insight into your weaknesses. Not them, of course. I have a no-killing-family policy.

11:38 A.M.
Cortex: Well, they'll need to put on disguises anyway. My sister has a cosplay outfit, but let me see if Mom and Dad have their superhero outfits buried somewhere in the walk-in closet. I'll message back when they're ready for you. Also, meet us at Ivanhoe's (no offense, but not ready for a villain to know where I live yet). It's an ice cream place. I'll send you directions.

V: Smart. I'd kill you in your sleep. Cool. I'll go tell Bernard.

12:05 P.M.
Cortex: They're suited up. Mom says she can use a break from the prep. My dad's green suit's faded a bit, and there's a tear at the knee. Otherwise (besides a few wrinkles) they look great. And, my sister stole my purple boots again ... so pink cowboy boots it is!

Super Secret Squad
July 5

Some Juan: 12:05 P.M.

Hey, guys! I updated the software on the headsets. Actually, updated the headsets, too. Little bitty earpieces now. It can identify voices and insert punctuation! It even reads text in your ear with the voice of the person who sent it! Want to try it?

V:

Cortex, I'm sorry. Bernard has to watch his friend's grandkid. He can only drop me off, not stay.

V:

Whoops wrong chat.

Cortex: 12:06 P.M.

Well, won't Himari be disappointed not to meet Bernard?

Cortex:

I mean. Her name isn't Himari. That's totally

a code name for my sister.

> **V:** ... Sure... Remember, no-killing-family policy. It's cool. Anyway, I'm super sorry about that. He can't get out of it. His friend is going on an assassination mission.

12:07 P.M.
Cortex: So, wait. How long does that last? Can you get home/you gonna stick around here until five? Because if so, my mom needs help setting up for the event.

> **Kevin:** Wait what event, bro? That why you sent me to Indy to get some tablecloths?

12:08 P.M.
Cortex: Sorry, Kev. Sent you to Indy because if I have to listen to the Rent soundtrack one more time, I'm going to start charging you rent to live with us.

> **Bernard:** The assassination mission ends at promptly eight if all goes well.

V: Ooo, Kevin, that's kind of evil. Don't put Cortex through that.

> **Kevin:** For you, babe, I'll turn henchman anytime ;)

12:09 P.M.
Cortex: OK, your rent plan starts tomorrow.

Bernard: There may be another assassination tonight because of you, young Kevin.

Kevin: Man, presidents get assassinated. I feel honored. And my mom said I'd never amount to anything. Take that, Kathy!

Some Juan: If you all are done, I have an idea. Why don't you use the new earpieces? Bernard can still talk to Himari through that.

12:10 P.M.
Cortex: I'm down. Himari's been hacking my account and reading all these messages, so she'll be excited to see her name on this thing.

V: What! You didn't tell me that.

Cortex: Eh, it's Himari. Little sisters are about as exciting as rocks.

12:11 P.M.
Bernard: Mine is, in fact, a rock.

V: ...okay, so, Juan, we'll grab the headsets—sorry, earpieces—and head over?

Some Juan: Sounds good. I'll be listening to see how it works.

Cortex: Cool. Message when you get to Ivanhoe's. We'll be standing in a very long line for ice cream.

Think you can cancel most of the background noise, Juan?

12:12 P.M.
Some Juan: Prepare to be amazed. I had to work with old tech last time. This is tech of my own design.

Bernard: I have heard it is the finest ice cream in Indiana.

Cortex: It's not bad. They have over 100 flavors. But, of course, Himari gets vanilla every time. Because ... Himari.

V: I like her. That's obnoxious. And I like anyone who is obnoxious to you.

Cortex: Well, she's obsessed with supervillains, so who knows? Maybe one day you'll train her.

12:13 P.M.
V: Perhaps. You better watch out. Anyway, we'll be at your house to pick up the tech soon, Juan. Peace out, everyone.

12:25 P.M.
Cortex: Update: Reached Ivanhoes. There's a line that could wrap around the earth. Five times.

12:26 P.M.

Cortex: Update: Someone got whipped cream in Himari's purple wig. She isn't happy.

12:27 P.M.
Cortex: Update: the line reached inside, but we ain't getting no ice cream no time soon.

12:28 P.M.
Cortex: Update: this is Himari. I stole his phone. Now I'm going to send every picture in his phone.

12:29 P.M.
Cortex: Update: this is Cortex. I stole it back when I read Himari's mind and waited for a time she was least alert. We're still in line. Himari is looking at the menu on the wall, but we all know she's going to get vanilla.

Some Juan: Why do we care about this?

V: We're on our way to Ivanhoe's. Be there in ten.

12:30 P.M.
Cortex: Update: one of the ice cream machines broke. Himari and I are playing mad libs while we wait. I'm concerned. All of her verbs are some version of "kill".

V: Himari, you are wonderful.

Cortex: Ooooh, "torture." She's branching out. Used it for a verb and noun.

> **V:** Neat. By the way, I've been doing all of this with voice text. This software is awesome!

12:31 P.M.
Cortex: Yeah, I was wondering how you managed to text and ride a dragon at the same time.

> **Kevin:** They're out of tablecloths.

Cortex: All of Indy? A whole city? Is out of tablecloths?

> **Kevin:** Yep. Oh well. Guess I better come home and get my showtunes ready to play for the party.

Cortex: No, wait. I need you to get me cups. For the party.

> **Kevin:** Dang it.

12:39 P.M.
V: We're landing in a nearby cornfield.

> **Cortex:** We're about to order. We'll meet you outside. Seating is crazy in here. Any favorite flavors?

V: Blood. Just kidding. Chocolate. Bye, Bernard! Love you! Have fun!

Bernard: You as well, Miss Vortex.

12:40 P.M.
Cortex: Awwwwww. And shocker. Himari got vanilla. But with strawberry syrup. I think the blood comment inspired her.

> **V:** I'm inspirational. Hey, I see it, I think. Is that Garfield holding an ice cream cone?

12:41 P.M.
Cortex: The orange cat? Yeah, Indiana is weird that way. Coming out to meet you guys. My parents are waiting inside to pick up the orders, but I have Himari with me. I'll pick up the speech-to-text thingies outside.

12:42 P.M.
Cortex: Hey, V! Oh good, thanks for the earpiece. This is Himari.

> **V:** Hey, Himari! Here, Juan gave me one for you, too.

Himari: Yes! Cal-Cortex! I mean Cortex! I can totally stalk you now.

> **Cortex:** You already do.

Himari: V, I've read so much about you. And, you know, of you. Like, that you've written.

> **V:** Yeah... um. Cool. Also, a little weird, but I admire stalking.

12:43 P.M.

Cortex: Wait, what have you written?

> **V:** Texts, dork. When she steals your phone?

Cortex: Oh, right. I thought she meant you wrote a novel or something. Now those writers creep me out. They know how to kill anyone.

> **Himari:** No, I meant your novel, under your pseu—

V: Anyway! Let's go get ice cream.

> 12:44 P.M.
>
> **Cortex:** Ah, Mom. Dad. Put these in.

Mom: Hey, Ca—sorry, I mean, Cortex. Took us a while to squeeze on out of there. Oh, is this the young lady you were talking about? Fantastic costume. Half my nemeses hired designers who used neoprene. Terrible fabric. Inflexible.

> **Cortex:** Mom. Stop winking at me.

Dad: Hello.

> **V:** Great to meet you, Mr. and Mrs. uh, what would you like me to call you?

Mom: Mr. and Mrs. Cortex is fine. I would tell you our superhero aliases, but I would rather not be taken out by a very young nemesis. Then again, could be a little better than this brain tumor I've got.

12:45 P.M.
Dad: Now—

Mom: It's fine, sweetheart. Just eat your ice cream.

V: Yeah, um. Hey, Bernard? Were you going to say hi?

Bernard: A pleasure to meet each and every one of you. My name is Bernard. It is simply a pleasure.

12:46 P.M.
Mom: You know, Bernard, your voice sounds very familiar. Have you done a lot of henchman work before? My daughter here is fascinated with villainous sidekicks, you know.

Bernard: I have been in the henchman business for sixty-five years, ma'am. I have assisted many villains, including Miss Vortex's parents.

12:47 P.M.
Mom: Sweetie, you've been holding her ice cream for several minutes. Give it to Vortex before it melts in the plastic bowl.

Dad: Here.

V: Thank you!

Himari: Oh my gosh, Mr. Bernard, I'm a huge fan. How many villains have you raised to be supervillains over the years? Like ten? Wow.

Bernard: I believe the number is nine, Miss Himari, but I am flattered.

12:48 P.M.
Mom: Get off your phone, we're having a conversation, sweetie.

Dad: Look.

Mom: Oh, her flight got in early. Cinder, a B-list hero, is flying in from Hawaii. Have a feeling she'll get inducted into one of the bigger leagues. I'm sorry, but we may have to take this ice cream to go and head to the airport. Vortex, are you joining us tonight?

V: I mean, as long as it's okay...

Mom: Oh, we don't get many villains at these things, so they'll enjoy the change of pace. Enough heroes' egos will make you dizzy after a couple hours.

V: Yeah, I've kind of noticed that with a lot of heroes...

12:49 PM.
Mom: Also, I ask that you turn off these speech-to-text things at the event.

Cortex: Mom, come on.

Mom: For a few reasons. I'd rather not have the information from the event be online where anyone can find it. If the media gets a hold of it before we publicize it, a number of A-list heroes will have my head. Or, at least, they'll have one of their nemeses decapitate me for them.

> **Cortex:** You sound like Himari.

Mom: But, also, I'm not a fan of technology, so I'd rather not have you all wired up tonight.

> **V:** That's fine, Mrs. Cortex. I can take yours and Mr. Cortex's. Himari, Cortex, you can keep yours for later.

Himari: Heck yeah!

> **Cortex:** Don't worry Mom. I'm shutting it off with my mind; don't give me that lo—

Super Secret Squad
July 5

Cortex: 11:02 P.M.

I think I'm starting to understand what my mom said earlier at Ivanhoes'. If I talked with Fluent for five more minutes, I would probably start using a list of PG-13 words. Ugh, I'm gonna sit. Feel like I've been standing for four hours.

V:

It was very difficult not to kill Great Guy. Scoot over.

Cortex:

Dang, V. Not so close. There's plenty of room on the porch swing. All right now let's get this baby going. Back and forth. Wheeeeeeeeeee.

V:

Haha stupid.

Cortex: 11:03 P.M.

Super excited to get Freezer's autograph. She said I could actually intern with her next summer! Do a little hero work and all that in Cleveland.

V: Nice! She's pretty cool. Get it? Heehee.

Cortex: Ugh, I get enough of that from Kevin, you weirdo.

V: Heeheehee.

11:04 P.M.
Cortex: Now you sound like Insanity. So, did you have fun? They seemed excited for you to be there. You couldn't even grab a cheese cube off a tray without one of them asking about your experience and trying to set you up with one of their kids who's trying to be a hero.

V: I mean, when they weren't people like Great Guy, it was pretty fun. I got a loooong list of potential nemeses under the age of twelve, hahaha.

Cortex: Oh gosh. So, when I was nemeses with Seizure, we made a pact not to fight other people. Are you thinking the same thing, or do you want to have a couple side heroes?

V: I've killed my last seven nemeses too quickly to get to that point... But I kind of like just having one.

Cortex: Me too. No pressure, though, hahaha. Have to bring my A-games to the fights.

11:05 P.M.

V: Heehee. Well, you haven't died yet, so that's about five times better than anyone else. Of course... I didn't pull out my knives the first time I met you. I guess taking it slow is a good thing. Get to know each other first.

Cortex: I mean, if you want to hash it out a second time, we have that huge backyard. And since we don't have pets, no one really makes use of it.

V: I don't know... it kind of seems weird to fight after being nice all day... I mean, you know, not fair to you when you must be tired out.

Cortex: Yeah, I'm kind of tired. Not used to staying up this late with all those people. My parents don't get introversion. Believe it or not, my dad's an extrovert.

V: Um... okay, if you say so.

11:06 P.M.
Cortex: Sorry my mom had to leave early. I know she was trying to get Great Guy and a few other people like him to steer away from you. It's just. She was feeling really weak, you know? She can't do a whole lot more of nights like this.

V: It's okay. She seems really great. I... I'm glad you let me meet them. Your family, that is.

Cortex: Yeah, they really seemed to like you. My mom says she's never seen anyone hang streamers so well. Mind you, we hire professionals sometimes. She said you used a little too much red, though.

> **V:** Haha! Well, compliment accepted. My new career: professional streamer-er.

11:07 P.M.
Cortex: I guess the disguises didn't make much sense because you saw photographs of all our family members hanging in the house. Oh well. Glad you have that no-family rule.

> **V:** Yeah. And I mean, you've been to my house, too. This whole disguise thing is a little silly, by now. I like your name, by the way. And your baby picture. Cute.

Cortex: Ugh, stop. Seriously why do parents take photos of babies in bathtubs? It will never go well for the poor things in the future. And it's not fair you got to hear mine but I don't know yours. Have you told any hero your real name?

> **V:** No. I... well, that's kind of how my parents died. Got too friendly with a hero. He used it against them. Found our house. Burned it down. Then it was just me.

Cortex: Dang. I'm sorry. You want to talk about it? ... Sorry, I don't think I've ever met someone who lost their parents and house in one day.

> 11:08 P.M.
> **V:** I mean, I'm fine, I guess. I learned a lot. When my master took me in and forced me to do stuff. Learned how to be a good villain. Glad I ended up finding Bernard. He was great friends with my dad. I... just wonder what would have happened if... you know. They were still around.

Cortex: To be honest, V. I think you turned out all right given the circumstances. If I lost both my parents, I probably would've ... I don't even want to think about it. Also, I'm glad you killed your old master. Honestly, I would break my old no-killing rule if he was still alive.

> **V:** Thanks, Cortex. And... it's Victoria.

11:09 P.M.
Cortex: Victoria? That's your name? That's so beautiful. It sure beats Caleb. Seriously, there's always like three in your homeroom class.

> **V:** Not if you're homeschooled. Heehee.
> I like it, though. It sounds... hero-ish.

11:09 P.M.
Cortex: My mom picked it from this dude in the Bible. She's Catholic, you know? Apparently he and Joshua wanted to get into this place called the

Promised Land. And they were spies and stuff. They saw all these big bad giants. The other spies were like, "No way in heck we can beat them." But Caleb and Joshua were the only ones brave enough to want to go into the Promised Land and face those giants. 'Course, had to wait forty years or something. Can't really remember why.

V: So I was right. It is a hero name.

Cortex: So where does Victoria come from? Besides ruling England and all.

V: Wish I knew. I was only ten... I think I kind of blocked a lot of stuff out, you know? Don't remember much. Don't even really... r-remember my mom's face.

Cortex: Oh, V. I'm so sorry. Please don't cry. We can talk about something else. Like listen to those frogs chirping. That's all I got. Why do frogs sound like birds? That's weird.

V: Ha. D-dork.

11:10 P.M.
Cortex: Quick. Punch me in the stomach so I can start crying. Hit me with granite.

V: What the heck? Why?

Cortex: It's just. I hate to see people cry. My dad cries a lot you know. Never have seen my mom tear up, but every single time the old man melts into saltwater ... it's rough seeing that happen to your dad.

> **V:** Caleb, you don't have to make me punch you to hide your tears. I'm freaking blubbering like an idiot.

Cortex: It's ok, you can't really tell out here since it's dark and all. Dang. Wonder how late it is.

> 11:11 P.M.
> **Kevin:** So ... did you guys mean to put this in the group text?

Cortex: Kevin, please tell me you're hiding in the bushes. Why the heck is your voice in my ear? I just had a heart attack.

> **Kevin:** 11:11 by the way. Make a wish ;) I'm staring at you guys from an upstairs window :)

V: I wish for you to fall out of that window.

> **Kevin:** Why? So I can fall for you?

Himari: Kevin! It was just getting good! Why did you interrupt?

> 11:12 P.M.
> **Kevin:** Bro, is your arm around her? I can't tell from this angle.

Cortex: Kevin, I swear, I'm going to burn your theater posters hanging in your room if you comment one more time tonight.

> **Kevin:** Not Kinky Boots! Anything but that!!!!!!!!

Cortex: That one will be the first to go.

> **Himari:** Kevin, does he still have his arm around her heeheehee?

11:13 P.M.
Kevin: I refuse to comment anymore. If Les Miserables goes I will be Miserables.

> **Cortex:** Sorry, V. I must've turned on the speech-to-text with my mind. The night air was so refreshing, it must've triggered something.

Himari: Yeah, I'm sure it was the night air.

> **V:** I-it's fine. I'm… just going to go wait out front. For Bernard.

Cortex: OK. Yeah. Good idea. We have to be at drama camp orientation early. You want me to wait with you?

> **Himari:** Oooooo

V: It's fine. I can kill anyone who messes with me. Bye, guys. I'm turning this thing of—

Now Nemeses :)
July 6

Cortex changed named to Caleb.

Caleb: 8:17 P.M.

Still scraping off black paint from your hands? Wish I would've known not to wear my favorite pair of jeans today.

Caleb:

Set looks good though. I took a picture when Mr. L went for a bathroom break. Sorry if it looks a little blurry, but you can still see the cardboard cut-out buildings. Could be New York. Or Detroit. Just no city in Kentucky. We hate those guys.

Caleb:

Kevin was born in Kentucky (Louisville).

V:

Ugh, it's like permanent or something. I'm proud of us. No one died today. Success. For you, anyway.

8:18 P.M.

Caleb: Yeah, well, came close with hanging up some of the lighting fixtures on the catwalk. Just about dropped one onto one of the counselors ... would've fallen twenty feet. And don't even get me started about wiring on those things.

> **V:** I'm glad you're good with tech. I'll stick to painting.

Caleb: It seems like it stuck to you. Good thing we did the other orientation things first. So let me get this straight. The kiddos have three stations every day: singing, acting, and choreography. Can I take a long bathroom break during that last one? Like, two hours? :)

> 8:19 P.M.
> **V:** We're dancing pros now!

Caleb: Also, how many kids did they say were in our group? There's, like, four groups, so no more than like fifteen, right?

> **V:** I think the legal limit is no more than eight kids per counselor?

Caleb: Oh sure. Because I'm a hero I have to know what's legal and all right? Well, sometimes ... I jaywalk! Oh no! Horror!

> 8:20 P.M.
> **V:** Wow. You dastardly devil, you.

Caleb: The other counselors seemed cool. The dude with the blue hair seemed into you ;)

> **V:** You mean the one with the Metallica shirt? He was kind of creepy.

8:21 P.M.
Caleb: So I was wrong to tell him that you were into him, right? Lol. Just kidding (or am I?). So ... remind me again why Bernard was helping today? Isn't there an age maximum for counselors?

> **V:** He's friends with Mr. L... somehow. And he likes theater.

Caleb: He is dramatic. I'll give you that. Plus don't all British people do theater?

> **V:** Stereotyping, much? I don't think he's ever been in a play. He just likes watching them. He's very classy, you know?

Caleb: Well, sure. He's British.

8:22 P.M.
Caleb: Got any plans before we meet up for realsies on Monday to be killed by fifteen kids?

> **V:** Well, Mr. L is giving us the day off tomorrow, then we do the finishing touches of preparing for the kids on Sunday. So... I don't know. I'll probably hang out with Fluffy, or Mr. Squiggles, or something.

Caleb: I was just thinking we haven't had a chance to fight in a while. Wanna try again tomorrow?

> **V:** Sure! Non-lethal combat? And where?

8:23 P.M.
Caleb: You just were up in Indiana. And I think I'll get my fill of Arizona. Wanna try a different state and figure it out from there?

> **V:** I like that idea. Um, do you want to try California or something? Fight on the beach? Epic sand flying everywhere?

Caleb: Yeah, remember that I hate the second episode of Star Wars. Well, like Anakin, I'm not a huge fan of sand. Kind of why I'm glad my family picked the midwest.

> **V:** Fair. How about, um... I don't know, what are you thinking?

8:24 P.M.
Caleb: What about Maine? They have really good seafood there. And beautiful scenery.

> **V:** I've never been there. Sure.

Caleb: Oh wait. No Maine's not good.

> **V:** Ummm why?

Caleb: I'd rather not get into it, but Maine doesn't have a lot of good memories for me. Let's not go there.

> 8:25 P.M.
> **V:** Okay... not sure why you suggested it then... how about Colorado? I've never been, but I hear it's pretty.

Caleb: Dude. Been to the Springs before (Colorado Springs). My mom, when she was stronger, liked to do a lot of skiing out there after some hero work to cool off.

> **V:** Ohh yeah that sounds cool.

Caleb: And it's not too far from Arizona, so Bernard won't have to strain himself. Can't believe he was lifting all that heavy wood for building the set today. That crazy man.

8:26 P.M.
Caleb: Seriously, how long do dragons live? He gonna go for a couple centuries?

> **V:** Well, he morphs into a dragon, so he's not a straight-up dragon. He just has dragon strength and all that. But he's pretty strong. As long as he takes his heart meds. That's the only thing not quite as strong as the rest of him.

Caleb: Makes sense at 85. So, want to meet at the base of Pikes Peak tomorrow? Huge mountain.

Purple and even covered in snow this fine July. Hey, purple!

> **V:** Ooo fighting in the snow! Epic. I don't have a coat, though...

8:27 P.M.
Caleb: When we meet up, we can buy you one there. Maybe they'll be on discount or something. I would go now, but most stores will be closing soon, and we live about twenty minutes away from everything.

> **V:** All good. Meet me there tomorrow morning around nine-ish Colorado time?

Caleb: Whoa! Morning. You sure you didn't inhale too many paint fumes today? Next thing, you'll be rescuing kids stuck in the snow.

> 8:28 P.M.
> **V:** I just hear the sun sparkling on snow is pretty.

Caleb: Man, getting poetic, too. Did Mr. L trade you for an evil clone? And by evil I mean good.

> **V:** I can still chop your tongue out if you want. Or fingers off.

Caleb: Still can message in here, so I'm fine with that.

> **V:** Ugh, mind powers.

8:29 P.M.
Caleb: Speaking of, when will you be comfortable with me using mine? I know I already do the tech stuff, but what about mind-reading? Anytime soon?

> **V:** Umm...

> **V:** Well, how do you feel about me in your brain? Cause I'll steal that power, you know.

Caleb: True. Lucky for you, you would know if I was using it. My veins sort of glow a pinkish purple when I read minds, so obviously it would be a dead giveaway.

8:30 P.M.
Caleb: I'll be cool with it when you are :)

> **V:** I mean... I guess we're actually nemeses now. So, yeah. We can use all powers.

Caleb: I'll warm it up when we're fighting on the mountain and stuff. Don't know if there's a whole lot of tech I can use in the area, and I don't really want to die on the second go-round, you know?

> **V:** Sounds good. Just a chill fight, you know? Literally. Haha.

8:31 P.M.
Caleb: Ugh, did Kevin steal your keyboard? Hey, V. How soon do you want to kill me? I need to plan for how many days I have left and stuff.

V: What the heck? What happened to "you'll never kill me?"

Caleb: I mean, you won't. But it's always good to plan ahead. Like, my mom is sort of on a death bent right now, so got me thinking a lot about mortality.

V: We haven't even found something to legitimately fight over yet. I need to try to take over the world first or something. Maybe I'll try to kill all the politicians or something.

8:32 P.M.
Caleb: To be honest, if you did the latter, I might turn a blind eye.

Caleb: Maybe I'll get back with Juliet so you'll hate me even more ;) Just kidding. OK, well my mom is needing me to vacuum the house, so I need to go. She thinks I spend too much time on this thing.

V: You literally control technology... okay, have fun. Maybe you can mind-control the vacuum.

Caleb: Lol. I'm not good at controlling more than one piece of tech at a time. And that would be a terrible idea. All the wires. I'd electrocute something if I tried that. All right. Night for now.

V: Only five-thirty here. I'm gonna go party with Mr. Squiggles. Tootles!

Now Nemeses :)
July 7

Caleb: 8:54 A.M.

Landing soon! I'm on the headset thingy because I don't want to fly the helicopter and operate tech at the same time. Mom's going to kill me for eating up the data on my phone.

V:

Same. On the whole, "I'm on my way and using the earpiece" thing. Not the your mom killing me thing, hahaha.

Caleb:

So, there's this really cool park nearby the mountain called Garden of the Gods. I think I'm gonna park there. It's not too far from Pike's Peak. And it's gorgeous here.

V:

Garden of the Gods? Epic. We'll be right there.

8:59 A.M.

Caleb: Cool. Landed. Not a whole lot of tourists here yet. Wanna meet up at a rock formation called the Three Graces? Or under the one that looks like two camels kissing?

> **V:** I've never seen kissing camels. Meet you there. Bye, Bernard. Thank you. Have fun with... who was it?

Bernard: Disturbia, Miss Victoria.

> **V:** Right. Have fun.

Caleb: Bum bum bee dum bum bum bee dum bum.

9:02 A.M.

Caleb: V? I don't see you. But guess what? Some tourist took a picture with me. I think they thought I was Dimension because somewhere in whatever language they said sounded like Dimens-o. But hey, I have a fan!

> **V:** You should have picked a more original costume. I see you.

9:03 A.M.

Caleb: Ah, see you now! You would think I could spy your black cloak against these red rocks or something.

Caleb: Hey, V! You look exhausted.

V: Getting up early two days in a row... Not used to it. Can't sleep before three in the morning.

Caleb: Yikes. You're going to be easier to defeat than a corpse. Sure you don't wanna bump it back a few days? Say, accidentally skip drama camp?

V: Mr. L would turn me into an actual corpse if we skipped. Come on! I want to see the snow.

9:04 A.M.
Caleb: OK, but even with that cloak, you'll probably freeze. Seriously, what's it made out of? The same stuff they make those Halloween costumes?

V: It gets hot in Arizona. But the whole cloak-and-red-eyes thing is too evil to pass up.

Caleb: Ah, makes sense. Hope you don't mind walking. There's a Super Store a mile out of the park.

V: Guess not. At least you have your purple boots today, not those cowgirl boots.

Caleb: Yeah, well doesn't help with all this red dirt. Seriously, how do the big league heroes make their costumes so pristine? I swear if I stretch too far, I'll rip something.

9:05 A.M.

V: Try black jeans and a black T-shirt under your cloak. Very comfy. Very practical. And combat boots are nice.

Caleb: Is all your closet literally black? How do you actually find clothes? I don't think I own anything darker than gray.

V: It's not *all* black. I have some purple.

Caleb: I guess purple is the kind of color that can work for villains and heroes. You don't have a lot of those. Like, can you seriously see a dark lord in sunflower yellow?

V: Heeheehee probably not.

9:06 A.M.
Caleb: Oh, I think one of those tourists recognizes you. The dude in the Crocodile Hunter hat. Look. He's pointing at you.

V: Uh, okay. That's weird. I guess I'll just kind of wave. Should I punch you or something?

Caleb: Who eats a hotdog at nine in the morning?

Caleb: Ummm V. He's waving very frantically now and clutching as his throat with the other hand. Now he's doubling over. Ummm.

V: Oh, gosh, he's choking. Go do your hero thing.

Caleb: Uh, um. Yeah, well, he doesn't appear to have a defibrillator in him, and according to his mind, he is very much choking. And very much freaking out. Umm. Uh. I don't know CPR.

> **V:** Honestly? This doesn't call for a defibrillator or CPR. Gosh. Watch and learn.

9:07 A.M.
Caleb: Where you going? V? Don't kill him!

> **V:** Excuse me, sir? Can I help you? Kay, I'm going to take that as a yes. Oof. Oof! Come on, spit it out.

Caleb: Ugh. Glad there was a bush to catch that nasty pink thing. Oh, good he's breathing again. His brain is giving all sorts of recovery and elated signals.

> **Unknown Source:** Oh, man. Wow. Thanks. I thought I was going to die by hotdog for a minute there.

Caleb: You OK, sir? Can we call someone?

> 9:08 A.M.
> **Unknown Source:** Nah, I'm good. Just had a little weiner problem. I'm good now. Thanks, um... I assume you're a hero?

V: Gross! No. Villain.

Caleb: Yeah. She totally is my sidekick. Ooof. Oww. V, why the ribs?

Unknown Source: Um... okay. Well, thanks hero slash villain people.

9:09 A.M.
V: Yep, no problem, okay, Cortex, let's go.

Caleb: Wow. I don't really know how to process that. I had literally no idea how to save him ... wow, better fight good today, Caleb, because that was a severe ego cut.

V: Are you talking to yourself?

Caleb: Wow. Didn't tell me you had super hearing. OK ... we should be reaching the end of the park soon. Ooooh, gift shop!

V: Dude, what? You can get a memento after we beat each other up. Come on.

9:10 A.M.
Caleb: Fine. The boring store is up the road a ways.

V: Gosh, V, get it together. You're killing your reputation.

Caleb: Ummm, did you mean to direct that at me? I heard "killing your reputation." Whatever you said before that. Zoned out. Well, there was this really interesting bird over there ...

V: Oh. Yeah. Neat bird. Oh! Look! A, um, trash can! I'm going to tip it over and litter! Bwahahaha!

Caleb: Aaaaaand now I'm picking it up.

V: Gosh dang it, that's boring. You were supposed to fight me.

Caleb: Over trash? Seriously, hit a tourist with one of these big boulders. I need better motivation than that.

9:11 A.M.
V: Geez, I was trying to come up with *something* to fight over. You better intercept that boulder, because that poor lady is literally doing nothing.

Caleb: Umm, V. Literally neither of us is going to be able to move any rocks here. These things are massive.

V: Watch me! Ha! Pebble to your arm!

Caleb: Oh what a world! Tell my sister she suuuuuuuuuuuuucks. Goodbye cruel world!

V: My work here is done. I'm going to go look in the gift shop without you.

9:12 A.M.
Caleb: Wait a minute. NOW you're going in the gift shop? You lame-butt.

V: Just to mess with you. Oh! I'm going to rob it! Bwahahahahahaha!

V: Bird!

Caleb: Make up your mind. What do you want? Wait up! Dang, she runs fast.

V: Cheerp! Chiiieer! Cheeerp!

Caleb: Are you trying to talk to them? How are you able to project your voice so loudly? No wonder Mr. L said you'd do good in the singing station at drama camp.

9:13 A.M.
V: Ooo, it's pretty over here. Hey, little birdie. Want a little cracker? Come here. Awww, that's it. You're so cuuuute!

Caleb: Where did you get a cracker? Do you literally prepare for these things?

V: Duh. Never know when you'll meet a bird. Now, shh! Look, she's hopping onto my finger. You beautiful thing. Look at you.

Caleb: Wait. How'd you get it to do that? Dogs literally whimper if I try to pet them.

V: What kind of hero are you? Shh, it's okay, baby. Big bad hero won't hurt you. Yes, that's right. So pretty. Have more cracker.

9:14 A.M.
Caleb: Just take a look at this place.
Who knew gods planted rocks?
It might even be prettier than Maine.

> **V:** Really? Heeheehee, birdie, that tickles!

Caleb: Yeah. I mean, all the Maine people may
come after me with lobster skewers and torches. But
... it just sucks when something beautiful gets all
ugly in your mind, you know?

> **V:** Here, put out your finger. What does that mean?

Caleb: I mean I'd rather not talk about i—he's
gonna fly away. Animals don't like me.

> **V:** Not if you do it right. Here. Take the bird. Read my mind, and you'll see how. I can't really explain it.

9:15 A.M.
Caleb: You sure, V?

> **V:** Yeah. It's not really something I can tell you. It's how you, like, mind-meld with them or something. They know what you're thinking. Show them you love them with all of you.

Caleb: Umm, ok. Promise I won't dig too deep.
Okay, okay, now I'm going to freak out the little bird
with my glowing veins. Okay, I think I see what you

mean now. Just gonna reach out my finger and—
hey! Hey, the claws don't hurt at all!

V: Nope! Here, let me just move your hands like this...

Caleb: Whoa. I feel like I just ran ten miles. What is that?

9:16 A.M.
V: Ahhh!

Caleb: V? You ok? Got a migraine or something? Why you holding your head? V?

V: Ahh! Oh... man... Caleb, I... I'm so sorry... Maine... you brought her there...

Caleb: Wait. Are you in my head? Ugh, I feel like I'm gonna pass out or something.

V: I don't mean to be!

Caleb: Seriously, my vision's in black and white now. Is the sky spinning?

V: Oh my gosh, I'll try to reverse it...

Caleb: Aaah, oh God I can breathe again. Whoooo whoooo, is this what air feels like? Lungs, I missed you. Wow. Did you just pump my veins with an energy drink? What is happening? My heart is beating so fast.

9:17 A.M.
V: Ah! Oh my gosh! What are you doing in there? Ah!

Caleb: ... augh .... Augh oh no. No, no.
I'm sorry. It was the energy spike.
I'm trying to stop it. Just need to breathe.
Heh uh heh... V. Why am I seeing Stroke?

V: No, don't look at that! No! No...

Caleb: I'm sorry. I tried to pull out, but it's like when you can't stop watching T.V. and you convince yourself you'll go to bed any minute, but you keep watching ... V, why didn't you tell me?

V: I'm... I'm really sorry, I had to... I had to do it. She was going to... kill him...

Caleb: No, no, no, I'm not mad. I just had no idea that *she* was your master. You always referred to her as a he and ... oh my gosh I dated the person who made your life hell.

V: B-but in Maine, you and her... wow, you actually really like, loved that girl... I'm so sorry.

9:18 A.M.
Caleb: Yeah, well, that wasn't really her, was it? I mean most people's secret identity's just a ruse ... I don't really feel like mine is.

V: I... just... gosh, I'm sorry, I'm freaking crying again gosh dang it.

Caleb: Yeah, that usually happens with the mind-reading thing. You learn to block out the empathy after a while. Oh, wow. That sounded villainous. Who freaking am I? Quick. Do a crime so I can be heroic and stuff.

> **V:** I can't get her out of m-my head... Caleb, I f-feel like I'm there... She's th-there with the... the knives and stuff...

9:19 A.M.
Caleb: Here. Hold out your hand.

> **V:** Why? D-don't read my mind. You d-don't want to see what she... what she did to me.

Caleb: Just trust me. We're gonna see something else, okay? All right it's coming out a little fuzzy. OK. Clearer now. You see them?

> **V:** Oh my... My parents! Mama! Oh my God... her face... is so gorgeous.

Caleb: I would say you have your dad's eyes, but red isn't a natural eye color, you know. OK, now tell me what you see. What are they doing?

> **V:** It's evening. We're sitting by the fireplace. But there's no fire in it, because, Arizona. Too hot. We're reading a book, like always before bedtime. He's reading the paper. Mama's showing me the pictures.

Caleb: OK, can you smell anything?
Hear anything? It's faint, but
tell me those things.

> **V:** There's like a citrus-y smell... my
> mom loved those essential oil things.
> She has a nice voice... smooth...
> soothing... kind of putting me to
> sleep...

9:20 A.M.
Caleb: Just tell me when you're ready for me to
release. It's not good to stay in a memory for too
long. It's kinda like a drug.

> **V:** I just want to stay here forever... but
> I guess... I guess I have to go.

Caleb: OK, I'm letting go. We can revisit it
sometime. All right, now do you know why we did
that?

> **V:** Um, no...

Caleb: To remind you that you're more than what's
been done to you. Just have to dig deep.

> **V:** Thank you.

Caleb: Oooof, wow. You don't give bad hugs.

> **V:** You neither. Dang it, I'm crying
> again, even though I'm happy.

9:21 A.M.

Caleb: Yeah, that sometimes happens to people. Oh, why is my back pocket burning up. Wow. Ummm my phone just got a billion texts from the Meta-Match thing. Think Juan has a new gadget or something for us to try?

> **V:** Let me see... wow, I have a million messages, too. Wait, what? We must have forgotten to turn our earpiece things off or something. Our entire conversation is on here.

Caleb: Shoot. Tell me it was on the PM and not the group text.

> **V:** Thank goodness, yes. Man. Don't need another... you know, Kevin and Himari thing.

Caleb: Yeah, let me shut it off before I accidentally switch it to the gro—

Archived Message "Bittersweet": July 1

Archived Message "Bittersweet": July 1 reopened July 7 at 9:56 P.M.

Cortex: 9:57 P.M.

Hey Sweet Tooth, ol pal. How's death? Sorry. Anyways, I just wanted to say that I had a wonderful day with V. I really feel like there's no villain I'd rather be paired with. She's already ten times better than Seizure. And smells better too. Today I noticed she smells a bit like vanilla. Did you ever find a hero that you just... you know, really connected with?

Cortex: 9:58 P.M.

I would almost say I liked her, but that would be weird, because she's a villain, right? Is there a word a hero can use to say he likes a villain? He crushes on someone he wants to crush?

Cortex: 9:59 P.M.

Nevermind. I'm lightheaded from having my powers drained today. I'm thinking too much about this. Glad I typed this message with my fingers instead of brain (don't think I have the energy to do any more powers today, anyway). Who knows how much Himari or V would ridicule me if they read this.

10:00 P.M.
Cortex: Goodnight, Sweet Tooth. May you find a nemesis wherever you are. And better yet ... a friend.

Now Nemeses :)
July 8

Caleb: 10:07 P.M.

V. Look, I know you don't want to talk, but please tell me if he's ok.

Caleb: 10:09 P.M.

I didn't know he was messing with the wiring when we were setting everything up. He was really quiet on the catwalk. It's so dark up there.

Caleb: 10:11 P.M.

I seriously wish I could take it all back. Please. I had no idea he was up there. Please tell me he did ok. Dragons can withstand fire and stuff. A couple hundred volts of electricity is kind of like that.

Caleb: 10:13 P.M.

At least let me know which room of the hospital he's in. I can come visit and bring a fruit basket or a basket of tea or something. What are some things Bernard likes? I wish I knew him a little better.

10:15 P.M.
Caleb:
V. Come on. Just tell me what I can do.

V: He's dead.

Caleb: What? No. That doesn't make any sense. He was alive when they wheeled him out on the stretcher.

Caleb: When? When did he pass?

10:16 P.M.
V: It wasn't the electricity... it was the shock it gave his heart. You know it wasn't doing that great.

Caleb: V, I swear I wish I could take it back.

V: I told you everything. He was literally the only person I had left. And you freaking killed him. Nice. Real nice. I guess you got me. Great job, hero. You win. Or can you really call yourself a hero? More like villain.

10:17 P.M.
Caleb: You're mad. It's completely understandable. Just let me know if I can do anything. I know you literally couldn't hate me more than now, but just let me know.

Caleb: Please.

10:18 P.M.

V blocked Caleb

Private Message
July 8

10:25 P.M.
Kevin changed group name to Roommate Goals.

Cortex changed group name to Kevin, I'm Not In the Mood.

Kevin changed group name to Sorry.

Kevin:

> Want to talk about it?

Cortex: 10:26 P.M.

> What do you think?

Kevin:

> That's a very dangerous question.

Cortex:

> Never mind.

Cortex changed name to Caleb.

Caleb changed PM name to Private Message.

10:27 P.M.
Kevin: Whoa, whoa, bro. I mean, I know your real name cause I live at your house and stuff, but what gives?

> **Caleb:** Makes sense, doesn't it? I broke the no-killing rule. I don't deserve a hero title anymore. I already changed my name in all the messages. The ones V hasn't blocked me from.

Kevin: Wait, what?

> **Caleb:** Seriously, where have you been? I got home a couple hours ago. I thought Himari would've told you by now.

10:28 P.M.
Kevin: Dude, what happened?

> **Caleb:** Kevin, you literally live a couple doors down. Come down the hallway and talk with me in my room.

Kevin: No way. You might have a two-kill streak tonight, and I don't want to take any chances.

> **Caleb:** Of course, I could just come into your room.

10:29 P.M.
Kevin: Nope. Locked the door!

Kevin: Who did you kill?

Kevin: Not V?

10:30 P.M.
Kevin: Tell me you didn't kill V.

> **Caleb:** I didn't kill V.

> **Caleb:** But I electrocuted Bernard on accident.

10:31 P.M.
Kevin: ...

Kevin: How do you do that ... on accident???

> 10:32 P.M.
> **Caleb:** Well, it happens when you're running through light cues with your mind, and some of the wires have been sparking and sputtering (really sketchy theater, by the way, smells like five years of dust). And when Mr. L sends Bernard on a mission to unravel these huge tangled piles of cords because he thinks it's an easy job for an old man to do, he does it. And so, when I try to increase the brightness of a light on stage, the thing sort of... he had a hold of the wire to that particular light ...

10:33 P.M.
Kevin: You fried him like a Twinkie.

Caleb: Yes, thank you for the acute observation.

Kevin: How did she take the news?

Caleb: She blocked me.

10:34 P.M.
Kevin: Daaaaaaaaang. Too bad. I thought you guys worked well together. Or against each other. This site is weird.

10:35 P.M.
Kevin: So. You gonna try to reach out to some other villains? Himari said a couple B-list villains swiped right on your profile. Almost Shadow Sabre level followings.

10:36 P.M.
Caleb: No thanks.

10:37 P.M.
Kevin: You'll get over her eventually, Cortex.

Caleb: Don't call me that.

Kevin: Why not?

Caleb: Because I'm not a hero anymore.

Private Message
July 8

Himari: 10:45 P.M.

Hey, V. I just heard. I'm so, so sorry.
I don't even know what to say.

V: 10:47 P.M.

You're already doing better than your
brother. He apparently has a million
things to say.

Himari:

Yeah, he's like that. He's hardcore moping right
now.

V:

Thought he would be happy. He
defeated a villain. Whoop-de-do.

Himari:

He didn't mean to. He would never do that to
Bernard.

10:48 P.M.
V: Yeah, and Octoman would never kill my parents. "Professional partners" and all. But he did. You can never trust heroes.

Himari: Hey, I know my brother is a pain in the butt, but he doesn't kill people. Especially not Bernard. And especially not someone you care about.

V: We're nemeses. Can't blame him. That's how it works.

Himari: He's been losing his mind all day. It was not intentional.

10:49 P.M.
Himari: V?

10:50 P.M.
Himari: V? Are you by yourself?

V: I have Fluffy. And Mr. Flappers. And Mr. Squiggles, and Gonzo, Chuck, and Carlos. Those are the sharks, by the way.

Himari: Pets don't count. Hey, I've always wanted to be a villain's apprentice. Not a henchman, of course. I'm not that cool. But maybe I could come stay with you?

V: You don't have to do that. I'm fine.

10:51 P.M.
Himari: No, really. You'd be doing me a favor.
Summer internship, you know? Not anything
permanent. I'm not trying to be Bernard.

10:52 P.M.
Himari: Also it would make my brother mad.

       V: Perfect. Come as soon as you can.

Himari: I'm taking the chopper. See you in a few
hours.

Private Message
July 9

Himari: 4:56 A.M.

Are you awake yet?

Cortex changed name to Caleb.

Caleb:

Yeah, bout to head out on a run, why are you messaging me on this thing? We have cell phones, you know.

Himari:

V's house has awful reception in the dungeon. Pretty cool dungeon, by the way. Anyway, Mr. Li... argh however you spell it... he said you guys don't have to help with drama camp. He feels bad about what happened to Bernard.

Caleb: 4:57 A.M.

OK, so many questions.

Caleb:
First, I thought you were at an anime convention. What the heck are you doing at V's house?

Caleb: Second, you need to be either a villain or henchman to private message on this thing unless voice-to-text picks up your voice. So unless you're leaning uncomfortably close to V, what's going on?

4:58 A.M.
Caleb: Third, please tell me you are returning the helicopter which I just discovered went missing.

Caleb: Fourth, which dungeon? The one with the rack or the one with the chains attached to the wall?

Himari: The rack one is her favorite. Anyway, I have henchman status now! I'm V's new intern. I'm kind of going to be here for a while, so... No returning helicopter at the moment.

4:59 A.M.
Caleb: Umm, ok first of all, you just finished your sophomore year of high school. So isn't that a little young to be up and leaving the house? Mom and Dad are going to be freaking out.

Caleb: Mom! Himari, for goodness sake, Mom. Have you thought about what this would do to her?

Himari: It's just for the summer.

5:00 A.M.
Caleb: OK, well congrats. Hope you enjoy the helicopter and a potential future in jail. Is that all you wanted to tell me? Because I've had plenty of other factors that pissed me off in the last twenty-four hours. You'll have to do a little better than that.

Caleb: Going on a run.

Himari: Gosh, you're moody. Fine. Have fun. Someone has to be there for V.

5:01 A.M.
Caleb: *sigh* You don't think I tried? She blocked me, Himari. But of course you already know that since you stalk all my accounts. Also, do not show her my PM with Sweet Tooth.

Himari: Oooo, hadn't read that one yet. Let me go look.

Caleb: No, don't. I'm deleting it.

Caleb: Dang it. Why don't they let you delete messages on this thing? I bet villains built this site.

5:02 A.M.

Himari: AWWWWWWW so cute! Imma tell V.

> **Caleb:** Don't you dare. I'll tell Mom and Dad what you're doing. They'll fly right over and force you to take the helicopter home. Also, have an alibi in mind?

Himari: Ugh, fine. I'm at an anime convention. It's all good. I got this covered.

> 5:03 A.M.
> **Caleb:** You're not at an anime convention all summer.

Himari: Let me worry about that. Crap, V is coming back. See you, bro.

> **Caleb:** Tell her she sucks.

> **Caleb:** Just kidding. Please do not do that.

Himari: Mkay, bye.

Private Message
July 9

11:23 A.M.
Himari changed name to Best Sidekicks Ever

Himari:

Yo, Kevin. You up?

Kevin:

Why are you up at this early hour? What's wrong with you people? I thought Caleb was the only dude who was insane and got up earlier than noon.

Himari:

Yeah, that doesn't work in high school.
Besides, it's like eight thirty here. I'm with V.

Kevin: 11:24 A.M.

Here as in Arizona? How'd you get there? And can you please kidnap me so I don't have to deal with your moody brother?

Himari:
I took the helicopter.
Is he still being a butt?

> 11:25 A.M.
> **Kevin:** Luckily, I was asleep and didn't bump into him this morning, but yeah. Last night was bad. He threw his costume in the trash and everything. Tore down all the posters of heroes on his wall. It's bad.

Himari: Ugh, he's so dramatic. V has been sulking in the dungeon all day. But that's a little more understandable. Bernard was everything to her.

> **Kevin:** True. Seriously, your brother's more a villain than she is at this point. I think he thinks so, too.

11:26 A.M.
Himari: What does that even mean?

> **Kevin:** Well, let's start with the fact he threatens me all the time. And, also, he's not very good at saving people. I sneaked onto his laptop last night when he was fast asleep to ... never mind what I was doing, but I read about his most recent fight fight with V. Some dude choked, and he had no idea what to do.
>
> 11:27 A.M.

Kevin: And then he killed Bernard. He doesn't have a great track record.

Himari: Not to mention the fact he keeps dating villains. Although, if it was V, I ship it. Anyway, I guess he's having some sort of identity crisis. I did that a few years ago. Everyone in the family is a hero, but I prefer the villain life.

Kevin: Yeah, this was a lot easier when I was skipping gen ed classes and had no idea superhero families were that big of a thing.

11:28 A.M.
Kevin: So what do we do? Because once he finishes with his hero posters, he'll come after my Hamilton one. The fifteen bucks it cost me drained my whole bank account.

Himari: Yikes. We need to get them back together, pronto.

Kevin: Agreed. Because as much as I appreciate the free housing, if Caleb turns villain, we know who his first victim is going to be.

Himari: Hmmm... we just need them to actually talk to each other. But they won't agree to that.

11:29 A.M.

Kevin: Yeah, she blocked him. So unless she initiates ... we all know that won't happen.

Kevin: Ooooh idea! We have this fun initiation in Phi Delta where the freshies think they're going on a blind date with one girl, but we actually set them up with guys in our frat dressed in drag. Fun, huh? Here's a pic of me on my date with one of the lovely "ladies".

11:30 A.M.
Himari: That's hilarious! But... what does that have to do with anything?

Kevin: Well, why don't we make them think they're going to a fight, or something (getting used to this hero lingo is weird) with another hero/villain ... but we set them up together.

11:31 A.M.
Himari: Ohhh, yes. What if I tell my bro I found a villain here, and you tell V you found a hero friend of Caleb?

Kevin: I could. You sure she hasn't blocked me yet?

Himari: Nah, she probably likes you more than ever. She likes anything that annoys Caleb right now.

Kevin: Oooooh good! I can talk about how he's driving me insane, too. Question: how will Caleb get to Arizona without a flap flap machine?

Himari: I'll use the helicopter to bring her to Indiana.

11:32 A.M.
Kevin: She might get suspicious if it's that close. What about Ohio or Michigan? Both of those are close.

Kevin: CEDAR POINT! I LOVE ROLLER COASTERS. WHILE THEY FIGHT WE CAN SPEND THE DAY AT THE PARK!

Himari: Yes! Yes yes yes! Okay, operation fix the moody super-people problems underway!

11:33 A.M.
Kevin: Also, can someone lend me seventy bucks for a ticket? I think Caleb cut off my allowance as an unpaid intern.

Himari: No problem. I got you.
There have to be some perks to having a family in the arms dealing business.

Kevin: Hahahaha. What?

Himari: Didn't you know? We make prosthetic arms.

Himari: JK, we sell top-of-the-line military equipment to governments friendly to the U.S.

> 11:34 A.M.
> **Kevin:** Whatever. What day should we have them meet up?

Himari: Maybe Wednesday? Give them a day to cool off a little, but not long enough for us to die from moodiness.

> **Kevin:** Me likee that plan. I'll hide in my room then and listen to Wicked under my blankets. Although it is getting really hot outside. How are you surviving in Arizona?

Himari: I get why V lives here, being a villain and all. It feels like the fires of hell.

> 11:35 A.M.
> **Kevin:** Well have fun, and good luck in your chat. Hopefully V won't send me that second place you mentioned.

Himari: Sidekicks away!

Private Message
July 10

Kevin: 12:01 P.M.

Hey, V! How's my favorite 22nd letter of the alphabet?

Kevin changed group name to BESTIES FOREVER <3

V: 12:07 P.M.

What are you doing, Kevin?

Kevin:

Begging you to kidnap me from this house of madness! Madness, I say!!!!!!!!!!

V:

Yeah, you're living with a jerk. Sorry you have to deal with that.

Kevin:

Thing is, I'm trying to connect with other heroes on this site. Hopefully I'll be out of it soon, but I thought, "Who hates Caleb's guts more than anything else and will understand my plight." And of course, the 22nd letter in the alphabet came to my head.

Kevin: That's you!

> 12:08 P.M.
> **V:** Yep, caught that. Are you asking me to set you up with a new hero? Because I don't really know many. Lots of villains, though.

Kevin: No way, babe. This hunk of meat is in high demand in the hero market. Got all these dudes in capes practically begging me to pour them coffee. Jealous? ;)

> **V:** I'd rather bash their brains then brew coffee.

12:09 P.M.
Kevin: But I don't want to loosen all ties, you know? Even though I got stuck with a crappy hero, he had a pretty cool villain. You wanna meet up with my new hero when the contract and W-9s are all signed?

> **V:** Yeah, I'd like that. But just warning you, I'm in a killing mood. The hero might not survive.

Kevin: Eh, that's fine. That means more internships for me (man, like, three in one summer). There's this cool guy from Ohio. Here's a screenshot of his profile. Whaddya think?

V: DynoMan? Explosives? Yeah, I'm down.

12:10 P.M.
Kevin: Cool, cool. And also, even though his costume literally has ticking time bombs attached to his belt, he's a rather chill dude. And totally cool with dying soon. Hence, the bombs.

V: Cool. I can help with that. Where are we meeting?

Kevin: This Neat-O place called Cedar Point. Also, the dude said he'd rather you not PM him. His last nemesis sent a virus on his computer, and he's wary about matching with anyone but sidekicks on this site.

V: Fair enough. I tried to do that to Cortex once. When we meeting?

12:11 P.M.
Kevin: Oh, late afternoon. This guy likes to sleeeeeeeeeeeep. How does 4:15 Ohio time sound for Wednesday?

V: Like, literally tomorrow? That's fast. Okay. I'll ask Himari to take me in the helicopter.

Kevin: Cool. Funzies. Wow. Amazing. Great.

V: Okay... well, see you then.

12:12 P.M.

Kevin: For sure. Also, wanna buy me some funnel cake afterwards? Spent all my funds on my last ticket to go :'(feeeeeeeeeeed the biiiiiiiiiiirds

> **V:** Good thing I like birds. You'll get your reward. Thanks for the set-up, Kevin.

Kevin: Oh ho ho ... set up indeed. See you tomorrow, red eyes ;)

Private Message
July 10

Himari: 1:05 P.M.

Hey, bro. Still moping around?

Caleb:

Hey, traitor. And, no. I did a lot today. Met up with a few friends. Ran ten miles. It's a great day.

Himari:

Glad to hear it. Anyway, do you feel like fighting? I networked with this cool villain who's looking for someone to fight.

Caleb: 1:06 P.M.

Not interested. I think my hero days are done. Besides, the garbageman collects the trash at three, so I'll have nothing to wear.

Himari:

Idiot. Pull your suit out of the trash. This is not really a question. The villain is trying to provoke a fight.

She's going to break the Wicked Twister at Cedar Point tomorrow. Kill a bunch of people. I can't do anything, but you can.

> 1:07 P.M.
> **Caleb:** OK, first off, no one rides the Wicked Twister.

> **Caleb:** Second off, this is really out of character for you. You sure V didn't put you up to this to send me to my death or something at a roller coaster park?

Himari: Butt. I don't want innocent people to die. Just because I like villainy doesn't mean I'm a murderer or something.

> 1:08 P.M.
> **Caleb:** *Sigh* which villain are we talking about? And honestly, I'll probably hurt the situation more than help. I don't know how to save people.

Himari: It's a rollercoaster, idiot. You can just mind control the controls or whatever. Anyway, it's DynaVillain. Here's a pic.

> **Caleb:** I don't know, H. She has a crazy resume. Seriously, she included her body count on her profile. It's in the three-digits.

Himari: So you're just going to let people die because you're chicken? Wow. You really are a villain.

1:09 P.M.
Caleb: Cut that out. You know I don't want innocent people to die.

Himari: Yeah? Then prove it. Be a man and save those people. Show me you aren't a villain. Save more lives than the one you lost.

Caleb: Gee, thanks for the reminder. Fine. Any tips for what time Dynawhoever she is is gonna arrive at Cedar Point?

Himari: 4:15. Tomorrow. Be there.

1:10 P.M.
Caleb: Let me double check with Kevin to see if he wants to come. He keeps complaining that I'm not giving him enough hours to fulfill the internship credits.

1:13 P.M.
Caleb: He rolled his eyes, shrugged, and said, "Fine. I guess I have nothing else on my schedule for tomorrow."

Himari: Sounds like Kevin. Gotta feed the sharks. Bye, bro.

Caleb: Please tell me you're not giving them human meat.

Himari: Of course not. That's not healthy for them. Peace!

Private Message
July 11

Kevin: 3:47 P.M.

We there yet, bro?

Caleb:

You didn't have to come. I thought I'd invite you and all since you've missed out on literally all my fights this summer.

Kevin:

Not that one time Sweet Tooth stabbed you. Ugh, that was awful. I want to vomit just thinking about it.

Caleb:

Why are you coming again? And why did you have me turn speech-to-text on?

Kevin: 3:48 P.M.

I have journals I gotta fill out each week for the internship. If I don't do anything interesting, my teacher'll fail me.

Caleb: And the speech-to-text?

Kevin: My, uh, teacher wants a transcript from the event. The prof's a big fan of superheroes and wants to analyze the sociological habits of hero-villain combat.

Caleb: Uh huh. I see.

3:49 P.M.
Kevin: What's with all the questions? I could ask you why you're wearing your dad's red suit. I mean, it fits well except it bunches around your calves. And there's the tear in it.

Caleb: Because I forgot about my other costume until after the garbage man picked it up, and designers can't turn out a new costume every other day.

Kevin: Why not?

Caleb: Well, with the number of up-and-coming heroes. It doesn't make much sense.

3:50 P.M.
Kevin: I'm bored.

Caleb: We're literally twenty minutes away.

Kevin: Let me play some music.

Caleb: Fine. But I'm going to turn these things off until we get there. No sense in your poor prof having to read through pages of Broadway lyrics.

4:10 P.M.
Kevin: We here?

Caleb: No, we're just pulling into a parking space that I paid twenty dollars for to admire polluted Lake Erie. What do you think?

Kevin: I think I smell five dollar funnel fries that you're going to buy me.

Caleb: Maybe after we stop the roller coaster. Why we heading to the beach again?

Kevin: Can't afford a park ticket. Besides, Wicked Twister is right by the water. You can control the coaster from that distance.

4:11 P.M.
Caleb: Dude. I would've bought you a ticket if you wanted.

Kevin: Nah, it's good, I have one.

Caleb: You what?

Kevin: Also, you might want to change your name on this thing. Otherwise my prof will know your secret identity. I think you can just say the command and it'll change.

Caleb: Change name to Cortex.

Caleb changed name to Cortex.

4:12 P.M.
Kevin: Whoa, I did not like the lady's voice who said that. Sounded robotic and Spanish.

Cortex: OK, almost to the beach. Come on, let's sprint this last stretch just in case.

4:14 P.M.
Cortex: Made it. Man, Kevin, you're slow. I'll wait up for you her-

4:15 P.M.
Cortex: Kevin, am I supposed to fight the creepy person in the cloak and mask over there?

Private Message
July 11

V: 4:13 P.M.

Okay, Himari. I'm in position. Can you hear me?

Himari:

Yep. I'm watching from over here. See me waving?

V:

Cool. This might get bloody. I don't know if you want to watch.

Himari:

Nah, it's good. How do you like the fireproof mask and costume?

V: 4:14 P.M.

It's fantastic, honestly. Where did you get it?

Himari:

Called in a favor yesterday. Obviously you're going to win, but I don't know how to help with burn wounds, so...

V: Thanks. Wait, is that the dude, that lame-o on the beach? That red suit is awful.

> **Himari:** I guess so. Dang, I guess he really does have a death wish or something. He doesn't look like he cares a whole lot about appearances.

4:15 P.M.
V: All right. I'm going to go provoke him. Threaten a civilian or something.

> **Himari:** Cool. Have fun! I want to see lots of gore.

Best Sidekicks Ever
July 11

Kevin: 4:15 P.M.

So when do you think they'll figure out who we set them up with? Turned off my speech to text thing, by the way, so he won't hear us.

Himari:

Same. I turned it off with V, until the right moment. Dang, she's going at him. Oh! Yep, that's a knife.

Kevin:

Glad he remembered the katana. Oh, and look. There's a lady in a bikini who is screaming. Classic. Also, what are you doing in Lake Erie, lady? That thing is nasty!

Himari:

That's disgusting. Wow! How many knives does she have? Is that a freaking sword?

Kevin: 4:16 P.M.

Maybe this wasn't a good idea. I mean, there are times I want him to die, but ... wait a minute, now they're trash-talking.

Himari: Classic. Oh, it was a distraction. He just went for the head. Brutal, bro.

Kevin: I know he has a killing streak, but come on. OK, so now they're just kicking up sand at each other.

Himari: Oh, gosh. Kevin, she's bringing out her poison knife. We need to intervene!

4:17 P.M.
Kevin: Yeah, and her eyes just darted to the tear in his dad's suit. What do we do?

Himari: I'm going to put us all in a chat. Prepare to scream at them.

Kevin: Over the sound of the Wicked Twister coaster, you bet!

Group Message
July 11

4:17 P.M.
Himari added Kevin

Himari added Cortex

Himari added V

Kevin: 4:18 P.M.

Cortex, stop fighting!!!!!!

Himari:

V! Drop the knife!

Cortex:

V?

V:

What the... Kevin? How are you talking in my ear?

Kevin:

I'm everywhere.

Cortex: He's behind those bushes by the fence.

V: What the heck? Cortex? I'm supposed to be fighting DynoMan.

4:19 P.M.
Cortex: Yeah, well I was under the impression I'm supposed to stop another Dyno-something from killing the Wicked Twister riders.

V: Kevin! You set me up!

Kevin: Heeeheehee yeah baby I did!

Cortex: OK, Himari. Where you hiding?

Himari: Yeah, not telling you right now. But heyyyy, we're all back together! That was a crazy good fight.

4:20 P.M.
Cortex: Ummm no we're not. Seriously, how did you think this was going to pan out? She almost killed me like five times.

V: And you're not out of the woods yet, bud.

Himari: Guys, stop it. That was an awesome fight. Don't you miss that?

4:21 P.M.

Cortex: I don't know. We haven't had a real one before. I kind of like to know who I'm fighting before I try to kill them!

Himari: So you hate her? And you want to fight her?

V: What kind of henchman are you?

Kevin: While you guys kill each other, can I head into the park now? I want to try the new Meanstreak installment.

4:22 P.M.
V: No. You're still in trouble.

Kevin: I can hop on the Wicked Twister and you can try to kill me there! Just let me die happy.

V: Cortex, were you part of this? Another trick?

Cortex: Ugh, no. I know when I've screwed someone over enough. And no, Himari told me I was meeting up with a different villain here. I wouldn't have fought that hard if I knew ...

Himari: Yeah, I take full responsibility. He didn't know. It was fun to watch, though. You guys are like, perfectly matched.

Kevin: Stop trying to be a hero, Himari. We both set them up.

4:23 P.M.

Cortex: Kevin, just go into the park. You probably have enough of a transcript to give to your teacher.

Kevin: Yeah, about that. We didn't record your fight. But you can see our commentary anytime.

V: Yeah... will you two give us a sec? Go ride a ride or something.

Himari: Yep. Signing off!

Kevin: Hey, I have an app with ride times. Dragster's not crazy. Wanna go? I'll take you sprinting away as a yes.

Private Message
July 11

4:24 P.M.
V unblocked Caleb.

Caleb:

Change name to Cortex.

Caleb changed name to Cortex.

V:

That's better. Couldn't hear you over the noise. It helps with this whole speech-to-text thing in our ears.

Cortex: 4:25 P.M.

Yeah, I forgot how loud some of those roller coasters get. Probably would've recognized your voice during the fight if they weren't making screaming noises.

V:

So... I guess I almost killed you. With a poison knife.

Cortex: What, no. Not even close. You were like three feet away.

> **V:** Yeah, well, they seemed to think you were in danger. Though you were fighting really well...

Cortex: No, you did really good, too. Seriously, gave me a work out for like a month. My abs and calves kill right now.

> 4:26 P.M.
> **V:** So I kind of did kill you. Heh heh.

Cortex: So... on a scale of one to Kevin how much do you hate me right now?

> **V:** Good hate, or bad hate?

Cortex: Mind if I sit? Ugh, sand. I don't know. I didn't know there were two kinds.

> **V:** Ugh, it does feel good to sit down. Um, I mean, good hate is like I want to be your nemesis. Bad hate is I either want to murder you or never see you again.

4:27 P.M.
Cortex: Oh, I guess that sort of makes sense. I feel like both kinds of the bad hate would suck. But I can't really decide which would be worse.

> **V:** Well... I don't exactly want to kill you as much at the moment as I did.

Cortex: But you don't want to see me again after this?

> **V:** I... Ugh! I can't even blame you anymore. Why can't it be someone's fault so I can kill them? That would be so much easier!

4:28 P.M.
Cortex: V, it's totally my fault. Just go ahead and kill me right now. You'd be doing both of us a favor.

> **V:** What the heck is that supposed to mean? I'm not going to freaking kill you. It wasn't intentional. And besides... I don't think I could.

Cortex: Right. It would be a waste. You wouldn't even be killing a hero.

> **V:** Stop talking like that! I don't need another person dying on me. We all make mistakes. I'm really sorry I blamed you. That was beyond villainous.

4:29 P.M.
Cortex: V, I don't blame you for being human. You loved him. I-if that were to happen to my m-mom. You're human. Not a villain. OK? Human.

> **V:** And you're human, too. You don't have to be perfect. Gosh, sometimes I hate this whole division thing. There's so much pressure to fit a certain mold.

Cortex: Yeah. I guess if we actually saw the face of the person we were facing, there'd be a lot less fighting, huh?

V: I'm taking this mask off.

Cortex: Me too.

4:30 P.M.
V: You look so much better without it.

Cortex: Yeah, you too. I didn't know you had freckles on your nose.

V: By the way, my eyes aren't red. Ugh, this sand. I'm taking out these stupid contacts. There.

Cortex: Green. Dang. Those eyes are really really green. Like Ireland could inhabit them.

V: Haha. Dork. I...

4:31 P.M.
Unknown Source: Caleb, what are you doing here? I thought you hated roller coasters.

Cortex: What? Oh, Ta—Juliet. Man, you had a hike to get up here.

Juliet: Yeah, brother's a big fan of the Maverick. Thought he would take me with a group of his friends. Would've invited you if I knew you'd be up here with—you guys just sitting and watching the lake?

Cortex: Nah, just talking. She and I bumped into each other on accident.

Juliet: Oh, sorry. I just thought it looked a little odd. Do nemeses usually hang out after they split?

V: You told her we split? I thought you guys weren't talking anymore.

4:32 P.M.
Cortex: Yeah, uh, well, we met up yesterday. She happens to jog early in the mornings, too, and well ...

Juliet: We're back together. I had some things to work through with my grandpa's death, but I'm better now.

V: Oh. Well, that's um, nice. Well, I have to go. I think the sharks are probably hungry. Have fun.

Cortex: Wait, V, what about Himari?

Juliet: Himari? Like, your sister Himari? What did she do now?

V: I'll find her. We have to go.

4:33 P.M.
Cortex: Oh, well, all right. You still want to talk on Meta and fight, or still looking around for other nemeses?

V: I'll have my henchman talk to your sidekick. Nice to see you, Juliet. Cortex.

Juliet: Bye.

V: I'm turning this thing of—

Archived Message "Bittersweet": July 1

Archived Message "Bittersweet": July 1
reopened July 9

Cortex: 2:03 P.M.

So, I can't tell if what I did today would count as something heroic or villainous, but at this point, I don't freaking care. Let me lay it all out for you, Sweetie.

Cortex:

Step One: Piss off V because you killed her grandpa and now she hates your guts and will never talk to you again.

Cortex:

Step Two: You freak out because now you have no idea whether you should hang up your cape or just go for villainy because you can't save lives for beans.

Cortex: 2:04 P.M.

Step Three: You look through the profiles of other villains at three in the morning and realize you never had it so good than you did with your last nemeses. Even if Insanity is the worst of them, you'll never pair with anyone quite like V. You know you won't.

Cortex: Step Four: To clear your mind, especially since your sister just stole your helicopter, you go for a ten mile jog before the sun rises. As you head up the hill, you can see another runner with her blonde hair swishing even in the dark early morning light. She looks like she's wheezing a bit and bent over.

2:05 P.M.
Cortex: Step Five: You realize it's Tamora. She'd mentioned something about asthma before. It's awkward. But you don't see a whole lot of runners out this time of morning, and it would be even more weird if you kept running without talking to her first. So you talk as she stops to walk because she can't run like she used to in high school.

Cortex: Step Six: So you talk. And she seems great. Ten times better. She's gotten better over the death of her grandpa. And then you think, hey, maybe V will be like that someday.

Cortex: Step Seven: Just kidding. You didn't freaking kill Tamora's grandpa.

2:06 P.M.
Cortex: Step Eight: Ten miles in, it's about seven, and you're both hungry. You stop by a local diner and sit. And talk. And eat. And talk. And now we're not eating. And now we're holding hands. And now we're kissing. And now we're back together.

Cortex: Step Nine: Isn't that great. So why doesn't it feel great? Why doesn't it feel great?
2:07 P.M.

Cortex: Step Ten: You will never have it good again. Because you're no good.

Private Message
July 11

Victoria: 11:35 P.M.

Hey, Bernard. I miss you.

Victoria:

I wish I could wake up every morning... well, late morning... and you would be there sipping tea, reading *The Daily Villain*.

Victoria:

Himari is living here now. I thought you might like that. You liked her.

Victoria: 11:36 P.M.

I'm so confused.

Victoria: You raised so many great villains. But you never killed anyone yourself. No matter who it was, your assassin friend, or whatever... you were just there for us when we needed you. Advice. Love, in your very proper way. Offering to torch Kevin. You'd be pleased to know that he's settled down.

11:37 P.M.
Victoria: You didn't deserve to die like that. But I know you would never blame Caleb. It wasn't intentional. There's no way he could have done anything differently without seeing the future. Unfortunately, that's not one of his powers.

Victoria: Something weird happened today.

Victoria: Himari and Kevin set Caleb and I up to fight. We thought we were going to be fighting other people. Long story short, he and I were talking. I unblocked him. It was going well, I think. He was all torn up about what happened, too. All the divisions between villains and heroes seemed so dumb in that moment.

11:38 P.M.
Victoria: Hopefully you can't torch people from the grave, because I'm going to tell you this. We took our masks off. I took out those stupid contacts. Sand in them, anyway, and they burn on a normal day. Well, he was looking in my eyes, and I... just couldn't look away. He was really close, and...

Victoria: Never mind. It's stupid. Anyway, his bleached-blonde girlfriend showed up. Apparently they're back together. He has horrible taste in women. She's not even that pretty. And she's, like, completely flat. Boring. Not that I care. We're nemeses, after all. Works for me if the girlfriend is lame.

11:39 P.M.
Victoria: At least I have my nemesis back.

Private Message
July 12

Cortex: 3:04 P.M.

Hey, happy Thursday. So … funny story. Umm, Juliet doesn't really want us to fight anymore.

Cortex changed name to Caleb.

Caleb changed PM name to Still Nemeses (fingers crossed)

V:

Hey! Um… is this another "yeah, never mind, we're not nemeses anymore" thing? Because the title of the group chat kind of… doesn't match.

Caleb: 3:05 P.M.

Soooo, like, when I was getting coffee with her and she was talking to me about all the reasons why it made no sense. I think she brought up how I needed to finish college and if she and I got into a long term relationship … a lot of it made sense. But, as soon as I left, I was like, "Wait a minute. No. I still want to fight V." So here we are.

V: So... what are you going to tell her?

3:06 P.M.
Caleb: I kind of hoped I didn't have to say anything to her. She's really good at persuading people of things. Like, I think she placed in nationals for debate this last year.

V: So you want to fight secretly?

Caleb: Yeah, kinda. I mean, we combat really, really well. Just think of the beach yesterday. The horrible stench of the polluted Lake Erie. Me kicking sand in your face ... good times.

V: Wow. You brought up all my favorite parts of that fight... not. Why don't we remember me almost taking your nose off with my knife? ;)

3:07 P.M.
Caleb: I mean, it is a big nose. It could use a trim. Yeah, I'd be down for a secret fight or two. Good thing Juliet's not my master so I'm not going behind her back and all (at least, she won't kill me for it). And my real master (my dad) likes you, soooo...

V: Ha! Well, my master just so happens to be dead. And as far as I know, even her master is dead, interestingly. Dropped off the grid a month ago. So I guess we're doing whatever we want.

Caleb: Wait, a master's master? Masterception?

3:08 P.M.

V: Yeah, there was this head honcho named Tempest. Don't know what his (or her) real name was, but the dude was in charge of like this giant killing-people empire. I guess Tempest wasn't into the whole villain-hero status quo. He/she/it wanted all the heroes dead. Really into world domination.

3:09 P.M.

Caleb: All those poor giants...being killed by that killing-people empire :) Poor Goliath.

V: Dweeb. So when are we fighting again?

Caleb: I'm free later today. This weekend is out because my parents scheduled orientation at Ball State. Mind you, they must've forgotten about drama camp performances when they signed me up for it.

V: At least something worked out in this awful week, I guess. I could crash it, if you want. Terrorize some freshies.

3:10 P.M.

Caleb: Sure! Maybe you can join us on our campus tour and act like you've gone there for years. Tell us all the wrong info.

V: I am totally down for this. But are we fighting today, too?

Caleb: Oh sure. Arizona or Indiana? Or somewhere else?

> **V:** Seeing as Himari still has your helicopter, I think I'd better come to you. Where do you want us to land?

3:11 P.M.
Caleb: Well, the helicopter pad would be a good start. Then again ... I'm trying to think of someplace you can discreetly land a helicopter without my girlfriend noticing.

> **V:** It's your family's helicopter. I doubt she'll be suspicious. We can make use of that massive animal-less backyard of yours.

Caleb: All right, I guess that works. Also, we rented Breakfast Club. And, Mom's making breakfast for dinner, wanna join us?

> **V:** For real? Heck, yeah. Himari and I have been eating Pop-Tarts and ramen the past few days. I freaking burn everything.

3:12 P.M.
Caleb: Yeah. Surprisingly, Kevin still eats those things in addition to whatever we give him here. Himari doesn't have a super sophisticated palate, so she'll eat anything.

> **V:** Cool. I'll go get Himari. She'll love this, too. We'll be there in a few hours.

Caleb: Nice, and if you have any orange juice or milk, Kevin just chugged the bottles. Like literally. The entire thing. He grabs them before anyone opens them and then suckles them and then says, "Oh, do you want some?" Seriously, tell me I won't end up like this as a college student.

> 3:13 P.M.
> **V:** Classic Kevin. Well, I don't have those, but I have children's tears and heroes' blood. JK. I'll bring some OJ.

Caleb: I'm cool with that as long as a Simpson doesn't follow. See you in a few. Hours.

Archived Message "Bittersweet": July 1

Archived Message "Bittersweet": July 1 reopened July 12

Cortex: 4:32 P.M.

Yo, Sweetie. Just found out something disturbing. Was hesitant to put it in here, but I needed to tell someone.

Cortex: 4:33 P.M.

OK, so I used to date Stroke, right? Well, if you didn't know, now you do. And, of course, I didn't know it was Stroke. I thought she was some girl who attended my rival high school.

Cortex:

So then, an hour ago, V mentioned something about masters having masters (I guess villains have some weird CEO hierarchy or something like we saw in retail). And then she got me thinking: Wait a minute. Didn't the master kill V's parents when she turned ten or something? If Stroke was roughly my same age, then she would've forced V to do all sorts

of awful things well before she reached her middle
school years.

4:34 P.M.
Cortex: To make matters trickier, in V's memories I
saw at Garden of the Gods, Stroke didn't look like a
pubescent girl when doing these things. So she had
to have been older. Then, I remembered how her
tan skin formed wrinkles around her eyes when the
sun hit her just right. And she did tire out more
easily whenever we did things like go for long walks
or even runs.

4:35 P.M.
Cortex: So, I researched dozens of articles online to
see what folks had guestimated for her age.
Wikipedia says she died at 26. Some other places
hazard a guess somewhere between 24 to 28.

4:36 P.M.
Cortex: Dude. I dated an old lady. And it was
illegal. Like, we only kissed (that was as far as we
went), but still. I feel like I need to vomit and scrub
my lips with soap for a week straight.

4:37 P.M.
Cortex: Don't tell V, Sweetie.

Cortex: Not that you could. But don't go all ghost
on me.

Still Nemeses (fingers crossed)
July 12

V: 8:04 P.M.

Is she gone yet?

Caleb:

Nope. Definitely plopping on the couch. Reaching for the plate of bacon.

V:

Uuugghhh. I can't blame your gf for coming over, but why did it have to be now?

Caleb:

I don't know. She likes to pop in at random times. She did this before we broke up, too. And, when a girl sees breakfast food, there's no turning her away.

V:

I would argue, but it's true.
Hey, nice soccer trophy.
Were you four? Five?

8:05 P.M.

Caleb: Yeah, it was before I got my powers and my parents made me quit sports ... wait, get out of my room. At least ... don't destroy anything.

V: Himari brought me up here. She wanted to show me stuff. Didn't know it was your room... at first. Now I do. Is that a teddy bear?

Caleb: Oh sure... Himari just likes to put my trophies in her room. And yeah. That's Brutus.

V: Awwww that's so adorable! I have a stuffed angler fish I've had forever. Angie.

8:06 P.M.

Caleb: She's giving me the stink eye for looking at my phone. Mind turning on speech to text? Have one of the earpieces in (the side she's not on).

V: Yeah, sure. Glad you can mind text. How's the situation?

8:07 P.M.

Caleb: Well, now she's going for the pile of cold pancakes. And eating them. Without syrup. What is wrong with her?

V: Noooo you have to have syrup! I'm glad we ate before she got here.

Caleb: And now she's snuggling close. I'm not really sure why. They're smoking weed in the movie. That's not terribly romantic.

V: You didn't pause the movie? Rude.

8:08 P.M.
Caleb: She would've gotten suspicious and … oh, I guess she has to go now. Got a text from someone. I think there's a family event she forgot about.

Caleb: OK she's getting up. She's hugging me.

8:09 P.M.
Caleb: It's a really long hug.

V: Dude, remember, no intimate relationship details.

Caleb: It's literally a hug. Like, we even hug our creepy uncles.

8:10 P.M.
Caleb: OK, now she's heading out the door. Did you hear the click?

V: Yup. Oohhh, what's this?

Caleb: What?

V: Mr. Muncie four and under beauty pageant. Didn't know that was a thing.

8:11 P.M.

Caleb: Oh no. Now you're going through my drawers. And yes, my mom took me there against my will when I was two. But clearly my looks were rugged even then.

V: Second place? Gosh, what happened since? Haha.

Caleb: I mean if you take the first place guy out, then I would be the most handsome man in Muncie.

V: Wow. Were they blind? JK. You were a nice looking baby. Cute bottom in the bathtub.

8:12 P.M.

Caleb: OK, how about you come downstairs and we finish the movie?

V: Himari may be asphyxiating she's laughing so hard. I better bring her down.

Caleb: All right. Also V ... I just remembered, we forgot to fight. We were supposed to do it when you got here an hour ago.

8:13 P.M.

V: Yeah, but then the pancakes were ready. Guess it will be a fight in the dark. Oooo, more epic, you know? But we have to finish the movie. Does anyone get killed? Maimed?

Caleb: Yep. All those things. How did you ever guess?

V: Detention is deadly. Woohoo! Coming down for some gore.

Private Message
July 12

Himari: 9:15 P.M.

Yo, Caleb. Thought you were gonna fight the girl. Looks like she's passed out on your shoulder. Did you kill her already?

Caleb:

Himari, why are you messaging me? We're literally in the same house.

Himari:

Don't want to wake up your little snuggler.

Caleb:

I think she just got bored because no one was dying on screen. When she gets up, I'll tell her she missed the most horrific deaths.

Himari:

Ooo, so you're just gonna let her sleep there? Oooooooo.

9:16 P.M.

Caleb: Duh. She loves sleep. If I wake her, she'll kill me.

Caleb: Although, I probably should get her up soon. It's getting late. The sun's going down outside. You guys need to get home before it gets dark.

Himari: I'm not flying in the dark. We already have this planned out. V is sleeping over with me. Slumber party!

9:17 P.M.

Caleb: What? I didn't know this was happening. Well, your party's gonna be incredibly lame because she's conked out.

Himari: For now. You should see how we party at midnight.

Caleb: Yeah? What all do you do?

Himari: Don't tell her I told you, but she thinks the sharks like going to the disco at midnight. There's a disco ball in their pool and she sings to them.

9:18 P.M.

Caleb: Duuuude. Can she carry a decent tune?

Himari: Yeah, it's kind of crazy. She's a soprano. Who would have guessed?

Caleb: Yeah, her voice is almost as deep as a dude's. All right, well she's cuddling even closer when I tried to move away. Any plan?

Himari: Get a room? ;)

9:19 P.M.
Caleb: OK that's a great suggestion. But I'm burning it where no one can ever see it. Want to try again?

Himari: Just like cough or something, so she'll wake up. I want to watch another epic fight.

Caleb: Ummm he-uh. He-uh.

V: Nooo, just mmm

9:20 P.M.
Caleb: If she grips me any tighter, I'm going to have difficulty breathing. Seriously, does she have the arms of a koala or something?

Himari: This is hilarious. I'm going to take a pic.

Caleb: No. Where are you?

Himari: You're not the only techie in the family. Hacked the security camera. Click. Nice. I'm sending it to you.

9:21 P.M.

Caleb: Won't Mom be disappointed. And please delete that.

Himari: Nope. Oh, crap. Hey, Mom, I was ju—

Still Nemeses (fingers crossed)
July 12

V: 10:59 P.M.

Caleb? I just woke up in... well, I assume it's the guest room. What happened? Did anyone die in the movie?

Caleb:

Oh everyone. You missed it. It was a massacre.

Caleb:

Uh, I don't know what happened. Maybe you got tired and stumbled into bed. Which guest room is it? The one with the painting on the wall? Or the one with the indoor waterfall?

V:

The waterfall. It's soooooo pretty. But how the heck did I get here? I don't remember anything.

V: Wait, Himari just sent me a pic.

11:00 P.M.
Caleb: No. Don't look at that.

V: Oh... that's awkward...
I didn't mean to do that...

Caleb: Oh it's fine. You were just trying to strangle me. Kind of like what snakes do. Sorry to disappoint, but I'm still alive.

V: Sigh. Alas, my plan failed. Wait, but how did I get here?

11:01 P.M.
Caleb: Expert sleepwalking?

V: Liar. I don't sleepwalk. Thanks, though. Nice choice on the waterfall.

Caleb: Hey, for all we know, Himari might've carried you up there. She plays tennis, you know. Huge guns.

V: Uh-huh. She's only like three inches shorter than me, and all. But we can go with that if you want.

11:02 P.M.
Caleb: So you wide awake now? Or thinking about heading to bed? Also, sorry we don't have a disco ball.

V: A disco ball... Himari! Ugh. Yeah, pretty awake, actually. I bet you're half asleep, though, lame-o.

> **Caleb:** Surprisingly, no. I'm usually out by now, but for some reason I have a lot of energy.

V: Up for a fight?

> **Caleb:** In the dark? We have a couple lights in the backyard, but it's gonna be hard to see. Up to you.

V: I like night fights. Killed one of my heroes that way. Won't kill you, though, don't worry.

> 11:03 P.M.
> **Caleb:** If you do, at least make it easy for my mom to clean up. All right, heading outside. Meet you out back?

V: Yeah. Hey, should we do voice-to-text so we can hear each other without yelling and waking people up? Then you can just talk with your mind and I'll be quiet.

> **Caleb:** Sounds like a plan. Yeah, the cicadas get chatty at this hour.

V: I see you. But you don't see me. Heeheehee

> 11:04 P.M.
> **Caleb:** Mkay, let's not have a repeat of the movie we saw tonight. It got creepy

at the end. You know. The part with all the gory deaths.

V: Ugh, can't believe you let me miss that part. I'll get you for that. Uh!

Caleb: Augh, V! Oh, so that's where you were hiding. Just behind the corner of the house. Wait. Augh. Augh. What are you doing?

V: Fighting. Come on, you have to block before I start actually hitting you.

Caleb: I can't see your arms. You're literally wearing all black clothing.

11:05 P.M.
V: Heehee sucks to suck. Thanks for the katana. And this. And this. Pickpocketing is fun.

Caleb: Come on. The katana is fine and all, but I need my wallet. It has all of twenty-four dollars in it. That's double Kevin's bank account.

V: Poor Kevin. I guess you'll have to catch me if you want it back.

11:06 P.M.
Caleb: V. V! I literally run ten miles a day. Give it to me you—haha, augh, augh. Forgot you had that free hand. Go easy on the stomach.

V: No mercy! I will beat you, foul hero!

> **Caleb:** Nay, dastardly villain! I shall protect this fine city from thee!

V: Your heroic speech is nauseating. Thus, I must now kill you. I would evil laugh, but I'm trying to be quiet, so just imagine it, okay?

> 11:07 P.M.
> **Caleb:** Fine. Then you won't hear my heroic guffaw because I can be even quieter than you!

V: Ah! Oh my gosh, stop! Tickling is off limits! It makes me scream! Stop, I'm going to wake up the neighborhood.

> **Juliet:** Not if you stop it right now.

Caleb: Oh, Juliet. Hi. Ummm, I was just teaching V how to—tell her V.

> **V:** Um. How to... find another hero. Because. You know. We don't fight anymore.

11:08 P.M.
Caleb: I thought you—you had a family thing.

> **Juliet:** I left something behind, but no one was answering the door. Saw plenty, V. So you can drop the act.

V: Uh, don't know what you mean. Can I help you find whatever it is you left?

> **Juliet:** My boyfriend, thanks.

V: Oh, heh heh. Found him. Right there.

> **Caleb:** Babe, listen, you're making a bigger deal out of this than you need to. We weren't even full-on fighting.

11:09 P.M.
Juliet: Hon, I don't have anything against your villain friend, but you're too young to be fighting yet. I don't want to lose you when you just graduated high school. Promise me you're gonna not do this for a couple years at least.

> **Caleb:** I—uh, I really don't know. Oh, babe your hands are freezing. Let me warm them for you.

Juliet: Thanks. Now about that fighting?

> **Caleb:** I can see it's really hurting you. So, I'll hold off. I promise. Sorry V.

V: What? Caleb, your eyes look kind of weird... are you feeling okay?

> 11:10 P.M.
> **Juliet:** Caleb? She calls you Caleb now?

Caleb: 'Course I'm fine, V. I'm just exhausted. My eyes get bloodshot if I stay up too late.

V: Okay... But Juliet, honestly, how is he going to fight later if he doesn't practice and build his resumé now? That makes no sense.

Juliet: V, please stay out of this. I'm trying to have a talk with my boyfriend. You can wait for us inside.

V: Um, okay... Caleb... you good?

Juliet: He's fine. Stop touching his forehead. Seriously, he's fine. Hands off.

11:11 P.M.
V: Gosh, chill. He can talk for himself, you know. He's like, really hot.

Caleb: I'm fine, V. Actually, you're the one who's not looking too hot. You sure you're doing ok? You just got all sweaty.

V: I... I think I might... oh gosh...

Caleb: V? V! Juliet, I think she passed out.

11:12 P.M.
Juliet: Maybe we should give her some air. I hear it's not good to crowd around someone who just fainted. Here, my hands are freezing again.

Caleb: All right. I'll let Himari know. Walk you to your car?

Juliet: Thanks, babe. You're sweet. Also, you mind turning off that earpiece thingy? Himari was telling me about it when you left for a bathroom break. I'd rather not have Himari read about anything I say to you at the car.

Caleb: Sure, Tamora. No prob—

Still Nemeses (fingers crossed)
July 13

V: 10:01 A.M.

Hey. Sorry again that I passed out. That was super weird. Himari and I got back safe.

Caleb:

Oh, good! Sorry, V. I don't know what happened. I meant to help you up after I walked Juliet to her car, but everything's all fuzzy. I think I might've passed out when I got inside. Not used to staying up crazy late.

V: 10:02 A.M.

Yeah... about that. Something definitely strange happened. Your eyes looked, like, red.

Caleb:

Bloodshot? Also, how could you tell? It was dark out.

V:

Not bloodshot. Like, glowing red. It was freaky.

Caleb: Wait, really? That's weird. You sure you're remembering things right? Like, the time I passed out with the Sweet Tooth incident, everything was kind of a blur for the rest of the afternoon.

10:03 A.M.
V: Maybe... did Juliet seem to be acting weird to you last night?

Caleb: Mmm, maybe a little. But she was kind of weirded out seeing you and me fighting. I don't know why she doesn't like you. Maybe she just doesn't like all villains after the Seizure incident.

V: Maybe. Hey, do you know much about her background? Where she's from and all that?

10:04 A.M.
Caleb: Umm, small town Indiana? Why? I think she's lived in Gas City her whole life.

V: Hmm. What about her family? Do you know anything? Where she went to high school? What she's doing for college?

Caleb: Whoa, whoa, whoa, is this a job interview or something? V, what the heck? Why are you so interested in my girlfriend?

V: I'm just curious. Looking out for you. You know. Hey, what's her real name? Maybe we can be friends.

> 10:05 A.M.
> **Caleb:** I don't know if I feel comfortable telling you her real name. It's one thing with no-killing rule for families. But, with girlfriends...

V: Honestly? You don't trust me at this point?

> **Caleb:** Yeah. I mean, yeah. All right. But you promise to extend the no-killing rule to friends? Friends and family discount?

V: Absolutely. I don't want to hurt you. Besides... I'm going, like, kind of vegan for a while, I guess. No killing. For Bernard.

> 10:06 A.M.
> **Caleb:** Wow, how honorable of you. Her real name is Tamora.

V: Hmm... hold up.

10:07 A.M.
V: Got a last name?

> **Caleb:** Tembrooke. Wanna know her social security next?

V: She on Facebook? I'm not seeing a Tamora Tembrooke in Gas City.

Caleb: Well ... she's not the biggest fan of technology. She thinks it distracts people from the present or something.

10:08 A.M.
V: Weird, since she's literally dating a dude with tech powers. I'm literally not finding her anywhere. You don't find that concerning?

Caleb: Umm no? We're in high school. We don't exactly need LinkedIn profiles yet.

V: Even I have an Insta for the sharks. She's nowhere. I'm just a little concerned after last night.

10:09 A.M.
Caleb: V. What is it you're trying to say?

V: Your eyes were glowing. She was being extremely possessive. I passed out. I don't do that unless I unexpectedly take on power from someone. Are you sure she's who she says she is?

Caleb: OK. It was dark. Hard to see. You were tired; you passed out on the couch. And yes possessive because that's what girlfriends do. Haven't you dated before?

10:10 A.M.
V: You already know I haven't. I just don't like her.

Caleb: Yeah. Why is that? Besides last night, when she was a bit uncool, when did she ever give you a specific reason to hate her? Seriously, Kevin's done crazier stuff.

V: I don't know. There's just something about her. And she doesn't want you around me.

Caleb: Probably because you're pretty and girlfriends get weird about stuff like that.

Caleb: I mean, you know. You're not bad looking and all. Even Kevin thinks so.

10:11 A.M.
V: I mean, I guess. Yeah. I'm just kind of paranoid, I guess. Sorry.

Caleb: No it's all good. And, I'm sorry I agreed to the no-fighting thing. Now that I think about it... I was really tired. I didn't know what I was saying. Maybe I can convince her to let us have a go in a couple weeks.

Caleb: You still crashing my orientation today? Or too tuckered out?

V: Oh, completely forgot about that. Yeah, I'll have to crash your party a different time. Man. What we really need to do is convince Juliet I'm not a threat. How, though?

10:12 A.M.
Caleb: Well, it would probably do you some good to wear pastels around her instead of the color of death.

Caleb: But ... she really likes hanging out with people. Quality time is her love language. Maybe arrange a time for all of us to get together to do... something?

V: Yeah. Maybe diffuse the... whatever it is. What about an Ivanhoe's run or something?

Caleb: Sure, sure. Yeah, I mean, nothing bad can happen at an ice cream store. Villains and heroes alike like it.

V: Right. When should we do this?

10:13 A.M.
Caleb: Let's give her the weekend to cool off. Besides, I need to spend time with family (before and after orientation). My mom thinks I log too many hours on this chat thing.

Caleb: Does Monday sound good? Let me check if that time works with her.

10:16 A.M.
Caleb: She says she's free, but she's curious as to why. What should I tell her?

V: Maybe you just want to have a romantic date. And then I show up and try to kill you. But totally fail. Because you're so strong and all. And obviously I hate you if I'm trying to kill you. So no threat.

> **Caleb:** Ooooh, I like that. So it shows we hate each other, but that I can totally beat you. She's mainly worried that I'm gonna die before our relationship gets serious.

> 10:17 A.M.
> **Caleb:** Let me see what time works best for her.

> 10:19 A.M.
> **Caleb:** Sooo, she wants to get there right when it opens. You ok with an early morning flight? Sorry. She likes to get up early like me.

V: Uuuuugghhhh nooooooo. Fine. What time does it open?

> **Caleb:** 10. Weird for an ice cream and burger place, but guess it makes sense. She and I jog at like five in the morning most days. She's starting to have a hard time keeping up with me. Apparently age has caught up to her. Lol. Old lady at eighteen.

V: Uuuuggghhh that's seven in the morning here. We're going to have to leave at like four or something. Uuuggghhh. At least Himari stole the jet this time, so it's a little faster.

> 10:20 A.M.
> **Caleb:** As in dad's jet? As in, the one vehicle neither of us is allowed to touch until we pry it out of his cold, dead hands? That jet?

V: Oh... She didn't tell me that. Whoops.

> **Caleb:** Uuuugh, I could've used that thing at least five times by now. It's easier to manage than the chopper, anyway. And sorry about the time. If it was with anyone else, I would've changed it. But she would get suspicious.

V: Fair. Okay, sounds like a date.

V: For you two, anyway. Which I'll crash.

> 10:21 A.M.
> **Caleb:** I know she sounds crazy clingy, but I think I know why. She was texting me about her grandpa. Apparently, he had lost his wife to a villain a couple years back. Collateral damage (they dropped a building on her). So, I guess she's shaken up about that. And also the whole Seizure thing. I'm not saying what she's doing is right, but she's just paranoid.

V: Oh, wow. Yeah, I guess that makes sense. Poor girl.

10:22 A.M.
Caleb: Yeah, maybe once she warms up to you, you could tell her about your past history with villains who didn't have the no-family rule. She might like you better for it.

V: Maybe. Maybe after you defeat me lol.

Caleb: We can talk about some details later, but I need to get ready for orientation. For some reason, they drew it out for two days. Wonder how big the campus is.

V: Whoa, intense. Okay. Have fun!

Still Nemeses (fingers crossed)
July 14

Caleb: 6:18 P.M.

Hey, Sweetie. Mind-messaging while we're returning back from Ball State. Goodness, that school's like a city. Didn't know Indiana had buildings that big. Have no idea how I'm gonna remember all the names to places. Makes sense why Kevin never went to half his classes; he probably couldn't find them. Everything sort of looks the same. Nice bell tower, though. Wish you were still alive because you had mentioned something about attending here. Maybe you could've showed me around while trying to kill me at the same time. If you don't, college will.

Caleb: 6:19 P.M.

So, is it bad if I'm not looking forward to my date with Tamora tomorrow? She wants to meet up after church at Cracker Barrel. Not only do I not want to go because that's a terrible cliche, but also, I don't know. I don't really look forward to these outlings.

Caleb: Like, when we spend time together and hold hands and stuff, I enjoy myself. But whenever we split and I get some time to myself ... I don't know. Maybe I hate her so much because I miss spending time with her? Does that make sense?

6:20 P.M.
Caleb: I hope she'll get a little more chill after Monday. When she sees me show how much I "hate" V and how I can easily win in a fight against V, she might let me keep my nemesis. If not, well, I'll just have to get better about sneaking around. :)

6:21 P.M.
Caleb: Speaking of V, planning to send her a gift. Ordered it on Amazon a couple days ago. It's a stuffed dragon. I know how much Bernard meant to her ... and it would go great with her stuffed anglerfish. Besides, she needs a little Brutus to help her get through this time (did I mention I had a stuffed bear called Brutus? Because I don't). I think she'll like it. It has gray scales like he did. It comes with a card, a fake piece of gold, and a dragon footprint on it. The card says, "You are the treasure I'm guarding." I mean she is a treasure, so it's not like it's lying. She's beautiful (turns the heads of any guy any place we fight ... even the non sketch ones), really talented (seriously, almost decapitated me), and super interesting to talk to. I know Bernard would've defended her to the death if needed.

6:22 P.M.
Caleb: You know something, Sweetie? I look forward to every fight with V. Even though we

forget to actually throw deadly weapons at each other half the time ... is it normal to want to meet up with your nemesis more than your girlfriend? Also, is it normal to find your greatest villain to be more attractive?

6:25 P.M.
Caleb: Hey, Sweetie. Funny thing. I don't remember changing my name to Caleb on your chat :) We weren't that chummy yet.

6:28 P.M.
Caleb: Oh, crap.

Private Message
July 14

Cortex: 6:29 P.M.

Kevin, do you know if there's any way to delete messages on Meta-Match?

> **Kevin:**
>
> Why you messaging me? We're in the same car.

Cortex:

Yeah, with my mom. Who hates technology.

> **Kevin:**
>
> Oh, yeah. That kind of sucks. Given your powers and everything.

Cortex: 6:30 P.M.

OK, I need you to tell me if you know how to delete messages. I don't think V saw anything yet. She usually replies when she does.

Kevin: Whyyyy? What did you tell her? ;)

Cortex: Stop that. I can't find a delete button anywhere. You of all people should know where it's located since you, of all the people I know, need to retract half the statements you say on the thing.

6:31 P.M.
Kevin: Here, let me see it.

Cortex: Fine, but don't be obvious about reaching for my phone. Mom can spy a bright screen from a mile away. Doesn't help you're sitting adjacent to her seat.

6:33 P.M.
Kevin: Coooooooooooooortex.

Cortex: Shut up.

Kevin: I haven't said anything yet.

Cortex: You will.

6:34 P.M.
Kevin: Can I be the best man?

Cortex: Absolutely not. You making a speech in front of hundreds of people? Pass.

Kevin: Well, who's gonna be your best man then?

Cortex: ...

Kevin: Do you even have any other friends who are guys?

6:35 P.M.
Cortex: Do you know how to delete messages? Yes or no?

Kevin: No. I leave them there to wave high and dry like a blazing red flag.

Cortex: Great, Kev. Thanks for all your help.

6:36 P.M.
Cortex: Sooooo, should I recant? Play it off as a joke? I could say you put me up to it.

Kevin: Yeah, that's a good way for both of us to die. And no. I'd rather stick around long enough for my mom to see me graduate. 'Course, you can kill me afterward before the student loans can get to me.

Cortex: I mean ... there are many ways she could interpret it. Maybe she'll see "attractive" as her ability to make objects gravitate toward her. Like a magnet.

6:37 P.M.
Kevin: Like a hero magnet :)

Cortex: Ugh, why do I go to you for any hopes of help?

Cortex: Should I say I meant all those things as a friend? That she's just like a sister to me?

Kevin: Would you be saying all those things about Himari?

6:38 P.M.
Cortex: Gross, no.

Kevin: Then, I think you have your answer. Maybe wait it out and see what she says. Or pollute her feed with a billion pictures of cats so she'll get annoyed and won't scroll up to read the messages.

Cortex: Finally, a decent suggestion. I'll do that.

6:40 P.M.
Cortex: Think 146 pictures of cats is enough?

Kevin: Paw-sibly. Heeheehee.

Kevin: I'll let myself out.

Cortex: Thank you.

Private Message
July 14

V: 6:26 P.M.

Ummm, Himari? Just got some weird messages from your brother. Does he ever call you Sweetie?

Himari:

Gross! No. Did he call you that? ;)

V:

No... It seemed like he was trying to message someone else. He was talking about me in the third person.

Himari: 6:27 P.M.

What was he saying?

V:

Um, some interesting stuff...
I don't know. I guess I'll just ask him...

Himari: Was he professing his love?

6:28 P.M.
V: Ha! We're nemeses. That's silly. I think he was maybe just complaining about me? I guess something about Juliet...

Himari: Send me screenshots?

V: Nah, it's fine.

Himari: OH MY GOSH WHAT DID HE SAY I HAVE TO SEE!

6:29 P.M.
V: Ugh, fine. I think it's nothing. Here, sent them.

6:32 P.M.
Himari: Duuuuuuude. That's the cheesiest gift ever. What a dork. But that's sooo cute. You have to message him back!

V: He obviously didn't mean to send it. Should I just ignore it?

Himari: What? V, please. Message him back. I can't stand that Tamora chick. Kick her out!

V: Himari! I'm trying to help heal the gap between her and me, not cause trouble.

6:33 P.M.
Himari: Cause trouble! Do it!

V: I'll think about it.

> **Himari:** Do it or I'm coming back from Petsmart without getting cat food!

V: Uugghhh fine. I'm going to check on Mr. Squiggles. Then I will.

Still Nemeses (fingers crossed)
July 14

V: 6:41 P.M.

Hey. Um, nice cat pictures. But why?

Caleb:

Because villains like cats? Here's another fifty of them.

Caleb: 6:42 P.M.

Loooooooooook at the cat pics. Look at them.

V:

You're going to make my phone crash. Why are you doing this?

Caleb:

Because I've finally found your weakness and will defeat you by it?

6:43 P.M.

V: Okay... Hey, by the way, do you know someone named Sweetie?

> **Caleb:** Ummmmmmmmmmmmmmm. No.

V: Weird. I got some messages from you addressed to that person...

> 6:44 P.M.
> **Caleb:** Oh. Lol. Ummm that was to Sweet Tooth. I sort of message my dead enemy sometimes. Yeah, don't read that. It's all trash talking and stuff. You'll get all jealous.

V: I kind of already did read it...

> **Caleb:** Isn't online text interesting? Without the in-person vocal inflection, there are multiple interpretations one phrase can have. Ha ha. Ha. Ha.

6:45 P.M.

V: You idiot, there's not many ways that can be taken!

V: Uh, sorry, Himari stole my phone. She just got back. I'm making her leave.

> **Caleb:** So is the weather still hot in Arizona?

Group Message
July 14

Himari added Caleb

Himari added V

Himari: 6:45 P.M.

Caaaaleeeb!

V:

Himari, what the heck?

Himari:

Not talking to you, V.
Talking to the chicken.

Caleb:

So you stole our jet, huh? That's right.
You better be saying you're the chicken
and you're talking to yourself.

Himari: 6:46 P.M.

Stop changing the subject!

V: Ummm I'm just going to leave this chat... You can message me in the PM if you want, Caleb.

V left the chat.

Caleb: I don't know if I trust saying anything to you in this, even if it's between us. You like to share everything with V.

Himari: Bro. You bought her a dragon? Come on, those texts... I swear I won't tell her. What's going on with you?

6:47 P.M.
Caleb: Nothing. I don't know. Nothing, I have a girlfriend. And it's a stuffed dragon. I could be getting it for our four-year-old cousin Eddie.

Himari: But you got it for her. Dang, if she's more fun to hang out with than Tamora, then just dump that chick.

Caleb: I mean... honestly, I kind of want to.

6:48 P.M.
Caleb: But this isn't the best time with her grandpa and Seizure and everything traumatizing that just happened to her. With her depression, do you know what that would do to her?

Caleb: And, when I spend time with her, like, all of these things seem to evaporate. It's only when we're apart that I want to break it off.

Himari: I guess that would be kind of mean. Okay. I guess I'm just your little sister. But I'm also V's friend. Up to you. I'm stepping out of this.

6:49 P.M.
Caleb: I mean, heroes and villains don't date. It just doesn't happen.

Himari: Seizure fell for a hero girl ;)

Caleb: Love interest and hero are two different things, Himari. Let's just forget this chat thingy happened.

Himari: Fine. But you better message V. She's asking me what we're talking about.

6:50 P.M.
Caleb: Tell her fairytales.

Himari: Idiot.

Still Nemeses (fingers crossed)
July 14

Caleb: 6:52 P.M.

So, my favorite fairytale is Red Riding Hood because they axe a wolf and she wears a red cloak.

V:

Okay... I only really like the Grimm's fairy tales versions. Everyone dies.

Caleb:

Yep. That's fun.

Caleb:

So. Yeah. How are all your sharks doing?

V:

Good. Being sharks. I think Gonzo is getting fat.

6:53 P.M.

Caleb: How come? You been feeding Great Guy to them?

> **V:** I wish. But human meat isn't good for them. I think he's been eating Carlos's food, too. Little bugger.

Caleb: Poor Carlos. Himari likes to eat my food.

Caleb: Speaking of food, how are we going to make the fight look real at Ivanhoe's on Monday? Because we've only had a couple real showdowns, and one involved me punching a window.

> 6:54 P.M.
> **V:** Yeah, and how are we going to make it look like you beat me? Because obviously that would never happen for real.

Caleb: Uh huh. Sure. Well, I mean, it's difficult to kind of go through a point by point fight on this thing. And we don't share phone numbers for obvious reasons. Even then, a call wouldn't be the same as, like, a choreography sesh with Mr. L.

> **V:** He's out of town this weekend, but maybe we could choreograph our own? Himari and I could come there. Good thing she has a credit card for all this jet fuel.

6:55 P.M.

Caleb: Yeah, but my parents might cut her off soon. They're starting to get suspicious about all these anime conventions.

Caleb: That's actually not a bad idea. We do have rooms in our house that Tamora can't easily get to. We could choreograph in one of those in case she accidentally crashes. Plus, you can see the real end to Breakfast Club.

> **V:** Yes! I want to see the gore. I'll tell Himari.

> 6:56 P.M.
> **V:** She's down. Wait, apparently your mom just called her... They found out about the jet. She's supposed to come home immediately and is banned from travel. She says she'll have to spend the night. Not that she's upset. Apparently the beds here are spiky? That's just the headboards. She just sleeps too crazy.

Caleb: Oh, dear Lord. Please pad those. If my sister wakes up with a spike in her head ... she is my parent's favorite child, you know. And of course she went and got herself banned. Classic.

> **V:** I'm sure they love you the same. For the record, you're my favorite sibling (just don't tell Himari.)

Caleb: Wow. Great. Um, thanks? Aren't you a little biased because you're my nemesis? ;)

6:57 P.M.
V: Bias doesn't make it untrue. Got to put this in airplane mode for safety lol. See you soon.

Caleb: OK, tell Himari to enjoy her last flight she'll be taking for a while.

V: Okay. Whoa, hold up. Your mom wants me to stay there for the weekend. Since I don't have a ride back. She says your dad can fly me home Monday evening. Is that okay with you?

6:58 P.M.
Caleb: I'm cool with it. Heads up, though, I'm out for a decent chunk of Sunday. Have a date with Tamora at Cracker Barrel. Think you can survive in our non-spiky house when I'm gone?

V: Yeah, we'll be good. Himari and I are apparently going to go to the pet store and get her a gecko? Hypoallergenic.

Caleb: That sounds dangerous. Have fun. See you later.

Caleb: Ask that gecko if it can get me some decent car insurance.

Still Nemeses (fingers crossed)
July 14

Caleb: 10:04 P.M.

So, sorry we had to turn on the speech to text things since SOMEONE DECIDED TO BLAST MUSIC IN THE BASEMENT WHERE THE WALLS ECHO.

V:

I can't believe Himari is putting up with that.

Caleb:

Oh, wait till he breaks out the Bye Bye Birdie. You'll want to cut off your ears. I'm glad he can't hear us.

V:

Why? Will he hear our anguished screams?

Caleb: 10:05 P.M.

Sometimes I feel like he's more of a villain than a sidekick. Anyways, I thought we would run through the thingy on Monday because I don't know how

long Tamora wants to hang tomorrow. Sometimes
dates—

> **V:** That's an insult to villains.

Caleb: —agreed. Sometimes her dates can last a
whole day. A whole date. Heeheehee. OK. So before
we go upstairs and plug in Breakfast Club, you want
to walk through the plan for Monday so it looks
real?

> **V:** So you guys are sitting there in one
> of those wooden booths, and I walk up
> and yell, "I found you! You will die!"

10:06 P.M.
Caleb: Sure, let's go for the video-game level of
realistic dialogue.

> **V:** Well, do you have a better
> suggestion? Usually I just straight up kill
> people with no intro.

Caleb: Actually, that might be better. Tamora's
really good at telling when people are lying. Tone of
voice and that kind of crap. So, honestly, don't say
anything. Just grab me and yank me out of the
booth.

> **V:** Okay, so I silently walk up to you
> with a deadpan expression and say
> absolutely nothing like a weirdo, then
> grab you and yank you onto the floor.
> Then what? I get in a good stab, just
> for appearances?

10:07 P.M.
Caleb: Well... I'd prefer not. But if you must. She's probably good at detecting lying if you fake stab me like people do on stage. Can we pick where, though?

> **V:** I mean, we could have you block the stab with your super awesome better-than-me moves.

Caleb: True. We do want her to think I won't die in these fights. OK, let's practice that then. I'm sitting on this box here for the Christmas ornaments. Pretend it's a chair—Kevin. Seriously? Singing in the Rain? And what's worse, you picked the number with the actress who can't sing. Himari, you pick the next track. Please.

10:08 P.M.
Caleb: Wow. Himari. Glad to see One Direction is alive and well. Please try again.

Caleb: You know what? This isn't going to improve. She went into Miley Cyrus mode. Let's just quit while we're ahead.

> **V:** Noooo! My ears! I need to punch something. Preferably you.

Caleb: Wait. I can control technology. What's wrong with me? There. How does Final Countdown sound?

> **V:** Yes! Intensity. Not as good as death screams, but pretty good.

10:09 P.M.

Caleb: So I'm sitting here. Enjoying my nice Trojan
Two flavor of icecream, and all of a sudden you
come up behind me. V. Oh, ok there you are. All
right and then you ... say nothing. So grab me out of
this seat. Ugh. Dang, V, where you been hiding
those arm muscles?

> **V:** Whoops. My bad. I'm trying to be
> chill.

Caleb: Seriously, I outweigh you by like fifty
pounds. OK, so then you go to stab me.

> **V:** Okay, I'm gonna go for the throat.
> Dude, move faster! I'm going to
> accidentally kill you!

Caleb: Sorry. OK, so I lean back as you swipe
forward and just barely miss the Adam's apple.
Wow. V. You really don't have to cut it that close.
Cut it. Hahahah.

> 10:10 P.M.
> **V:** Dweeb. Now what?

Caleb: OK, let me think. I'm alert. Adrenaline
pumping. I feel like I would try to get the knife out
of your hand or tackle you. Any preferences?

> **V:** Do both. Grab the wrist and take me
> down. Looks cooler.

Caleb: Oh, ok. Like, I can see that no problem with Seizure. You sure Tamora will be fine with me planting you into the floor?

> **V:** Well, that makes it pretty obvious you're stronger. Then, boom, fight over. Because you're that awesome and I'm that weak. Ugh, I hate saying that.

10:11 P.M.
Caleb: Again, it's acting. It's like a play. OK, so I'm gonna tackle you now ... I ... not really sure how to do this. Should we just do it the first time in the ice cream store?

> **V:** You're going to mess it up. Just go for it. You're not going to hurt me.

Caleb: I feel weird with Kevin and Himari watching.

> **V:** Um, you feel weird fighting? Because they're watching? That makes no sense.

Caleb: Never mind. Just maybe stand like a football player, with your legs apart, so it won't hurt as much when you fall. Like that, yes. OK ... here goes nothing.

> **V:** Oof. Dude. Now you're just hugging me. You have to actually knock me over.

10:12 P.M.
Caleb: It's just weird. I don't usually tackle people unless I'm mad at them or something. Like I want to

tackle Kevin ninety percent of the time. That
sounded weird.

> **V:** Ugh. Allow me to demonstrate. Look
> out!

Caleb: Oooof, dang, V. OK. OK. I get it. If you can
do it, I can do it. It's just business right? Just
acting.

> **V:** Yes. And I didn't even hurt you. I'll
> be fine. Need a hand up?

Caleb: Thanks. All right, your turn.

> 10:13 P.M.
> **V:** Oof! Whoa, yes, good. But you have
> to grab the wrist at the same time. I can
> still stab you.

Caleb: OK, fine, I'll remember the wrist thing. All
right, what next?

> **V:** You have me totally pinned. So, like,
> you won. I can call for a truce or
> something.

Caleb: That soon? I feel like fights have to last for
as long as a Demi Levato song or something. Like
the one Himari is playing right now. Seriously, she
doesn't usually do this genre.

> **V:** I think she's just trying to bug you.
> Okay, idea. I get my legs up and kick
> you off me.

Caleb: Now we're talking. She would've called it a bogus fight if we ended it there. OK, so I'm away from you now. Next step?

> 10:14 P.M.
> **V:** I can swipe at you with the knife again. Or what if I throw it at you?

Caleb: I would say swipe unless you have incredible aim. Would rather not take too many chances on a fake combat.

> **V:** Obviously I have incredible aim. But you might deflect it into a civilian. Fine, I'll go for the torso.

10:15 P.M.
Caleb: So I jump back and run into a table since it's crazy cramped in there and plant my back against the table as you nearly miss my head or something. Let's try that movement. Here, I'll sit up against this ornament box, swing the knife at me, and I'll duck. Nice. Yes.

> **V:** Now I'm exposed from that swing, so you should punch me in the gut.

Caleb: OK, but not for real, right? But, I feel she'll detect a fake-ish one, you know? Punches make a certain sound when you do them right.

> **V:** Nah, just go for it. Bernard taught me how to take a punch right so it doesn't do damage. But let's not do it right now. It still hurts.

Caleb: Yeah, I'm fine with leaving that till later. Who knows? Maybe I'll figure out something less painful that does the same trick. OK, so you double back from pain and I ... push you out the door?

> 10:16 P.M.
> **V:** Do an awesome twirl thing and put me in a chokehold.

Caleb: Oh, I like that idea better. And then I choke you until you say, "OK, fine. You da bestest hero. None can defeat yoooooou."

> **V:** Nope. I'm just going to say nothing like a weirdo. Because that is apparently the plan.

Caleb: Well, but how do I know when to stop "choking" you?

> **V:** Can I at least say something a little more epic?

Caleb: "You da bestest epic hero." See, there's an epic in ther—ooof wow. See I kind of wish I had a Bernard because, holy shiznozzles, that was. That was a punch. Right to the gut. Thanks.

> 10:17 P.M.
> **V:** Whoops! I'm so sorry. I really am trying to be gentle... I just get excited. Just a play punch.

Caleb: That's fine. I'll get you back on Monday. OK, so what would you rather say in the choke hold?

V: "Ugh, please let me go!" Then you drop me. Gasping for air, I say, "Why do I even try to fight you? You always win." Then I limp off.

Caleb: Maybe overkill at the end, but I guess that's better. I don't know. All of this makes me feel gross inside. Should we really do this Monday?

V: Well, if we want to fight, and you don't want to get rid of—I mean, yes. We do.

10:18 P.M.
Caleb: I guess keeping my nemesis is a worthy cause. All right, I'm gonna shut off the music with my brain powers. Wanna head up to finish Breakfast Club?

V: Yes! I hope someone's head gets chopped off!

Caleb: Oh yes. They do. It's epic.

V: Nice! I'm gonna turn this thing of—

Super Secret Squad
July 15

Caleb: 12:03 A.M.

Ow. What are you whacking me in the ear with that stuffed dragon for? It's too late in the evening for pain.

V:

It was supposed to be the head. Bernie is unhappy because you lied. There was no gore!

Caleb:

V, it's a high school drama set in the 80s. What were you expecting?

V:

Honestly, not gore, but it's still fun to whack people with dragons. I'm so glad he got there right before Himari and I left. Right at the door in his Amazon box!

12:04 A.M.
Caleb: Yeah? Does Mister-Give-Caleb-A-Headache-At-Twelve-In-The-Morning have a name?

V: I just told you! It's Bernie. Because he's itty bitty Bernard and so cuuuute!

Caleb: Awwww. Sorry I didn't hear you above the, "Don't you forget about me!" Also, what a boring family. They couldn't even stay up to finish the thing. Mom made the lame excuse of Mass tomorrow.

V: I'm shocked that you're awake, Mr. I-Have-the-Sleep-Habits-of-an-Eighty-Year-Old.

Caleb: I don't know. I'm usually exhausted by now, but for some reason ... I don't know.

12:05 A.M.
V: Mind if I take the contacts out? I know it's kind of gross, but they start irritating me late at night.

Caleb: No, V. You must keep them in forever. Yes, take them out. I have contacts myself, you know, for seeing things.

V: You do? Hold up, let me take these out. Okay, let me see. Oh, yeah! You do. Sneaky.

Caleb: Surprisingly, when they're not red, people don't notice. Isn't that crazy?

V: Heehee, you're just jealous yours aren't cool.

12:06 A.M.
Caleb: No, yours are warm. Cool colors include blue, purple—hey, Bernie, stop whacking me in the head!

V: Sorry, can't control him. Heeheehee!

Caleb: Ahhh. Ahhh. He's eating me alive! What a world! Don't you forget about me, world!

V: Wow. Nice dead face. Tongue out. That's very accurate.

Caleb: Would you give a speech at my funeral?

V: Sure. This idiot died by stuffed dragon. Darwin award to him. Heeheehee.

12:07 A.M.
Caleb: Man, my mom will love it. You're laughing a lot more maniacally tonight than usual. Do you just get this way in the ungodly hours of the morn or...?

V: Who says "the morn?" You really are eighty.

Caleb: Well, whenever I talk to Tamora, I'm apparently eight. So I guess I'll stick with eighteen and be happy with it. Hey, you okay? You look sad all of a sudden.

V: No. I'm not sad. I'm fine.

12:08 A.M.
Caleb: You sure? Was it the popcorn? Sometimes Mom puts in too much butter. And Himari is kind of lactose intolerant and things go badly very quickly.

> **V:** No, I like dairy products.

Caleb: What then, V? You were laughing like Insanity a minute ago. You ok?

> **V:** It's dumb. I was just thinking about if the plan didn't work. I... can't really imagine not being nemeses anymore.

12:09 A.M.
Caleb: Aww, V. Of course it'll work. And even if it doesn't, you think I'm going to listen to the mean, old girlfriend and not fight with the best villain I've ever had? No way. Rather break up with Tamora first.

> **V:** Really?

Caleb: Sure. She's lame. Doesn't even swipe knives at my throat or hit my head with stuffed dragons. Can you picture a marriage like that? Or even a long term relationship.

> **V:** I mean... I would need someone who was chill with being whacked by stuffed dragons.

Caleb: Clearly. Like, when dating sites ask you things you look for in a potential partner, that's the first thing. Yeah. I swear. I'd rather be nemeses with you if it came down to it.

> 12:10 A.M.
> **V:** Yeah... not that I can really imagine some dude I wouldn't murder... but I think I'd choose being nemeses over that.

Caleb: Glad to hear it.

Caleb: But seriously, V. Are we ever going to get, you know, real fighting? Like, where we try to kill each other and stuff? Because I have no desire to get to that point. Is that bad?

> **V:** I hope not. Because I don't either. I—oh!

12:11 A.M.
Caleb: So, um, that was ... you know for you not dating guys, you're really good.

> **V:** I mean... I don't have anything to compare it to... but you're kind of... amazing.

Caleb: Whoooo, umm. Not sure what to say ... that's a first.

> **V:** Then don't say anything, doofus.

12:13 A.M.

Caleb: Wow. You seriously haven't kissed any guys before?

> **V:** Just cute sharkies on the top of their little heads. Heehee.

Caleb: Lucky sharks.

> 12:14 A.M.
> **Kevin:** So what the heck did I just wake up to?

Caleb: Haha, oh my word. I'm crying. There are actual tears.

> **V:** Um, you okay? What the heck? What are you laughing at?

Caleb: K-kev, he's ... h-he's in my ahahaha. Oh, it's so late. So, so late.

> **V:** Um... what?

12:15 A.M.
Caleb: So, you know how sometimes I accidentally send the wrong messages to certain groups or turn on group messages with my mind? Somehow always when you're around. Anyway, take a wild guess at which group text the last ten minutes was transcribed on. Hint: It's a Secret.

> **V:** Oh my gosh. Noooo. Oh, no. I'm gonna die.

Caleb: See. Normally I'd be embarrassed. But at this point in the night, you could stab me and I'd still be laughing.

> **V:** I might for turning that thing on. Ugh. Let me turn mine on. Kevin? Don't read ANYTHING.

Caleb: Yeah, might as well tell him to stop listening to Broadway songs while you're at it.

> 12:16 A.M.
> **V:** Noooo. And Himari is in this one, too. They can be deleted, right?

Caleb: Haha. Nope!

> **Kevin:** Don't be with that bozo, V. Be with a real man.

Caleb: So, Juan? He's also in this chat, right? Hello, Juan!

> **Some Juan:** I was just going to ignore it.

V: Noooooooooo. Why is my life so awkward? You suck.

> **Caleb:** All right, the stuffed dragon torture is beginning again. Signing out for no—

Still Nemeses (fingers crossed)
July 15

Caleb: 1:05 P.M.

So, I don't get it. They don't have crackers in these barrels. Or barrels. We do have a plow above our table, sooooo, that's interesting.

V:

Is she that boring? I feel like I probably had more fun at Mass, and I don't even know Latin.

Caleb:

Well we have this interesting game on the table involving a triangle and pegs, so I'm having the time of my life. Yay. Yipee.

V:

What is she doing?

Caleb: 1:06 P.M.

Mostly looking at the kitchen door annoyed they haven't brought out the biscuits. See, I'm more of a pizza guy. This home cooked food brings in too

many people on Sundays. Introvert needs to hide.
I'll scurry under the plow.

> **V:** Cheese pizza. Mmm. By yourself. In
> a dark room. No pepperoni, though. No
> meat.

Caleb: As long as there's sauce, I'm down. Oh,
she's talking now. I'm nodding occasionally and
grunting to make it seem like I'm listening.

> **V:** Hate to ask this, but why did you
> date her in the first place?

1:07 P.M.
Caleb: Oh, she's reaching for my hand now. She
likes to do this a lot. She says she's a huge fan of
physical touch or something. Seriously, how do her
hands get so cold in ninety-degree heat?

> **V:** Dude, the whole relationship-details
> thing...

Caleb: Yeah, V. I don't know if I should be PMing
you while I'm on a date. I feel like that's kind of
rude. Don't you?

> **V:** Yeah. I guess. I feel bad that you're
> pretending to still like her until she's
> emotionally stable enough to handle it...
> then she's going to be messed up again.
> Ugh, she bugs me, but poor thing...

1:08 P.M.
Caleb: Umm, what the heck are you talking about?

V: ... What we talked about last night. She needs someone right now. But then you're going to tell her you don't think it's working.

Caleb: Did you have a conversation with Kevin and mistake it for me? Seriously, what isn't working? I think it's working just fine.

V: Um... we talked about this face to face last night. Pretty sure I didn't kiss Kevin.

1:09 P.M.
Caleb: Honestly, V, last night was a complete blur. Kind of like when drunk people get all fuzzy, I don't remember much about it. Just disregard whatever I said because I was too tired to filter and actually think.

1:10 P.M.
V: That's not funny.

Caleb: I wouldn't joke about something like that. V, I have a girlfriend. Whatever happened, forget about it. I'm not dropping Tamora any time soon.

1:11 P.M.
V: Wow. You must have been really drunk. Or I hit you way too hard on the head. Gosh. Have fun on your date. Hate you too.

Caleb: Sure, whatever floats your boat, or yacht, or whatever villains ride on the water. I'll see you when I get back.

V: You're disgusting. Bye.

Private Message
July 15

V: 10:09 P.M.

Hey, Bernard. I'm having a crisis.

V:

I was going to tell the stuffed dragon Caleb got me. I named him Bernie. But Himari is right here so that would be totally weird.

V:

Anyway, this is super embarrassing, but I think I'm getting too emotionally involved with Caleb.

V:

I mean with my nemesis. Cortex. The hero. The anti-villain guy.

10:10 P.M.

V: This hasn't happened before. I always kill them too quickly. But he and I hang out literally all the time. I know his family. I'm friends with his sister. I stay at his house. I... well, we won't talk about last night. Apparently he hardly remembers it. Somehow. Anyway, this relationship is way unprofessional.

V: We never even wear masks anymore. We don't even fight. Not really. Just kind of mess around.

V: I wish I could find something awful about him. Like that coworker I killed, who had fighting dogs. He was easy to kill. Kind of an accident, actually. I was just releasing the dogs to bring to the house, but then he snuck up on me. I left the police to take care of that one. Probably good. Fluffy wouldn't have liked all those dogs.

10:11 P.M.

V: Or the other coworker. Probably shouldn't have killed him at work, but I had to help poor Courtney, you know? No one believed her. But he had her cornered in the back room... He deserved it.

V: Oh, yeah, and that gangster/ mob boss dude. He was going to shoot that kid.

V: And most heroes are just foes in a mask. We kill each other. That's what we do. No problem there.

10:12 P.M.

V: But Caleb doesn't wear a mask. And I can't come up with a reason why he deserves to die. Sure, he's obnoxious sometimes. And he kind of sucks at rescuing people. (He's good at fighting villains, though.) And he has awful taste in women. Why the heck is he still with that girl? He said... well, nevermind. At least he sticks with his poor choices. Not really a player (even though sometimes he pretends he is one.) Unless he does what he did to me to a bunch of girls.... No, I know he doesn't. Stroke and now Tamora. He's a one girl sort of guy.

V: I'm incapable of hating him. Can't even bring myself to hurt him. I could have killed him a million times. And... he thinks I'm fun, and pretty, and talented. (He didn't mean to tell me that; apparently he messages dead people, too.) That part wasn't part of his apparent "drunken stupor" or whatever dumb crap that was.

10:13 P.M.
V: I have more fun with him than anyone, even Himari. He gets me. He's sensitive, sweet about everything that happened to me. We fight really well. Honestly I think we could trash-talk forever.

V: Also, he's really attractive. I love his big old doofus grin.

V: Gosh, I'm glad you're not really reading this. That would be super embarrassing.

10:14 P.M.
V: But he's still with his stupid girlfriend! Why is he still with freaking Tamora?

V: I mean, he said really nice things about me, (and other stuff) but he's still with her. So... apparently he doesn't like me? He was willing to send me packing pretty quick when Tamora didn't like me.

V: Maybe this is my fault. Tamora can probably tell. That's why she's so possessive. The poor girl has been through so much, and here I go making her out to be some sort of villain. Just because I'm jealous of her.

10:15 P.M.
V: This is not going to work, Bernard. Villain. Hero. Girlfriend. I'm a villain. I kill people. I'm supposed to take what I want and leave destruction in my wake. I'm certainly not supposed to care about a hero.

10:16 P.M.
V: I think there's only one thing I can do.

Group Message
July 16

10:01 A.M.
Himari added Caleb.

Himari added V.

V: 10:05 A.M.

In position, Himari?

Himari:

Yep. I've got my corner booth. Eyes on the targets.

V:

You on mind-text, Caleb?

Caleb:

Yeah, good thing, too. It's loud by the picking-up food area. Seriously, how long does it take for two ice cream sundaes?

10:06 A.M.
Himari: At least you get some. I don't have time. I have to pay attention.

Caleb: Tell you what. If this all works out, and you make sure V and I look like we're legit fighting, then I will get you a large of whatever. But we all know you'll get vanilla.

> **Himari:** With red stuff on top. New favorite.

V: I'm so proud.

> 10:07 A.M.
> **Caleb:** OK, got the goods. Gonna slide into the table with my lady friend. Waiting on your cue, Himari.

Himari: Go time.

> 10:08 A.M.
> **Tamora:** Oh, Caleb, look! I didn't know V was in town. She's right behind you. Hi, V! Coming for one of the famous Ivanhoe's' sundaes? Caleb, honestly, turn around. I know it's loud in here but come on.

V: Coming for vengeance. Get up!

> **Tamora:** Sorry, dear. I couldn't hear that. The line usually starts over there.

V: Gah. Cortex, I've come to kill you. Get up and fight me! Ugh!

> **Caleb:** Uhhh...

10:09 A.M.
Tamora: Oh, that's hilarious. I can't take you two seriously. I'm gonna snort ice cream if you keep making me laugh.

> **Himari:** Caleb, get up! Fight her! What are you doing? Stop staring at Tamora, idiot!

Caleb: It feels weird to let go of her hand and punch V. Wait, is that what I was supposed to do first? I'm getting the order mixed up in my head.

> **Tamora:** But seriously, V. What brings you up from Zona? You're not going to fight my boyfriend, are you?

V: Here to destroy him, actually. Get up, Cortex! Why are you like a rock all the sudden? Chicken?

> 10:10 A.M.
> **Tamora:** Well, I won't stop you two, I suppose. Go ahead, babe, show her who's boss. Let's start with the right knee. It's weaker than the other one.

Himari: There you go, get up, wait, what are you doing? That's not the plan!

> **V:** Augh! What...?

Tamora: OK, babe, now you just kicked her knees in, go for a stomach punch. Mean it. There you go.

> **V:** Augh, what... Ah! The katana? Whoa!

Himari: Looks really convincing, but a little intense, bro. Ease up.

> 10:11 A.M.
> **Tamora:** OK, well she doesn't leave a whole lot of weak spots in the cloak, but try for the neck. I know it's hard to aim with it, sweetie, but make me proud, ok?

V: Easy, make it look convincing but not—augh!

> **Himari:** Caleb! You just sliced her neck! Chill!

Tamora: Not that deep. You could do better than that. OK, so while she's grasping at her new wound, that opens up her side. Kick that.

> **V:** Augh, Caleb, stop. Stop! Too much!

10:12 A.M.
Tamora: All right, she's down babe. This is it. Go for the femoral artery. I know you didn't do well in anatomy class, so just make a decent gash in the thigh. Should do it.

> **V:** Caleb! Caleb, stop!

Tamora: Babe, this has gone too far. Are you actually going to kill her?

> **Himari:** Oh, thank God. V, she's gonna make him chill.

Tamora: Auuuuuuuuuuugh!

> 10:13 A.M.
> **Himari:** V, what the heck! What did you just do?

Caleb: Wha-what the—Tamora? Tamora. Oh, God. Tamora. No, no, no, no. Please tell me there's a pulse. Himari! Freaking call an ambulance. Don't j- just stare.

> **Himari:** I'm calling!

V: No, stop! Don't pull the knife out—

> **Caleb:** Hardly bleeding. Does it really matter? We all know what it means when humans stop bleeding. Here's your knife back.

10:14 A.M.
V: I can explain...

> **Caleb:** Get out.

V: No, hold on. Caleb, she wasn't who you—

> **Caleb:** We had one rule. We literally made it when we started talking. You

were supposed to leave her out of this. What did she ever do? So what if she hated you? I have plenty of people who can't stand me, and I don't go throwing knives at them.

10:15 A.M.
V: I wasn't going to! It wasn't that she hated me, it was—

> **Caleb:** I don't care what it was or wasn't. Get out. Go home. Leave me alone.

V: Caleb—

> **Caleb:** Don't touch me!

V: Really! I-I j-just... you don't under-

> **Caleb:** Just go.

Himari: Oh my gosh. You're just going to let her run away? What is going on? Oh my gosh... I'm turning off this freaking thin—

Private Message
July 16

Kevin: 11:25 A.M.

So I heard it went well.

Caleb:

Kevin, don't make me lodge a knife in you. Still have the thing from Ivanhoe's.

Kevin: 11:26 A.M.

All right, but your mother wants to know where V went. She's supposed to take her today in the jet.

Caleb:

Don't know. Don't care.

Kevin:

Come on, Caleb.

Caleb: Don't "come on" me. Last time I checked, a villain hasn't killed both of your girlfriends.

11:27 A.M.
Kevin: Well, the first turned out to be a villain who probably would've killed you.

Caleb: Not helping.

Kevin: When do I ever? And you murdered Bernard. So I guess you two are even.

11:29 A.M.
Kevin: Please don't kill me.

11:30 A.M.
Caleb: It's not a fair comparison. Bernard was an accident. She just threw the knife at Tamora. With no warning.

Kevin: From what I heard from Himari, it seemed like self-defense. You were going really hard, bro.

Caleb: Then, she should've lodged the knife in me. I wouldn't have minded. Tamora just stood to the side.

Caleb: And V said she had incredible aim. I don't care how much pain she was in. Tamora and I were three feet apart. No way she could miss that shot.

11:31 A.M.

Kevin: OK, so maybe she aimed on purpose. I thought you'd gotten sick of Tamora. At least from the post-Breakfast Club talk anyway.

> **Caleb:** Bro, it was crazy late at night. I could've said I was a dragon and believed it.

Kevin: You seemed wide awake to me.

> **Caleb:** Whatever. I need to know why she did it. On purpose.

11:32 A.M.
Kevin: Easy. Just pull up her message and ask her.

> **Caleb:** I blocked her.

Kevin: 'Course you did.

> **Caleb:** What else would you do when someone just traumatically killed your girlfriend? In front of a bunch of screaming customers?

> 11:34 A.M.
> **Caleb:** Exactly.

Kevin: Can't help you except to say unblock her and ask.

> **Caleb:** We had literally one rule: me and her. She'd leave family and friends out of it. I asked her at least three times to specifically not hurt Tamora.

Kevin: No offense, but she's a villain. Their word isn't trustworthy.

Kevin: And even if she does keep promises, maybe she had a good reason to take her out.

> 11:35 A.M.
> **Caleb:** Be glad I'm a hero, Kev. I might have taken you out with that last comment.
>
> **Caleb:** There's never a good reason to murder someone. Heroes never do.
>
> **Caleb:** And for her to target Tamora, who couldn't defend herself... I don't care if I didn't love Tamora, she was still a friend. I'd known her longer than V.

11:36 A.M.
Kevin: So what you gonna do about it?

> **Caleb:** For goodness sake, I'm a hero. We can't let this crap fly. If a villain murders an innocent person, we have to fight back. And she's my nemesis, so that makes her my responsibility.

11:37 A.M.
Kevin: Should I set up the fight? I can message Himari or V.

> **Caleb:** Not sure. I don't think we actually know how to combat for real. We've just seen the movies ... maybe I

should ask other heroes on Meta-Match how to deal with this. Sure the site's got plenty of dark-hooded heroes with murdered girlfriends.

11:38 A.M.
Kevin: Whatever you say, boss. Still think it would be better to talk with her.

Caleb: I'm not sure I trust anything you think, Kevin.

Kevin: Smart.

Private Message
July 16

Cortex: 12:03 P.M.

Hey, Dimension. I'm not sure if you're still active on this thing because you retired. But, I have a problem with my nemesis. I really look up to you as a hero and wondered if I could get some advice. Tried to get your cell from my dad, but he wouldn't give up any contacts even if a villain was pointing a laser gun at his face.

Dimension: 12:10 P.M.

Greetings, Cortex. I use the site on the occasion that a weaker villain may want to tussle once or twice. Good resume booster for them. What can I help with.

Cortex:

Wow. You got back to me faster than I expected. Dimension, my nemesis just killed my girlfriend. Any ideas what to do next?

Dimension: 12:11 P.M.

Sorry to hear. Lost two or three to a nemesis myself. I thought it was rather obvious, but set up a time to fight him or her to avenge your love?

Cortex: Her. And normally I would... but she's different. I don't—I don't know if I could do that. See, I would want to do some significant damage to whoever did this sort of thing. Broken legs, fractured spines ... nothing deadly, but enough to put them out for a while. But I... I couldn't do it myself. Not to my nemesis.

12:12 P.M.

Dimension: Cold feet, eh? Can't blame you. In my earlier days, I always apologized after every punch. But did you really love this girlfriend enough if you don't want to at least snap your nemesis's arm?

Dimension: Don't tell me you're one of those pacifist heroes.

Cortex: No. It's hard to explain. But I really want to know how you got over fearing that you'll hurt your enemy too much.

12:13 P.M.

Dimension: I must say, I'm not proud of my solution. Keep in mind, I was fresh out of college with strange ideas about the world and how it should work ... I hired a guy to do the job for me.

Cortex: A mercenary?

Dimension: An assassin. Wish we'd have Angie's List or Yelp back then because from what I heard he made a rather grotesque job of it. Poor nemesis agonized for several hours before succumbing to a painful demise.

12:14 P.M.
Cortex: Yeah, maybe don't use that solution in my case?

Dimension: Again, not proud of those days. However, hiring another hero to do the job might help.

Cortex: I'd rather not sneak up on her with another person. That's villainous. Me watching from afar as someone else breaks her arm.

12:15 P.M.
Dimension: Villainous, villainous. Cortex, the only difference between heroes and villains are cape colors and backstories.

Cortex: I don't believe that.

Dimension: At least take another hero with you. So if you chicken out, he or she can swoop in and finish the job.

Cortex: If I do that, V will need to bring another person with her to the fight. It's only fair.

12:16 P.M.

Dimension: Fair. Ha. If you fight fair, you never win.

Cortex: Remind me why I have a poster of you hanging on my ceiling?

Dimension: Fine, kid. She can bring another villain with her to the fight. But if you want to bring another factor to the fight, at least multiply that number by ten. Make it somewhat worth the watch.

Cortex: Like, ask a bunch of heroes to come?

12:17 P.M.
Dimension: Sure, run into plenty of them on this site who don't have the guts to do some real damage to their villains. Get a band of those together so you can all take care of each other's burdens.

Cortex: I'll think about it.

12:18 P.M.
Cortex: And, Dimension? You're wrong about heroes.

Dimension: Give it time.

Announcement Board for Heroes on Meta-Match

Title: Getting Together a Band

Date: July 16 (12:45 P.M.)

Cortex: Hey, everyone. Name's Cortex, but you can literally see that a few words over. I want to get a band of heroes together to fight nemeses who we have hesitations about hurting. My villain just killed my gf, but don't have the courage to do any harm to her. Send me a quick PM if you're interested. I live in the central Indiana area, but have transportation if the majority of you want to fight elsewhere. Make sure your villains know about the fight, too. We want to make this as fair as possible.

 Comment   Like   Share

Private Message
July 16

Shatter: 1:23 P.M.

Hey, hero dude. Saw your post in the announcement board. Wondering if you still needed heroes for a team.

Cortex:

You're the first to get back to me. Got a score to settle?

Shatter: 1:24 P.M.

Eh, villain killed my parents. But of course, the villain can summons creepy crawlies with his mind, so that makes him a little hard to battle when you're deathly afraid of them.

Cortex:

I see. Maybe we'll get someone on the team who has a large can of bug spray. Remind me of your power? You never said.

Shatter:

Everything I touch shatters into little pieces.

Cortex: Oh.

1:25 P.M.
Shatter: Yeah, it makes maintaining most relationships difficult.

> **Cortex:** I feel like that sounds more like a villain's power.

Shatter: And a villain's backstory? Parents killed? True. But I figured, hey, might as well try something different. Doesn't help I got a bunch of tattoos, got a buzz cut (why do people feel like girls can't rock this?), and like to wear dark makeup. Most people read into it all wrong.

> 1:26 P.M.
> **Cortex:** I'm starting to think we'll never be able to tell villains and heroes apart nowadays. So, tell me, Shatter, is Indiana too much of a hike for you?

Shatter: Live in Massachusetts, but can make a trip if needed. Let's wait out where the others are from. Isn't it crazy most of the people I run into here are from the U.S.?

> **Cortex:** Maybe it's in our Settings or something. I'll have to tinker with that. Thanks, Shatter. I'll put you in a group text when we get another handful in here.

Shatter: No prob. Thanks for including me!

1:27 P.M.

Cortex: Don't forget to invite your villain. Remember, we want a clean, fair fight.

Shatter: Lemme see what I can do. He likes to send bugs over software, too though.

Private Message
July 16

Deaden: 1:54 P.M.

Yo, got another spot on that team of yours?

Cortex:

Before I answer, please explain your power. And consider a name change because no parent is going to let their child say their favorite superhero is Deaden.

Deaden:

Right, right. An explanation: I can mute one of the senses of my enemies. So, like sight, hearing ... smell is kind of pointless unless you really want them to have a miserable time in a bakery.

Cortex: 1:55 P.M.

That's interesting. Just one at a time?

Deaden:

Yeah. Get a massive headache if I overshoot and go for two. Usually I try sight or feeling, but hearing has its perks, too.

Cortex: Right, especially if your villain is on headset with a henchman. OK, so speaking of nemeses, did yours do you wrong?

Deaden: Oh yeah. You see that sweet motorbike in my profile pic?

1:56 P.M.
Cortex: The neon green one that matches your suit? Nice helmet, by the way. It looks like it's completely made out of dark glass.

Deaden: It is. Anyway, my villain stole it.

1:57 P.M.
Cortex: ... and, he or she ran over your mother with it?

Deaden: No! But my mentor gave me that thing. After he died ... it just means a lot to me, OK?

Cortex: I mean, I won't try to make your tragedy seem, well, less like a tragedy, I guess. What does your villain do, anyway?

Deaden: Oh, Hemlock? She doesn't have any powers. Really good at combat though.

1:58 P.M.
Cortex: No powers? And they still let her become a villain?

Deaden: You'd be surprised at the number of heroes and villains who don't have powers now. Not every guy has to shoot lasers out of his eyes, you know.

> **Cortex:** True. Where you located at? U.S.?

Deaden: Canada. Nova Scotia area.

> 1:59 P.M.
> **Cortex:** Aren't Canadians really peaceful?

Deaden: Have you ever seen a hockey game?

> **Cortex:** Fair enough. Invite your villain to the fight, and I'll keep you updated.

Private Message
July 16

V: 2:00 P.M.

Hey, Juan. I need help.

Juan: 2:04 P.M.

I've been watching the Meta-Match news feed. Interesting choice, there. I know that whole thing happened with you two, but seems like he wasn't ready for you to take out his girlfriend.

V:

It wasn't like that. I need to get back to Arizona somehow. I'm stuck in Indiana. Do you know anybody?

Juan:

Most people take a plane.

V:

I just killed a girl. It's all over the news.

2:05 P.M.

Juan: Fair enough. I can ask around. I have some friends in the area who might let you borrow their aircraft. It's going to cost a lot, though.

V: Money isn't a problem if they're willing to wait until I get home to send a check.

Juan: All right. I'll let you know. By the way, why did you kill that girl?

V: She tried to kill Caleb.

2:06 P.M.

Juan: Dios mio. Did you tell him that? Looks like he's getting a squad together to kill you.

V: I noticed. No, he blocked me.

Juan: There's this thing called in-person interaction.

V: Did you forget about the part where he wants me dead?

Juan: Fair. You know, I usually just go with whoever pays, but do you want me to tell him?

2:07 P.M.

V: Would you? Oh, Juan, thank you! Please tell him that she was a villain named Tempest. She was mind-controlling him. Tempest used to be Stroke's boss. Head of the whole villains-assassinating-heroes ring. I didn't realize it because she dyed her hair and she was definitely wearing contacts, and I'd only ever seen her in person twice. But the way he so quickly changed his mind about things, and that one time I passed out, not to mention her "kidnapping" by Seizure. No way a kidnapper just lets her hang out in the house. Those two had a fling a while back. Guess they got back together. But then was her signature move. The femoral artery. She told him to do it when he was fighting me. You bleed out and die in minutes, but everyone thinks they'll be fine because it's just a leg wound. And then she got up, and had a hand on his shoulder, and I saw her start to pull a knife out of her belt, and she had this look in her eye, so I threw the knife and killed her. Oh, gosh. I just realized. Caleb knows a bunch of heroes. She probably read his mind to get information about them. That's why she did it. The Shadow Assassins! Juan, heroes are in trouble! If she gave them that info... oh my gosh! You have to tell him all of that!

> 2:13 P.M.
> **Juan:** That was quite the villain monologue. But, I'm sorry, I can't tell him that.

V: What? Why?

> **Juan:** You know how we met. Through the Shadow Assassins. You know I work for lots of people. They're one of my biggest customers. And... it turns out, they've offered me a lot of money to

find out how much you know. Looks like just about everything.

V: Juan! We left the SA! We got out!

> 2:14 P.M.
> **Juan:** Well, you left, anyway. I was always more of an independent contractor, you know? Sorry. It's nothing personal. But I'm going to have to shut off all communication on your device. Can't have you contacting anyone. This whole hero-gathering is going to be great for the SA. Huge ambush. Well done.

V: No! I can pay you! I can pay you even more!

> **Juan:** Actually, you can't. I've hacked your accounts, of course. Diverted your funds, now that you can't do anything about it. I suggest ditching your phone. It's tracking your location. The SA are coming for you. Can't have you stopping the occasion, you know?

V: Juan! No!

> 2:16 P.M.
> **Juan:** Sorry. Again, it's not personal. But here's some good news. I just messaged the SA. If you keep the phone, I'll text you one piece of information once I know.

V: What's that?

> **Juan:** Where the showdown will happen. Not that they expect you to survive until then.

V: Fine. But you better send it to me as soon as you know.

> **Juan:** Of course. I'm a man of my word. I only hope for your sake that you are still alive to receive my message.

Private Message
July 16

Lucid: 2:40 P.M.

Saw your post. I'd like to join.

Cortex: 2:41 P.M.

Sorry, just got back from helping my mom carry in groceries. Power and where you live?

Lucid:

You still live with your mom?

Cortex:

Sure, most high schoolers stick around for a little while.

Lucid: 2:42 P.M.

You looked older in your profile.

Cortex:

Ummm, thanks? You look about mid-twenties in yours. Also, what's with the long skirt and leaves in your tangled white hair? It reminds me more of an elf than a hero.

Lucid: Do you want people on your team or not?

2:43 P.M.
Cortex: Sure. Power?

Lucid: I make people's greatest nightmares come to life.

Cortex: Wanna be less vague?

2:44 P.M.
Lucid: No, that's what I do. I sense their most recent nightmare—a serial killer chasing them through a mall with a knife, public humiliation by indecency, etc.—and I access their brain stem (or wherever the heck dreams come from; don't know anatomy, just sense it) and cause them to think the nightmare is really happening.

2:45 P.M.
Cortex: Dang, this site needs to filter heroes and villains better.

Lucid: Come again?

Cortex: It's just I already have someone on my team who can hurt someone physically (literally causing them to shatter to pieces) and someone else who can kill one's senses. If you tag along, we can take out a whole human.

2:46 P.M.
Lucid: Isn't that the point?

        Cortex: No.

Lucid: Remind me the lesson, then.

        Cortex: Probably to teach the villains not to cross us again.

Lucid: So ... we do so by hurting them.

        2:47 P.M.
        Cortex: You never talked about your villain.

Lucid: Don't have one. Freelancing.

        Cortex: Well, you need one for the fight. I refuse to outnumber my villain.

Lucid: Wow. Didn't think they had heroes as stupid as you since the 30's. Fine. I'll go scrounge for a throwaway bad guy on this site. Happy?

        2:48 P.M.
        Cortex: Ecstatic. I think I'm gonna call it quits after you. I have a feeling working with other heroes feels a lot like high school group projects.

Lucid: Yeah, well, I'm not exactly jumping up and down to be with you either, jerk. Also, I live in Oregon. Try to pick a closer spot to me than god-awful Gas City.

Cortex: I'll see what I can do.

Private Message
July 16

Caleb: 4:07 P.M.

I don't want to talk a lot. Just wanted to let you know, I'm getting a group of heroes together. We're planning a fight (haven't hammered out the details of where and when yet). And we're coming after you. Usually, I wouldn't want to. But you killed Tamora, and we had literally one rule. I can't let that slide. I wanted to warn you ahead of time. These heroes are bringing their villains. And some sound like they will bring a lot to the fight. You can bring a couple of your own if you want (heaven knows some of these heroes want to knock some teeth out). I always like to give my villains a fairer advantage. Please don't say much in response because I don't want to hurt you more than I'm going to. I just need to know if you're in or not. If not, we need to figure out some other way to avenge Tamora. Got it?

V: 4:09 P.M.

Of course. I don't know why you're upset. You didn't even like her. But I'm willing to fight. Let me know when and where. I can kill you too.

4:11 P.M.
Caleb: Great. Please don't hold back; because I won't. I'll let you know as soon as my team settles on a time and place.

4:12 P.M.
V: Good. Let me know as soon as possible.

6:54 P.M.
Caleb: How does Wednesday in Vegas sound?

V: We will be gambling our lives in Las Vegas. I like it. When shall we meet?

Caleb: 6:30 a.m. Las Vegas time. Meet at the fountains at the Bellagio.

V: Good. The waterworks will be external as well as in the eyes of the heroes.

6:55 P.M.
Caleb: Did Kevin hack your account? That was animated movie level of cheesy puns.

V: I look forward to your demise.

Caleb: OK. Glad to hear it. Over and out.

Caleb blocked V.

Private Message
July 16

Juan: 7:00 P.M.

It looks like you had a great conversation with your boyfriend. He most likely hates you more. Anyway, I found out the time. 6:30 a.m. in Vegas at the fountains at Bellagio.

V:

You messaged him as me? Juan! Why are you doing this?

Juan:

I just helped you. Now you better ditch that phone. The SA are only five miles away from you.

Juan: 7:08 P.M.

Looks like they made it to where your phone last pinged. You still alive?

Juan: 7:10 P.M.

Pity.

Best Sidekicks Ever
July 16

Himari: 7:08 P.M.

Kevin! I just got to V's house. She's not here. And she's not answering her phone.

Kevin:

Wait. You left Indiana? When? You sneaky banana.

Himari:

Hopped a plane as soon as I could. Something isn't adding up here. Has she messaged Caleb?

Kevin: 7:09 P.M.

Maaaan, your family is loaded. Mind donating to Kevin's College Fund? And I don't know, bro. He's barely talked to me. I tried to get him to reach out to her, but I think he messaged Dimension instead. He had mentioned something about a team.

7:10 P.M.
Himari: Okay, I'm working on hacking his
messages. Hold up.

7:12 P.M.
Himari: Oh my gosh, V is going to die. He's got a
team of heroes who seem more like villains. But
apparently he messaged her... and she's chill with it?

> **Kevin:** I don't really keep up much.
> She's hard to figure out. But, yeah, they
> seemed close until the Ivanhoe's thing,
> so that sounds a bit wonky.

Himari: Yeah, really close. I really didn't need to
read that whole chat. My brother's an idiot. But
where do you think she is? I just feel like she had to
have a reason or something. She's just a little
butterfly with really sharp claws.

> 7:13 P.M.
> **Kevin:** Weird analogy. I dig it. So ...
> lemme think. I tried to run away from
> home when I was seven. Got a whole
> suitcase of G.I. Joes and five bucks
> worth of change. Sorry, got nothing.
> Does it look like she's been in the house
> as of late? Are the sharks still alive and
> well, or do they eye you like a tasty
> snack?

7:14 P.M.
Himari: Kevin! They're sweet sharks. I don't know.
She set up an automatic feeder before we left. But it
doesn't look like she's been around. They're

unusually needy for pets right now. She hangs out with them all the time, and they get lonely when she doesn't.

> **Kevin:** OK, didn't need a documentary. So she's probably still in Indiana. No way she can catch a flight after murdering someone. It's been popping up on social media all day.

Himari: Yeah, she's been on an FBI list for a while. Villain probs. Argh. I don't know what to do.

> 7:15 P.M.
> **Kevin:** You're asking me? I struggle with grilled cheese on the frat kitchen stove.

Himari: Sigh. Well, I guess I can try to hack her account. That will be hard, though. My brother is awful about security, but she had Juan work on hers.

> **Kevin:** Man, yeah, Juan's pretty good. Good luck breaking into her bank account of messages.

Himari: I know that seems stupid, but villains' real identities are their most prized possession. Because, you know, government and stuff always looking for them. The FBI aren't a huge fan of heroes and villains.

> 7:16 P.M.

Kevin: Whatevs, sister. I'm going to watch a bootlegged copy of Dear Evan Hansen. Let me know if you find anything.

Himari: I will. And if you can, keep my brother from doing anything too stupid.

Kevin: Again, putting your faith in the wrong person. But ok.

Archived Message "Bittersweet": July 1

Archived Message "Bittersweet": July 1 reopened July 17

Cortex: 10:06 P.M.

Hey, Sweetie. I know you liked to work alone, but did you ever team up with someone? Did you ever get pre-fight-day jitters where your toes feel numb and you've visited the bathroom four times in one hour?

Cortex:

I don't know if I can do this.

Cortex: 10:07 P.M.

The longer amount of time I spend away from Tamora, the less I feel attached. I don't just mean that in the, "She's gone to a better place, best let go." I mean, I remember everything I disliked about her. Does that happen often with dead people?

10:08 P.M.

Cortex: Of course, don't get all warm and fuzzy either. I only knew you a couple weeks and couldn't decide whether I hated or tolerated you. I don't remember much except you sliced my face and gave me a cool scar. So, I guess I recall the good things with you passing. But, something happened today that scared me.

Cortex: They had her funeral. For a small town, a lot of people showed up. That's the community here.

10:09 P.M.

Cortex: Her parents chose to have an open casket. Don't know why. Maybe because V only stabbed her in the chest and you could easily cover that up with a floofy purple blouse. Her face still looked perfect. Waxy, with blush and eyeshadow (why do they make up the corpses, anyway? What are they trying to hide? That they're human?).

10:10 P.M.

Cortex: Sweetie, when I looked in that casket ... I felt what I always imagined I would feel toward a nemesis. Hatred. Pure hatred. The kind that makes the veins in your neck explode with fire and your lips purse from pain.

Cortex: Why?

10:11 P.M.

Cortex: Sure, she was clingy. And controlling. 10/10 wouldn't date her again. But, why when the pastor talked about all the little children inheriting the kingdom of God, or something having to do with

someone so young going to heaven, why did I feel
... relief? Like, she was lead in my chest, and V
somehow knocked her off of me?

10:12 P.M.
Cortex: Been thinking about death. Heroes don't
often die in the movies, but I've heard about plenty
of fights-gone-wrong. The kind Hollywood studios
don't pick up. I don't know about Lucid's villain, but
even when I tried to make it fair, I feel like we have
a strong advantage over V.

Cortex: What if she dies, Sweetie?

Cortex: What if she dies?

10:13 P.M.
Cortex: I will not feel relief at her funeral.

Private Message
July 17

Scourge: 11:17 P.M.

Himari! It's V. Please answer!

Scourge: 11:18 P.M.

Himari, it's me! Please answer. I need your help. Caleb is in danger!

Scourge: 11:19 P.M.

Please, he's going to notice his phone is missing and Juan will probably track it. I was captured by the Shadow Assassins. I guess today they decided I really didn't know anything about other heroes' whereabouts, because they're going to kill me tomorrow. Or brainwash me. I don't think they've decided yet.

Scourge: 11:20 P.M.

Gosh dang it, Himari, respond! Caleb is walking into a trap! The SA are going to ambush the heroes when they get there for the fight!

Scourge: HIMARI! IT'S V! Dang it, he's coming. He sees the phone. Tell Caleb. Don't let him go. And tell him I'm sorry. I wish I had time to tell him the truth but asdf adstogvuh'bijnkol

11:25 P.M.
Himari: V! Oh my gosh! Are you okay?

11:26 P.M.
Himari: V! Please answer. Oh my gosh, I'm so sorry. I was in the other room. Where are you? What's happening?

Scourge: Who is this?

Himari: V?

Scourge: I don't know, I was just walking down the street and this creep stole my phone. What even is this app she downloaded? I called the police. She dropped it as she ran away.

11:26 P.M.
Himari: Wait, so who are you?

Scourge: My name is John. Oh, the police want this phone for evidence.

Himari: Wait!

Himari: Crap.

Best Sidekicks Ever
July 17

Himari: 11:27 P.M.

Kevin! V messaged me!

Kevin: 11:28 P.M.

Listen, usually I'm up at this time, but do you know how early we have to fly tomorrow?

Himari:

I got the weirdest message from V. Let me send you the screenshots.

Kevin:

Shoot. Who the heck are the Shadow Assassins? Baller name.

Himari:

I don't know. But what was that?
A weird attempt to avoid the fight?

11:29 P.M.

Kevin: People get cold feet before big events. Marriages, killing your best friend, that sort of thing.

Himari: But why would she make up such a weird story? I couldn't track the phone. I've been working on it while messaging you.

Kevin: True. And V isn't one for lying. The only time she did something shady was when she killed Tamora for no reason.

Himari: I wish I could message this John guy more, but apparently the police took the phone. Let me look at this "Scourge" profile. That was really fast to make a new profile.

11:30 P.M.

Kevin: Yeah, sounds like a fun guy. Definitely would fit in well with the middle ages.

Himari: Pretty detailed bio. Fights with a whip. Makes sense. Wait, he's been on here since 2017. Did she hack a profile?

Kevin: Or she learned to time travel. I like my explanation better.

Kevin: Wait, Scourge. Seen that name before. I think they mentioned him in an online comic. Or something. Yeah, if I recall right, that dude's bad business.

11:31 P.M.
Himari: Huh. Interesting account to hack. I'm going
to do more investigating. Besides, I have to set up
all the earpieces for the "heroes" tomorrow.

> **Kevin:** Oh, did he put you to work on
> that? Yeah, don't know why. He can
> control tech and everything. But the
> way he's been talking about it ... I feel
> like his heart isn't in it. Reminds me of
> when Stacey Higginbotham played
> Dorothy my senior year. That
> production was not wonderful and
> couldn't be salvaged by even a wizard.

11:32 P.M.
Himari: Okay... well, if you can, talk to him. And
I'm going to keep trying to hack V's profile. No
success, and it's been twenty-four hours. The
software I ran took forever and did nothing.

> **Kevin:** Try my best. He's locked himself
> in the room all day. So non face-to-face
> it is!

Private Message
July 17

Kevin: 11:33 P.M.

Heyyyyyy best friend. Wanna call off the fight tomorrow and be friends with everyone?

Caleb:

...

Caleb:

Don't know if I can. All the heroes bought plane tickets already. Some already flew to Vegas. And knowing their powers, I don't want to tick them off. Besides, we're all supposed to be working together to defeat each other's villains. I won't even have to fight V.

Kevin: 11:34 P.M.

Yeah, and let some other guy finish the job. Nice. Real heroism.

Caleb: You are one to talk Mr. Bootleg everything and never give more than ten percent effort.

Kevin: Hey, I never claimed to be a hero. You did.

Caleb: I'd like to call it off, but V seems eager to combat. Basically, everyone wants to do it but me. And the voting system in my house works that majority wins.

11:35 P.M.
Kevin: Screw democracy. This isn't Ancient Greece.

Caleb: Isn't America a democracy?

Kevin: I don't think anyone knows what America is.
You gonna call off this fight or what?

11:36 P.M.
Caleb: Sorry, Kev. Too late to back out. But I'll let her win if that's what you want.

Kevin: That wasn't what I meant.

Caleb: No, I think I've made up my mind. If it comes down to me or her making it out alive, I wouldn't want it to be me.

Kevin: Just get some sleep. You're not thinking straight. Don't let the hero get to your head.

11:37 P.M.

Caleb: Actually, Kevin, I'm wide awake. I haven't thought this clearly since ... the night we kissed.

Kevin: Ugh, why did I ever let you kiss me.

Caleb: You know who I meant. I don't even hug you, bro!

11:38 P.M.

Kevin: Hee hee hee. At least think about calling a truce at the start of the fight.

Caleb: I'll try. But it'll get shot down.

Caleb: And Kevin? Couldn't have asked for a better sidekick.

Caleb: Who would work for free. If I paid you, that would be a different story.

11:39 P.M.

Kevin: Eh, I'll take it.

Private Message
July 18

Cortex: 12:01 A.M.

Hey, Bernard. I guess I'm on a roll with talking to dead people tonight. Probably because the thought of death decided to keep me up. So... speaking of, is the afterlife peaceful? You roaming around Heaven with a bunch of dragons, scorching the likes of the Kevins up there?

Cortex: 12:02 A.M.

Bernie ... (she named the stuffed dragon I got her that), why does she want to fight tomorrow? I don't get it. She and I kissed, and you definitely wouldn't have approved. And then, all of a sudden, she stabs my girlfriend and is all like: I REGRET NOTHING!

Cortex:

But I don't want to kill her.

12:03 A.M.

Cortex: Do me a favor, Bernard. If she does die later today (gosh dang it is it that late?), take good care of her. She's probably more of an angel than most of the people you're seeing up there. I don't even want to fight tomorrow, but it seems weird to back out now.

12:04 A.M.

Cortex: And if I die, please burn me to a crisp. Well-done. None of the meat should be pink.

12:05 A.M.

Cortex: I don't know if I believe in Guardian Angels, but please somehow help her to win the fight today. I'll do my best (because she can tell when I half-heartedly do something), but please somehow turn things in her favor. I don't want to go to another funeral this week.

12:06 A.M.

Cortex: Gonna catch a couple hours of sleep before I fly out. Wish me luck.

Cortex: Actually, no. Wish her luck. Or whatever you have up there.

Private Message
July 18

Hypnia: 5:30 A.M.

Vortex. Are you almost to Las Vegas?

Vortex:

Yes, mistress. I will be touching down shortly.

Hypnia:

Excellent. Your comrades will be joining you in front of the Bellagio.

Vortex: 5:31 A.M.

Yes, mistress.

Hypnia:

When the battle begins, I want you to attack the hero Cortex. He is weakest against you. You must kill him.

Vortex:

Yes, mistress. I promise, I will make you proud.

Group Text
July 18

5:52 A.M.
Cortex changed group named to Vengeance.

Cortex:

So where you all at? I thought we planned to meet thirty minutes ahead outside the hotel. All I got here with me is Kevin.

Kevin:

Are there any sidekicks I can hang with or am I awkwardly third wheeling again?

Shatter: 5:53 A.M.

I accidentally touched my sidekick.
I don't have one anymore.

Cortex:

Wow. Suddenly, I'm feeling less self-conscious about my past record with Bernard.

Lucid: Who?

Cortex: But seriously, where you guys at? We need to go over the plan.

Deaden: So sorry. Canada is not close to Vegas.

Cortex: You still flying, bro?

Deaden: The plane is taxiing. We'll be deboarding soon.

5:55 A.M.
Cortex: Oh, I see Lucid on the other side of the drop off circle. Hi, Lucid! Can you hear me?

Lucid: Yes.

Cortex: Sleep well?

Lucid: I control nightmares. What do you think?

Cortex: I'm thinking our group should meet by the fake Eiffel tower near our hotel. I think the fight would be cooler in fake France.

5:56 A.M.
Cortex: Oh nice, good to see you Shatter. I'd shake hands with you, but we all know how that would go.

Shatter: Yeah, I don't shake hands with heroes. Only villains. Which is ironic, haha.

> **Cortex:** Yep, so y'all bring your villains with you, or should we expect them to show up later?

Shatter: Um, hopefully? Villains are unpredictable.

> **Cortex:** I would just rather not do the fight if we're unevenly matched. If no one shows up, you guys wanna call it off and just have a fun day in Vegas?

5:57 A.M.
Kevin: Smooth.

> **Deaden:** I'm sorry, but I would much prefer to fight. Ya know? Flew all this way.

Lucid: I did not miss my great aunt's wedding to avoid a fight. I was going to be throwing punches at either event, so ...

> **Cortex:** Oh, all right. Maybe we'll have a better idea at six thirty. You heading into the airport, Deaden? Customs might hold you up, and if you don't show, I guess we'll have to forfeit. Darn.

Deaden: Don't worry. I'm from Canada, not Mexico. I'll be there soon.

5:58 A.M.
Cortex: I mean, who picked this early time, huh? No way we can fight. I'm having difficulty keeping my eyes open.

Shatter: You did. You specifically said you get up every day this time of morning.

Cortex: Well look who's lucid all of a sudden. Sorry, I'll let myself out. Guess I can't fight because I'm making awful puns.

Lucid: Are you scared, Cortex? It's okay. We'll do great!

Kevin: Yeah. Listen to the flower girl who sounds like she sucked helium.

Cortex: Kevin!

5:59 A.M.
Kevin: Sorry, bro. I'm thinking the fight needs to happen.

Cortex: Who's side are you on?

Kevin: My teacher who says she'll give me an A if I give her a full-fight transcript.

Lucid: Obviously Deaden won't show until toward the fight time. Want to give us a rundown and have him read the speech-to-text on the way over?

Cortex: You sure you're cool with that, Deaden? We can push the fight back a couple days if you feel unprepared.

Deaden: Don't worry. I was talking to them and I think we're good friends. They're just going to let me through. So nice, ya know?

6:00 A.M.
Cortex: I don't. All right, so the plan is we do a sort of face off thing when all the villains and heroes show up. We want to form a clean, straight line, Instagram worthy, people. And then, we each choose someone else's villain to fight. Anyone here a fan of bugs?

Shatter: Just not me. Definitely not me.

Cortex: Well, clearly. That's your villain who can summon bugs. Lucid, Deaden? Either of you down for some insecticide?

Deaden: I like the little creepy crawlies. I can take those.

Lucid: By deadening their senses? Sounds like a waste of a power, but all right.

6:01 A.M.
Kevin: Wow. I thought she was hot before, Cortex, with her elf ears and tangle flower hair. But now, I'm not so into the snooty.

Lucid: I can hear you, you know.

Cortex: OK, and Deaden, you said your villain didn't have any powers but excels in combat skills. Any takers?

Shatter: Oh! I can.

Cortex: So Deaden takes Shatter's villain. Shatter takes Deaden's. Lucid, what does your villain do?

6:02 A.M.
Lucid: Makes them elated beyond measure until they grow hysterical and can't fight.

Cortex: Well, I have a decent funny bone. So you and I will swap. You fine with taking V? Just don't let her touch you, or she'll absorb your powers.

Lucid: Well, you've given me no other options, so yes.

Cortex: OK, now that we've established who grabs who, what's the plan if someone falls or needs help?

Lucid: From what I've heard about the villains, I don't think that'll happen. Heroes always win in these scenarios.

6:03 A.M.
Kevin: Guys, the water is so cold in these fountains. What gives? It's hot in the summer.

Cortex: Kevin, get out of there. OK, well I still think we should figure out a plan in case one of us doesn't make it.

Shatter: Um, kill the villain who did it? Seems pretty straightforward.

Cortex: Wait, you guys don't have no-killing-your-villain rules? What are you? Postmodernism?

Deaden: I thought the point was to kill them.

6:04 A.M.
Cortex: Well, I wasn't hoping to give an Ethics class, but here we go. How are heroes better than villains if we both are taking each other out?

Shatter: We're heroes, they're villains. That's what's different. Come on. Let's warm up.

Cortex: Ugh, wait, no. Guys, do you just kill every person you face? How have you not ended up in jail? Heroes are usually the ones to provoke the fight, you know. So you can't claim self-defense.

Deaden: They're villains. Villains don't have those kind of rights. You're allowed to kill them. They're bad guys.

Cortex: OK. First, remind me never to team up with anyone ever again. That includes you, Kevin. Yes, you who just submerged your whole head into the fountain. And second, I will not participate in this fight unless you all promise, to the best of your ability, not to kill the nemeses.

6:05 A.M.
Shatter: What!

Lucid: I mean, I suppose I just swiped right on this villain, so we haven't exactly developed a hatred yet. This time, Cortex. This time.

Deaden: Eh, for now. Deal.

Cortex: Fine, warm up it is. Anyone have any signature moves you'd like to share with the group?

Shatter: Um, I walk up and touch people. Oh, yeah, I can't promise the no-killing thing. They always die. Sorry.

Cortex: All right, maybe we'll make an exception for Shatter. But seriously, your power doesn't count as your signature move. You gotta have choreography. You gotta spin and sway as you kick them in the face.

6:06 A.M.
Deaden: Are you a dancer, eh?

Cortex: No, it's just ... I've had training with professionals. Like once ... it doesn't matter. We need it to look cool. Half the fight isn't fighting. Otherwise it would look messy and no spectator will want your autograph afterwards.

Kevin: So like a Broadway number!

Cortex: No, Kevin. It's nothing like that.

6:07 A.M.
Kevin: Sure it is! When you practice a dance number over and over again. Even in West Side Story, the fight is super blocked. And in Newsies, and Wicked ...

Cortex: OK, forget signature moves. Why don't we take a lap around the place and do some stretches. If you don't mind, Kevin, I think I'll turn off this thing until we get to ten till. Would rather not have a script of us just breathing heavily all the time.

6:20 A.M.
Cortex: Do villains always come late? I thought they were the ones who set ticking time bombs.

Deaden: I'm right down the street. Yes, but we always get there before it goes off.

Cortex: OK, I guess we should've called a later meeting. Sorry. I show up early to everything.

Kevin: I forgive you, Cortie.

Cortex: I am not sorry that Kevin fell asleep on the ride over and hummed in his sleep. And also he ate a donut while we ran and yelled at us to go faster.

6:21 A.M.
Cortex: Anyone down for a game of Mad Libs?

Shatter: Wait, I see Deaden. And is that a villain?

Cortex: Depends. Is he or she wearing black, red, or green?

Shatter: Black.

Lucid: Mine just messaged. Said he'll be here a minute late. Tsk, tsk. First fight, too.

6:22 A.M.
Cortex: Imma turn the chat off for a game of Mad Libs. Turn it back on at 6:29?

Lucid: You do you.

6:29 A.M.

Cortex: Shatter, that the dude who killed your parents? The one with the spider tattoo on the forehead?

> **Shatter:** Yep. Deaden, take that creep down.

Deaden: Will do.

> **Cortex:** Wait, we have to wait for everyone to show. Mine and Lucid's villains haven't appeared yet. Weird.

6:30 A.M.
Deaden: Is that scrawny kid Lucid's villain? That already makes me laugh. Can we start and your villain can join the fight late, Cortex?

> **Cortex:** Then Lucid will miss out on all the fun.

Shatter: Hold on. Does she wear a black cloak? There's a girl like that coming from that direction.

> **Cortex:** That's her. Battle formation! Kevin, go hide somewhere.

Kevin: I'm good at that. I'll do that, boss. You won't be disappointed in me.

> **Cortex:** No promises.

6:31 A.M.
Deaden: Hi, villains. Good to see ya. We going to get this going?

Maybe Vortex: Yes. Let us fight.

> **Cortex:** Wow, V. Your voice sounds weird. Kind of like Siri. Except creepier. OK, before we get started, villains, we've paired you up with a different hero, so you'll have someone unbiased fighting with you. Shatter's villain, yeah the one playing with a centipede, you'll go with au—!

> **Cortex:** V? What gives with the throwing knife? You're supposed to fight Lucid. I hadn't gotten to that. Oh my gosh. How many knives do you have? You work for CutCo or something?

V: Enough talk. I will kill you all.

> 6:32 A.M.
> **Cortex:** OK, someone needs to fire whoever's writing her video game dialogue. Kevin, does she sound normal to y—eahhhhh! Lucid, please, attack her!

Lucid: I mean, this has been rather entertaining.

> **Cortex:** Please, that one just nicked my ear.

Lucid: Fine. All right, red eyes, let's see what's been plaguing your sleep lately.

V: Only your existence.

6:33 A.M.
Cortex: Ugh, this is worse than Kevin. Auugh crap. That one got my cheek. Dang. And I was just healing from the Sweet Tooth one.

Lucid: Um, problem, Cortex.

Cortex: Want to be more specific?

Lucid: There's something odd happening in her head. I can't access the part that makes nightmares. It's like it's blocked off.

Cortex: Can you unblock it?

Deaden: I'm bored. Shatter, let's fight them!

Shatter: Yes! Aaaaaahhhhh! To battle!

Cortex: Have you guys been watching this whole time? Seriously? What kind of team are you?

6:34 A.M.
Kevin: You look great! I can't see you from my hiding spot, but I believe in you!

Deaden: Eh, she's pretty. I mean, pretty intense. Ya know? Little crazy though.

Cortex: Well, Lucid can't get to her, and now she's chasing me around the fountain chucking knives. Wanna switch with someone, Deaden? She could use a patch of blindness right now.

Deaden: Umm, a little busy.

Shatter: You guys are distracting me! Can we turn these off?

6:35 A.M.
Kevin: Guys, Himari has had a breakthrough! Either she's discovered how to improve her kick serve or it actually pertains to this fight. I'll keep you posted.

Cortex: No, Shatter, we need to keep them on. How else are we gonna be updated about the fight? OK, I think Shatter just turned hers off.

Kevin: So...it's not about the kick serve.

6:36 A.M.
Kevin: So, Himari hacked Scourge and figured out his location. The same one V sent it from.

Cortex: Try that again in English. Augh! How does she run so fast?

Kevin: Some dude who's part of this bad league called the Shadow Assassins. Legit, huh? He apparently was with V or something before the fight.

Cortex: What?

    Kevin: Wait, Himari's messaging me. In all caps too. Whooohoo, man. She's very excited about something.

Cortex: Wanna pick up the pace? She's doing the poison ones now, and I can't afford a scratch.

    6:37 A.M.
    Lucid: So, I can't help Cortex at the moment, but I just took out my guy. Too easy, too. Poor thing. Looked like a middle schooler.

Cortex: OK, why don't you help out Shatter and Deaden, so one of them can relieve me of, holy crap that was close.

    Kevin: Well with one villain down, you guys should be good to go. Sorry, I think there's something wrong with Himari's connection. Update loading.

V: Assassins! To me!

    6:38 A.M.
    Kevin: Awww, does their villain group have a nickname?

Deaden: Auugghhh! They're coming out of the water! And from the sky. They're a—aaaauuugghhhh clunk

> **Cortex:** They? Who is they? Oh—shoot.

V: Bwahahahahaha!

> **Cortex:** Well, Deaden and Shatter are off headset. Any word, Lucid?

> 6:39 A.M.
> **Cortex:** Lucid? Kevin?

Kevin: Yo, I got that update. Wanna hear it?

> **Cortex:** Ummm, a little busy with the horde of assassins surrounding me. I'm trying to read their minds to predict their moves, but there's so many of them. I don't read more than, like, five minds at a time.

V: You will die, fool!

> **Kevin:** OK, so I'll tell you anyway so you can't go to your grave thinking I'm a completely useless sidekick. So you remember Juan? As in never mind I'll find Some Juan like you?

Cortex: Yes—ugh. There aren't a whole lot—ugh —of Juans in Indiana.

Kevin: So apparently he's tight with the Shadow Assassins. And he kind of led them to V. Which could explain the creepy robot voice.

6:40 A.M.
Cortex: You couldn't have—ugh—started with—ugh—that? I'm getting pummeled out here!

Himari: Kevin, you're so slow I hacked this chat before you finished! Caleb! I think they brainwashed her!

Cortex: Yeah, well—jeez—as enlightening as this man-talk is. If you haven't noticed the group of—augh—dudes forming a circle around something in a—ugh—fetal position. Yeah, that—ugh—is me.

Himari: I can't see you, idiot. But, using the field around you, I just hacked their headsets. They're Juan-made, too. Oh, not good. It looks like you're the only hero left alive.

Cortex: Headsets. As in the ones that can make squeaky-eeee-dolphin noises when you—ugh—get bad feedback? Watch this.

6:41 A.M.
Cortex: OK, so I broke out of the circle when they went to grab their ears. So, got a bloody nose, a bruised chest with possible detrimental damage, and a cut bleeding lip. Anything else I missed?

Himari: Hold on, got V's feed. Someone is telling her what to do. Look out! Where was she hiding a sword?

Cortex: I mean, maybe I can read her mind. I've been sort of focused on the twenty other assassins, but since they're now chasing after me and not kicking me, I can get more selective.

Himari: Good! Oh! Nice! I just got her feed linked to ours. You can take a listen too.

Hypnia: Good, Vortex. Stab for the chest.

6:42 A.M.
Cortex: Whoop. Can't tell how hard it is to run backwards and duck out of the way of a sword aimed at your chest. So, weird thing about her mind. I'm having a hard time reading it. I think I'm starting to see what Lucid talked about. Ever try to talk to a brick wall?

V: You are a brick wall. Prepare to fall like Jericho.

Cortex: Wow, creepy lady giving V feedback, didn't know you knew your Bible stories, but that's, I guess ... comforting.

Hypnia: He can't kill you, Vortex. Go straight for him. Slice his neck.

Cortex: Oh, dude. I'm so stupid. I can freaking turn off your headset. There. Now who's roaming blind? Or deaf. I don't know. Why are superheroes so much better at quips in the movies?

V: You will die. Take that!

6:43 A.M
Cortex: Ugh. Well, I'd hoped that would. Ugh. OK, if V kicks me anymore, she's gonna snap a rib.

Kevin: I believe in you.

Himari: Yeah, she's dead set on killing you. Oo! Camera! Apparently that's how that lady knew how to tell her what to do. She was watching this video. Like a mini GoPro. Man, you look awful.

Kevin: Be yourself! You can do it!

6:44 A.M.
Cortex: Yeah, pretty sure I've swallowed a tooth. Any ideas how to shake the other guys? I've been doing the feedback thing for a while, but they've taken them out and started after me again. If my ribs are cracked, they're gonna puncture a lung. And I can't r-run much l-longer.

Cortex: Shoot, they're rounding up again. Guys, my chest hurts so much, I can't take another punch. I don't know how V did it.

Cortex: Guys, anything? Ugh.

Himari: You were the best brother ever. I love you. I can't listen to this! I'm turning it off. I love you. I can't see the screen anyway.

6:45 A.M.
Cortex: Ugh, oh, God. Ugh. Himari, d-don't. Ugh. Oh, God. God, please.

Kevin: I'm sorry, Cortex. I need to shut it off. Love you, man. You took it like a champ. But I can't—I can't hear this to the end.

V: Yes. Hold him down. I want to kill him myself.

Cortex: V-v, n-no. Please. Oh, God, please.

V: Are you going to beg? Cry? Something? I like it when they do.

6:46 A.M.
Cortex: I-I don't c-care if you kill m-me. I'm gl-glad it's m-me and not y-you.

V: What are you talking about, fool? How should I kill you? Hmmm. Choices.

Cortex: Quickly. Or not at all. I-I like the second op-option, heh-ugh.

V: Ha. A joker. Hmm. One more good kick to the ribs. Or I could slit your throat. Hmm. So many choices. I like the blood, though. Throat it is. Here, love. Tilt your chin up. Let me help you. Agh!

6:47 A.M.
Cortex: N-no, let m-me help y-you.

V: Let go of me! What are you doing?

Cortex: V-V not v-villain. Not—ugh—not hero. Human.

V: What are you putting in my head? These aren't my thoughts... are... they...

Cortex: G-garden of the Gods, and b-birds, and the f-first fight in the sk-sketch coffee parking lot. It h-hurts to t-talk. Ugh.

V: Oh my... oh my gosh... Caleb! What! How...? Oh my gosh, look at you!

Cortex: H-hot, right?

V: Hush. Duck.

6:48 A.M.
Unknown Source: Vortex, what are you ahhhh!

Cortex: D-dang. Sh-she kicks hard.

V: Keep your head down. I'm throwing knives.

> **Cortex:** H-hurts to, but an-anything for you, babe. L-look out behind. G-guy with gun.

V: Ah! There. Rude. Guns aren't sportsmanlike. Uh!

> **Cortex:** They're v-villains. W-what's da plan. Oooh things are g-going black and fuzzy a-all at once.

6:49 A.M.
V: Hey, stay awake for me. Ah! Take that. Auughhh! Oh my... augh!

> **Cortex:** F-fine. But I take you on r-real date because you're princess and oooh you s-sure Lucid isn't alive? I feel like I-I'm in a dream.

V: Okay, maybe you should go to sleep. Oof! Ten more. Uh!

> **Cortex:** Night-night V. I'll tell the B-Breakfast C-club to have a massacre just for you.

V: Hey, cut it out. You're fine. Don't be a—uh!—sissy. Keep it together, Caleb. You're gonna live.

> 6:50 A.M.
> **Cortex:** But d-dying so easy. Hurts l-less. Please?

V: It doesn't—oof!—hurt less for me. Stay alive for me, okay?

> **Cortex:** Mkay, I take you to b-bowling alley f-for date. That's s-sexy. Those b-bowling shoes. Mmm.

V: Wow. You are really out of it. Uh! Whoa! Die, you butt!

V: You still in there, Caleb?

> 6:51 A.M.
> **Cortex:** M-maybe.

Unknown Source:
wwwwweeeeeeeeoooooooooooo

> **V:** Now the police get here? Thought they liked to leave us be. Must be because the hero's dy—I mean, a little injured.

Cortex: We g-go to jail? I-I hate the color orange.

> **V:** Uh! Nope. No jail. Just assassins running away.

Cortex: Yay.

> **V:** Oh, gosh. I have to get you out of here. Officer! Help, he's dying!

6:52 A.M.

Cortex: Office-r. Sh-she love of my life. Imma d-date dis girl.

> **V:** Oh my gosh, dying you is so embarrassing. He needs an ambulance!

Cortex: Hey, V. Imma sl-sleep now. T-turn off headset thingy? OK, I t-turn it off.

> **V:** Okay, you do tha—

Private Message
July 18

11:17 A.M.

Caleb changed Private Message name to Birds of a Feather

Caleb:

So, lip's busted pretty good. And since you guys were fans of the throat punch, I guess we're going to do mind chats for a little while.

V:

Looks like it. Weird. Why is it picking up me talking?

Caleb:

I'm experimenting with the tech. Guess I'm getting a hang of the software. A bit late now... Ooh, my arm feels cold. Haven't had an I.V. for a while. On a scale of one to Kevin how bad do I look?

V:

Here, let me pull that blanket up. Well, the fact that you're alive makes you definitely not a Kevin to me.

11:18 A.M.

Caleb: Wait?! Did Kevin die?! Why didn't you tell me—oh, oh, ok, I see now. Sorry, emotions are kind of shooting off in all sorts of directions. I feel the horrible combination of loopy and in uncomfortable pain.

V: Those drugs aren't making you even close to as loopy as you were earlier. Do you remember much?

Caleb: Everything kind of entered a tunnel after I did the whole mind magic on you. Takes a lot out of me, and I didn't have much in me to start with.

V: Well, you missed some entertainment. By the way... how much did you see in my head?

11:19 A.M.

Caleb: Not a lot. Just kind of most of the date—er, fights—we went on. I couldn't explore because I was kind of fighting for my life and all that. But, if you want to fill me in, I'm confused as heck about what's happening most of the time.

V: So... at least you don't hate me right now... not sure why you don't though. You don't even know, yet.

Caleb: Oh, dude, no. How could I... what do you mean yet? Just because I lost a tooth and cracked a rib, or two, or three, doesn't mean I'd hate you.

V: I still killed your innocent girlfriend, in your mind. So, how are you okay with me now?

11:20 A.M.
Caleb: Well, it's weird. I was at Tamora's funeral, but for some reason I felt immense relief that she had passed. I don't know if you've ever felt that way before when someone died. Maybe your master. But, yeah, I kind of got over it within twenty-four hours. Wanted to call off the fight, but you seemed into it. But now it makes sense with the whole brainwashing thing.

V: Well, the way you're feeling is going to make way more sense in two seconds. Feel okay to do a little memory diving? It will be much quicker than telling you.

Caleb: You sure? I might pass out, though. Still regaining my energy. Eh, what the heck. I'll wake up in a few hours.

11:24 A.M.
Caleb: Why do I always date ladies who lie about their age? And turn out to be mindless killers?

V: Hahaha! She had to be like thirty, you freak.

Caleb: I guess that makes sense now with the getting out of shape on runs and sounding crazy mature for an eighteen-year-old. But dang. Is there a personality type I'm going for ... please tell me you're eighteen.

> **V:** Yep. I do kill people, though. So, there's that.

Caleb: Well, you're not mindless. You have a beautiful mind. And face too. And arms and sense of clothing choice and I could keep going.

> **V:** Arms? Of all the things. Heehee you doofus.

11:25 A.M.
Caleb: So wanna break down this Shadow Assassins thing? It sounds super cliché, by the way. So you better believe Hollywood will pick it right up.

> **V:** Basically, there's villains and heroes, and then there's the Shadow Assassins, like extremist villains. They want all the heroes dead. They're not interested in nemeses, just dead heroes. I think they have some sort of master plan to take over the world after all of you are dead, but that part was fuzzy.

Caleb: Sounds like a sequel. So, no one but us made it out of their little party in front of the Las Vegas hotel thing?

> 11:26 A.M.
> **V:** Unfortunately... no. Well, Kevin did. He came to see you a while ago but

then said you were too ugly to look at and left. I think he's getting food.

Caleb: Classic Kevin. Kind of glad he did squat at the fight today. Otherwise we'd have to promote him to hero. Seen Himari lately?

V: Planes coming into Vegas have kind of been rerouted. Apparently the fact that a bunch of villains got on planes... your family is going to take a while getting here. TSA is freaking out.

Caleb: Naturally. Oh shoot! My family. I don't want my mom to see me like this. She can only take so much, you know?

11:27 A.M.
V: Oh, trust me, she wants to see you. She's called me at least five times already. They have my number now, by the way.

Caleb: Why them and not me? So, I changed the group name. Hoping it sticks a bit longer than the other ones. You know where I got it from?

V: Wait, let me look. Aww! Yes. Colorado, of course. And you have to ask for my number.

Caleb: Or I can just steal Himari's phone and send you my favorite songs. I think I have another one with Sunshine in the title if you want to listen :)

11:28 A.M.
V: You're lucky I don't punch invalids.

Caleb: I think you got your fill for the day. So what happens now? By now I mean when we leave the hospital. And they cut this weird tag thingy off my wrist. And everything doesn't smell sterile or have awful pink wallpaper anymore.

> **V:** Well, you're staying here for a little bit, anyway. After that... I'm not sure. I don't think I really want to kill heroes anymore. Obviously, I can't fight you, but I'm not fighting anyone else.

11:29 A.M.
Caleb: And honestly, after working with the team of heroes today ... rest in peace, guys ... I don't know if I'm cut out for hero work. Like, I suck at it. But what do you do when you've been planning to do one thing your whole life?

> **V:** Well. Maybe you get to know your former nemesis better. And play with sharks. And go to college and find a new thing to do.

11:30 A.M.
Caleb: Right. College. Even after the fight and everything today, I feel like that still sounds more intimidating. But graphic design sounds fun. No math, at least. And very few casualties. I guess we're lucky we can change our lives at eighteen. My mom and dad always talked about giving up hero work to try another business, but too late in the

game. No wonder Dimension got all bitter. He didn't major in graphic design. His kerning needs serious help on his outfit.

> **V:** Heehee. Maybe you can design my book covers someday.

Caleb: Wait, you write books? Let me guess, murder mysteries?

> 11:31 A.M.
> **V:** No! Okay... sometimes. But also children's books.

Caleb: Oh dear Lord, that sounds frightening. But, I guess I can test my hand out for the next Dr. Seuss. So, we have jobs figured out. What about ... you know, other things?

> **V:** Like what?

Caleb: Like what we're going to do with Kevin when he's living in the attic at forty years old.

> **V:** Ha! I don't have an attic. Sounds like your problem.

11:32 A.M.
Caleb: Wait a minute, V. I didn't say anything about it being your attic. Why would he be living there? ;)

> **V:** You realize when you do that the weird robotic voice says "winky face."

Caleb: ;) ;) ;) ;) ;) ;) I can't actually wink. One of my eyes is swollen. The other one keeps tearing up.

> **V:** Stop it heeheehee. It's okay. You still... have a great personality. Winky face.

Caleb: You suck. So when I get cleaned up, how about a date? And no, I don't mean like the fourth of July or Monday or anything else Kevin would respond to that question.

> **V:** Duh. At least then we don't have to bemoan the fact that we "forgot to fight."

11:33 A.M.
Caleb: Although, if you want to do a little choreography once in a while, in sketchy coffee parking lots where the power goes out, I'd be down.

> **V:** Is that not what dates normally look like? Heeheehee.

Caleb: Yeah, people are really lame. Sometimes they just talk and hold hands and don't try to stab each other. So where am I taking this weird Shark Princess?

> **V:** Shark Princess. Ha! I like that. Well, somewhere sketchy, obviously.

11:34 A.M.

Caleb: You and I got plenty of places like that by us. And somewhere there's a lot of space to throw knives.

V: Ooo, yes! And we have to explore the secret rooms at my house sometime.

Caleb: And actually see Vegas instead of a hospital in Vegas. I must be one of the first patients here without an alcohol poisoning problem.

Caleb: So basically we're describing a bunch of dates. And basically we're saying we're gonna go on them. So... that makes us... ?

11:35 A.M.
V: Oh shoot! The house! I just remembered something! The sharks! Mr. Squiggles! Fluffy! Mr. Flappers! Juan took my funds! I don't have... like, anything. Where am I going to put them? Will I rehome them? What am I going to do? Carlos is always eating Gonzo's food and Fluffy needs special snuggles and—

Caleb: Whoa, whoa, V. Do you even have to ask? My family will take care of you. It might be difficult hauling them up to Indiana, but have you seen the size of my house? We need some excuse for half the rooms we have.

11:36 A.M.

V: Wha... oh my gosh. R-really? You're m-making me cry.

Caleb: Quick, punch me, so I can too.

V: Then I'd cry more, stupid, because you'd probably die! Hahaha.

Caleb: I'd kiss you to make you feel better, but the busted lip would probably make it feel like you were making out with a fish. So ...

11:37 A.M.
V: Well, sounds like there will be plenty of time for that later. Heeheehee.

Caleb: Can't wait. Super sorry about this, V. But I think they pumped my brain full of lead. Even if both eyes were working, I'd have difficulty keeping them open.

V: That's okay. I'll let you know when your family gets here. Sleep well.

Archived Message "Bittersweet": July 1

Archived Message "Bittersweet": July 1 reopened August 2

Cortex: 8:03 A.M.

Hey, Sweetie! You'll be happy to know in a few days I can finally get up from the couch. Losing muscle mass sucks, bro. V says she wants to go on a date as soon as I can get moving. As fun as movie nights are, cuddling isn't really much of a thing because of the whole three-cracked-ribs ordeal. Also, movies seem to be the one thing we're not agreeing on. For some reason, she hates Disney princesses. Go figure. Probably because she's more gorgeous than them. And can sing better too. At least, from what I hear when she makes the rounds with the sharks.

Cortex: 8:05 A.M.

I'd considered getting rid of this account but decided to keep up with a few villains. Wanted to track the activity of the SA, but they seem to have stayed low for now. Himari hasn't had any leads either. And she's drowning in summer homework for her Junior Year of classes. Glad that's over with. School starts in roughly two weeks, though, so kind of sucks I spent a good portion of summer unable to get up.

8:06 A.M.
Cortex: I've decided to major in graphic design and go out for sports. Intramural ones. No one really cares if you have skills in those because it doesn't really count for professional leagues or whatever. Dad got all huffy, but I pulled the whole Dad-I'm-so-sad-because-I-have-busted-bones-and-face, and he relented. What were your parents like, Sweetie? I'd always gotten the impression the parents of villains are awful, but from the stories V has told about hers ... sitting by the fireplace, reading children's books.

8:07 A.M.
Cortex: She's actually a very good author. Her children's books are darker than the typical Shel Silverstein, but Himari read them to some kids she babysat. They seemed to enjoy them. They feel more real than most of the stuff I read as a kid. I feel like an author needs to go through what V did before they can write as well as she does. The best authors are villains, then.

8:08 A.M.
Cortex: Sweetie, I keep wondering if you had a hero, like I had a villain like V, how you would've turned out. Would you need therapy and be chatting with dead people like me? Probably. But, would you also have someone who makes you feel like a hero even when you know you're a villain? Definitely.

8:09 A.M.
Cortex: I don't think I'm going to return to this site for a while. Kevin left because his internship hours ended, but we plan to meet up once a week over wings. Himari's off to school soon, and even Mom

and Dad are thinking about getting part-time jobs in Gas City. Everything's changing, and I think it's time to say goodbye to Meta-Match. At least, farewell to you. Friend and Human.

Private Message
August 4

V: 12:03 A.M.

Hey, Bernard. Caleb and I actually just got back. His mom is definitely talking to him right now, lol. About bringing me home at a reasonable hour. Heehee. Didn't even scold me. Poor guy.

V:

Yeah, so I live with Caleb's family now. Which is a little weird. But I'm going to go to school at this little college nearby. Great writing program. And the sharks and all the pets love the attention. Good thing Fluffy is hairless so his mom doesn't get allergic. And, I get to be with Caleb constantly.

V: 12:04 A.M.

But don't freak out. We behave. His mom makes sure of that, lol. Most embarrassing ground rules talk of my life.

V:

Anyway, we just had our first official date. I feel like it was the best day of my life. Not in like a wow, that was incredibly romantic way, (even though it was), but in a "I made it and we're alive" way. I almost lost him, too, in Vegas. And then I would have had absolutely no one. It doesn't even feel real. Bernard, his family is amazing. They act like I'm part of their family. How did I ever get so lucky?

12:05 A.M.
V: I found out that I like real dates. We saw a movie, which was fine, I guess. Still not a huge movie fan, but I like to watch them with Caleb, because he does, and it's cute. And I can tease him about his movie choices. But apparently you're not supposed to laugh in the theater. Unless it's "an appropriate laughing moment." What does that even mean?

V: Then we went to that coffee place where we had our first fight. I don't even know if that was really coffee. But we watched a deal go down and that was fun. And there was a really high dude who forgot his pants. He got kicked out. That was funny.

12:06 A.M.
V: So we should have driven home, but it was dark, and we could see the stars in the parking lot, and forgot to get in the car... So that's probably when I made Caleb lose track of time. It's nice that he doesn't have a busted lip anymore.

V: What I'm trying to say is, I think everything has changed. And it's good. Thank you for looking after me all those years, Bernard. I probably made you go grayer than you already were. But I wanted to let you know... I don't think you need to worry anymore. I think I'm okay.

V: Also, if you have any control over these things, don't torch Caleb with lightning or anything, okay? Thanks.

12:07 A.M.
V: I love you, Bernard.

Private Message
August 5

11:23 P.M.
Cortex changed name to Caleb

Caleb:

Hey, Dimension. Remember me? I'm a kid you met at a party. The dude you tried to avoid while swiping at a cold shrimp cocktail. You were my hero, man. I followed you in all the comics. Saw all three of your movies (third one seriously needed help. What was the director thinking?). Even binged the T.V. show which was great the first season, OK the second, and then introduced the fifth dimension in the third and just kind of went downhill from there.

Caleb:

Yeah, that was me.

Caleb: 11:24 P.M.

I remember you used to go onto talk shows, and they'd ask you, "What does being a hero mean to you?" And honestly, I can't remember your answer. Probably because it wasn't real. It wouldn't stick to you like the words of V's children's books do to the kids Himari visits. And I know those names mean nothing to you, but I don't care. I'm just going to rant.

11:25 P.M.
Caleb: But I remember you at my parents party. Your eyebags were so purple, they matched your suit. And I remember coming up to you with a pen and paper asking for an autograph. And you just stared at me for a moment with these steely gray eyes and said, "Find a new hero, kid."

Caleb: And then, of course, Mom had us pose for an awkward picture after that because she didn't hear what you said. And then proceeded to post it on every social media site possible.

11:26 P.M.
Caleb: And then you proceeded to tell me what you thought was the difference between heroes and villains. Cape colors and backstories. I'm here to tell you, you were wrong. Not because there are more differences, but, in fact, almost none.

11:27 P.M.
Caleb: Dimension, I met this amazing girl who throws knives and sings to sharks. She wears a black hood, but God, she'll kill you when she wears a purple dress to the movies. And then she'll kill you with laughter when she leans over to you and asks why no one else spruced up for the occasion. She bleeds purple and red.

11:28 P.M.

Caleb: She dances and dies a little each time she sees me get to hug my parents. And even when they open their arms to her, it's not the same. Sure, she can have Christmas and brined turkeys at Thanksgiving with someone who isn't an aquatic creature. But she hasn't had this for a decade. And not even a dragon can heal all ills.

11:29 P.M.
Caleb: My V, she's a treasure. And no wonder a dragon guarded her for so long. And no wonder no one could see the gold and green until she took the contacts out of her eyes. And no wonder I didn't deserve to have her until I understood how little I deserved to have her.

11:30 P.M.
Caleb: And you want to know something else, Dimension? She's a villain.

Caleb: You heard me right. A villain. A villain with a body count that is nearing one hundred. A villain who has a weird obsession with scars and blood and electric eels and the rack.

Caleb: A villain who saves the lives of girlfriends even when those girlfriends turn out to be villains. She's a little monster who rescues men choking on hot dogs and can get a little bird to land on her finger when no other hero can.

11:31 P.M.
Caleb: Want to know something else? Probably not, but I don't care. She's ten times the hero you ever were. Twenty times for me, of course, because I

literally can't even save toast from burning. She cares more deeply about things than any Great Guy could, and loves harder than anything you can imagine on T.V.

11:31 P.M.
Caleb: So, I admit it, once and for all, Dimension. And you'll be the last one to hear anything from me on Meta-Match for a long time.

Caleb: I have fallen in love with a villain.

Caleb: I have fallen in love with a hero.

Caleb: I have fallen in love with a human.

11:32 P.M.
Caleb: And most importantly ... I have fallen in love with a friend.

Hope's Acknowledgements

I'd like to thank my Lord and Savior Jesus Christ who has been the hero of my life when I was a villain for quite a long time.

Of course, I'd love to thank Alyssa. It's always a breath of fresh air to find someone who can accept how weird you are, let alone stick together to write an entire book. I can't think of anyone else who I would like to endeavor this project with. You are so tirelessly hardworking, and you write incredibly. If no one can see that, bring them here so I can punch them (yes, I'll bring out the villain side of me just for them).

To my family, James, Carlee, Amanda's support group (y'all know who you are), and Cyle's Henchfolks (same goes for here).

To Cyle and Tessa who hear endless pitches and receive an unfortunate amount of emails from me. Thank you for tirelessly working with me to present the best story I can to the readers.

To Mrs. DiPaolo, Professor Taylor, Mrs. Riordan, Dr. Johnson, and the endless array of teachers who deserve a significantly higher wage for all the work they do. Teachers are the real super heroes, people.

To Loki, who deserved a better death (just sayin').

To Daredevil, who I wish could see this acknowledgement but, alas, can't.

To DC, thank you for wonderful T.V. shows, and to Marvel, thank you for excellent movies. You've helped us to inspect the complexities of three-dimensional characters and what the true meaning of friendship, justice, and mercy should look like (and how even heroes fail to grasp that sometimes).

To being verbs, which I used way too much of in this book. I was afraid of you before this book because high school teachers would dock points if I used you. But, apparently, people implement you a lot in conversation, so I hope my editors didn't hate me too much on this project because of you.

And to all the fans of superheroes and supervillains who flipped all the way to the acknowledgments sections. All two of you. Thank you.

Hope Bolinger is a literary agent at C.Y.L.E. and a graduate of Taylor University's professional writing program. More than 700 of her works have been featured in various publications ranging from HOOKED to Writer's Digest. **Her boarding school drama Blaze** (Illuminate YA), released in June 2019, and the sequel, Den, released July 2020.

She's a theater nerd, occasional runway model, is way too obsessed with superheroes, and may be caught in a red cloak, fairy wings, or a Belle costume in her downtown, for no reason. Her favorite way to procrastinate is to connect with her readers on social media (@hopebolinger). Check out more about her at hopebolinger.com

Alyssa's Acknowledgements

I don't have a body count like V, but I definitely needed a hero. Thank you, Jesus, for being that for me.

Hope, you know you're on here. I respect you and look up to you. It's an honor to work with you. You really are a hero, and writing with you is so much fun.

Mama, Daddy, Steph, thank you for living with my weirdness. For understanding when I give you vacant stares because I'm thinking about stories. Steph, for being the best nerdster. Mama and Daddy for encouraging me to dream and do what I love.

To Cyle's Henchfolks, our first supporters on this project, a big thanks. To the Pizza Squad: y'all are the best, especially for being supportive of your two crazy writer friends.

To J-Dawg, who was willing to listen to my ridiculous stories ever since fourth grade, a big shout out.

And an especial thank you to Professor Linda Taylor, our prowrite matriarch. You are an inspiration, always there for us, always encouraging. You're a hero.

And to all the Taylor University professional writing students: y'all are crazy talented. Thank you for inspiring me.

Alyssa Roat grew up in Tucson, Arizona, but her heart is in Great Britain, the inspiration for her YA contemporary fantasy *Wraithwood*. She is the publicity manager at Mountain Brook Ink, a literary agent at C.Y.L.E., a freelance writer, and an editor with Sherpa Editing Services. She holds a B.S. in professional writing from Taylor University. She has also worked for Illuminate YA Publishing, Little Lamb Books, Zondervan Library, and as the online editor and a staff writer for *The Echo News*. Over 200 of her works have been featured in various publications, from newspapers, to national magazines, to anthologies. Her name is a pun, which means you can learn more about her at www.alyssawrote.com or on Instagram, Twitter, and Facebook as @alyssawrote.